# The Song of

*About the author*

Colin Mackay works as a night-watchman at weekends in Edinburgh but otherwise devotes all his time to writing. He has had two plays performed; his poems have been published in a number of magazines and *Chapman* have published a collection, *Red Ice*. His experiences embrace those of the classic writer working from hand to mouth in London, but recently have borne fruit in his ever-increasing literary output.

*About the artist*

Alyson MacNeill is a young artist living in Crail. She has already illustrated several books, many of them classics, for a number of distinguished publishers.

Colin Mackay

# The Song of the Forest

*with wood engravings by*
*Alyson MacNeill*

**Flamingo**
Published by Fontana Paperbacks

First published by
Canongate Publishing Limited 1986

This Flamingo edition
first published in 1987
by Fontana Paperbacks
8 Grafton Street, London W1X 3LA

Flamingo is an imprint of
Fontana Paperbacks, part of
the Collins Publishing Group

Made and printed in Great Britain by
William Collins Sons & Co. Ltd, Glasgow

*for*
*Richenda,*
*Patrick, and Jacqueline*

# Prelude

## *The Riders*

That night the riders came and grazed their horses in the forest at the place known as Wolves' Crag where they made their camp. They were forty hard, cruel men. Some wore armour of metal rings sewn onto thick leather shirts; others wore jackets of bearskin so shaggy they looked like the very beasts themselves. They spoke and laughed with harsh voices. They had come from burning a village in the north where they had killed the headman and raped the womenfolk in the embers of their smouldering homes. Tomorrow they would scout out the village in the glen on the other side of the forest. That strath had not been raided for many a year. Sour and bloody as they were, they relished that rich strath; sour and bloody, nursing their grievances, they laughed and made coarse music in the night that lay around their campfire, and none but the trees and homes of the forest's children heard their song.

Come under the branches, stranger, and hear the story of those trees.

# 1

## *The Forest*

The straths of Scotland were made by giants thousands of
years ago before the time of man. They carved them out
with ploughs of ice harnessed to the rushing white clouds,
then they strode over them with storm pouches full,
scattering grains of snow on the yawning rocks, and the
snow sprouted from the rocks as water, down every cliff
and hillface it leaped singing, and wherever it touched the
gritty soil seethed into life in a thousand glens. And when
the giants saw that their work was finished, they stood on
the land that was theirs, and raising their faces to the
sun with the wind in their green hair, they became the
mountains, and the hollows where their feet had trod
were called lochs, and forests of new birch and pine and
alder grew about their massive thighs, and the waters of
their creation sang through them and beyond, down to
the distant sea.

In those days the forest did not know the tread of humankind. It was a wild, beautiful land that grew in the slow backward step of the ice: great black woods whose children were the bison and the antlered elk, the reindeer from the tundra and the wild boar who worried the roots with his tusk; the lynx and the wolf hunted there, the brown bear clawed the bark of its trees, and the beaver worked the daylong water's bank. They heard the sound of darkness, they heard the seasons play the forest as a harp. Neither the fisher heron on the lochside nor the antlers belling from the hill knew of the spear or feared the coming arrow. The giant woods stood waiting, under the thatch of heaven and the white footprints of the sky, their calm still unburdened by the terror of creation.

Then the folk came in slow migrations from the south. Prodded by the constant uterine flow of humanity, they came in coracles over the wide water, they came clad in deerskin and unshaven, came gradually in twos and threes, both man and woman heavy with child, came in small families of generations and marriage laws, seed and womb, hunter and fisher, trekking northward to the land of the long light of summer and the dark winter sleep. They were the first and silent ones whom history has forgotten, though they too knew the meaning of longing and of sorrow, and experienced death and transfiguration to their full. Others came among them then who left the first kitchen middens and the mystery of them to haunt the grey coast; then came the people of the stones, the builders and planters, the herders and potters, the builders of tombs, those who dotted the mountainsides with their broch forts, and putting axe to tree-root named the straths for the first time.

There they made their homes, by the waters, in the forest glades, by the coast of the northern sea, and they hunted the bison with wolf skins on their shoulders, and took the elk for his antlers and the reindeer for his hide.

They put plough to mother earth, at first in reverence and to druid chant with sacred animals pulling a creation of gold across her bosom; then in anger and in greed, taking sharp metal to the mother's flesh and digging stones from her body, trampling the green girdle beneath their feet.

Then they looked at the vast forest with awe. O, how strange it was! Goban the White Stallion galloped there, they said: Goban who had built the world sometime before the coming of the folk, sang the legend handed down by the oldest ones in the dim storytelling firelight of winter evenings; Goban white as the moon and stronger than a thousand mighty warriors; Goban who was chieftain of all beasts, whose hoofs thundered by day on the wild hills of Morven, whose boiling mane flared the night through the woods of Balquhidder to the twisting glens of Atholl; and they invoked the horse-lord for his wisdom and his protection, the folk who had come to dwell in Strathnaver and Strathmore, by Garry and Tay and Tummelside—through all of which galloped Goban, great and invisible, majestic as a god.

Who was Goban? The peasants knew him; the riders knew him too. Perhaps his thundering was that of the cooling wind in the brown branches, perhaps the cascade of his mane (for the simplest mind seeks its reasons) was the swirl of falling leaves. For autumn came even to the happiest land, and with it came the ring of iron on living timber as folk sought to strengthen turf walls and fence their village against the howling of the hungry wolf and the snapping of his jaws in the short days. And so men hurried from the field and the forest clearing, women and boys brought their beasts within the stockade, and the village in the glen was a place of preparation, even as the badgers of the wood were preparing their setts. "Listen," said the sentry on the drystone tower that guarded this length of the strath overall. Two big men raised helmeted heads towards the sky. They listened. In the field a young woman leading an ox turned and listened also. *Listen!* "The song of the forest," mumbled Black Finella, who had seen more years than anyone could mind on. She mumbled it alone to the cat by the peatstack in her hut. In the field the ox blew into the young woman's hand. The sentries on the tower resumed their pacing.

*Listen!*

It is the month of the red roaring when the rutting stag gives voice; it is the time of migration, of the silver geese music, and of the coming of the redwing. At middle pitch the redwings call *see-ip*, in flight, *see-ip*, and the snow thrush answers harshly, *tchak-tchak*; highest of all, the goldcrest—*see, see, see*—so thin, so nearly inaudible; and the trees creak and groan, the rings of their age turning within them. The Song of the Forest, they call it, those who stop and listen. Over the marshland by the loch and riverside wails the gull; the golden leaves of the birch whisper together in the crisp air; the red squirrel disturbs the acorns on the forest floor; the fox trots lightly along the hill path: the Song of the Forest, they call it, those who stop and listen.

Then comes the drifting mist. It hangs in thin tapestries over the deer in the yellow fields; the tall trees vanish slowly into the folds of its grey cassock. The sentry on the tower strains his eyes—Could raiders be out there? He does not know. He curses the cold sky spiders that have spun this chilling web about his watch. In the village, folk see to their roofs—for now the storm comes, as they knew it would, lashing the treetops till the woods are black with it, till even close to the trunk in the inmost forest under the tier upon tier of branches where the earth is ever warm and brown with dead needles, even there its stinging soaking constant rain prickles at the bracken like badger hair.

The terror of creation is on the folk. The sun is being hunted by a hungry wolf! Day is captive in a cave of water walls! Day is gone from us, the sun is gone, the world is dark!

"Ah," says Black Finella to the cat who sits by the smoking peats, "the stag bells, autumn rains—and now the winter will snow."

Snow. They hide from it in winter, the folk of the village; the soldiers in their tower; the old priest, Mungo, who rubs his cold knuckles in the little kirk; the red-faced Shirra, lord of the towersmen, stretching by a roaring fire; even the outlaw riders in their wandering bands lay in plunder in the autumn and hibernate winterlong. But the forest never sleeps: its song is heard in the coldest, darkest hour. When all but the evergreens are leafless, and the cold air creeps on the pine branch, it hums to the sound of the capercaillie, to the darting titmice who poke for food among the tree crannies, to the calling *pruk*, *pruk* of the dry-throated corbie on the crag, to the nightly *hoo* of the watching owl. Winter is the day when cobwebs of frost hang on the lichen of the forest bed, and the mossy wall of the Shirra's tower glistens like a palace of crystal. Winter is the night of the running fox on the forest path, the mating time when the vixen screams and the dog yaps in the clear air. Winter is the coming of the snow. Black is the sky then, white the earth; black the gaunt trees that straddle it, white the frozen moonlight on a loch ringed with ice. And the louping wolves come out of the forest: hunger-driven they cross the snowfield under that same moon and scour the glens of the strath, sniffing round the stockade, trying to muzzle a way in between the staves to the fatness that waits within. Snow, snow. The very bears leave the forest then, they wear coats of white on their lumbering backs, they stand on their hindlegs under the trees, and the trees shake over them their silver shawls. Snow. Solitary men trudge in it like the heavy shadows of their own dancing breath, horses are hidden by the steam of their nostrils, women chip bucketloads of icicles for water, children fight with icicle swords. O snow! dress of the forest, robe of the mountain, fleece of the tingling sky! Over it all the ringing cry of the buzzard—*pee-oo*, *pee-oo*—the buzzard who glides on wings that scarcely move. O snow.

And old Finella, blowing into her peats, counts the snows of the past and says, "Och, this is nothing to the likes of yon."

Then slowly the grey skies begin to recede. The black masses part and small patches of pink cloud fringe the lengthening day. The frozen water-leap begins to *drip*, *drip* slowly at first, then with increasing speed *drip drip drip* on its dried *drip* rocks *drip* by reeds wintered hard and harsh as spears. The lochside fisher rests his hand on the ice and feels the water surge below. He winks to the little boy who stands beside him. No need to chip a hole now, he says. It is coming. *Drip* goes the ice, *drip* from the trees, icicles fall tinkling from the rooftops. On the meadow the snow is dissolving into puddles. The night is milder. The tower guard sniffs the air like a young deer. In the forest the badger wakes in his warm sett and sniffs it also. Mungo in his cloak snores peacefully from time to time. Before dawn there is the white haar of the thawing snow. The loch crackles and sighs with the breaking ice, the gurgling water rises to a roar as the hill burns break free and send lumps of frozen foam spinning over their gleaming boulders. The trees are rustling in the sough of the green wind. The chaffinch and blackbird join the call of the capercaillie. *Doo-doo-err-rr* croons the swan. The haar fades away, the sky is snell and clear. The sun flickers on the deep red heather of the mountain and the brown and rose madder of the meadow. The peaks are capped with placid cloud, the heather of the pinewood greens towards its blossoming.

Above the unfurling bracken the willow warbler calls *pee-pee-pee*. Sparrows twitter about the village eves. The white night has gone, they cry. Light floods the world. The strath girls are singing as they drive the beasts out to pasture, and in the wooden kirk folk chant the Easter hymn. *Surrexit Dominus de sepulcro.*

## 2

## *The Hunters*

One day through the spring forest walked a woodcutter whose name was Wat. He was poorly dressed in brown rags and his feet were wrapped in straw, yet he smiled. The winter hunger had left little enough fat on his bones, yet he smiled because the forest smelt so sweetly full of life, and it would soon be the time of flowers, and because the Shirra's sons had promised him a slice of the day's kill in return for his wood.

Wat walked jauntily with the gait of a man who knows his business, as fine he did. Thus every year he worked in the forest. He knew the trees, many of them, and gave them names. He cut with care and knowledge, and only in places where life would always grow anew. At secret spots he made a stack of his cuttings and returned the next day with a sledge to pull them back to the village and the Shirra's tower. In spring he did good business. There were always roofs to repair, hen coops the fox had torn at, the stockade pole brother wolf had broken down, forbye the Shirra's fire—for men of lordly kind would not be contented with mere peats as the common folk were. And for all these things, folk turned to Wat, and Wat answered them.

Axe on shoulder through the green gloaming he went. Another foot would have stumbled, for this far in the forest was a jungle of waist-high heather with only a few tracks made by bears that sought the silver of running burns. Suddenly a current of fresh air brushed his face. He looked around. Six paces off a yellow beak capercaillie was sitting at the foot of a pine tree. "Ech, brother, it's lucky for you I've no a bow on me, or you'd be in the pot," said Wat. The bird sat silently looking at him a moment, then burst through the undergrowth in a flurry of grey and black feathers. Wat took the axe in his hands. Slowly, his thoughts on the iron cooking pot at home, he crossed to where the bird had been, and stood listening. Well, the creature had not gone far. Just beyond those nearest trees seemingly. Wat knew the way of the capers, that they loved the thickest undergrowth, and that, for all their great size, they would near wait till a man put his foot on them before exploding through the bracken with a heart-stopping *whirrr*. He fingered the blade of his axe and crept through the screen of pines.

It was near the place called Wolves' Crag.

No two-legged creature could have a greater sense of the canny than this man of the woods. Above a sharp ridge, where the trees cleared the bright morning sky, Wat glimpsed two black shapes, corbies that soared and circled and cawed loudly. "An unco noise, yon," he thought, and thinking it, suddenly stilled into complete immobility. Aye, an unco thing, yon. The corbies cawed over the treetops, and Wat raised himself onto a big hummock that stood head-high above the heather. As he did so, a family of hoodie crows rose from the other side of the ridge. He saw raven and crow together swoop out of sight over the trees, and then back again into his patch of blue, circling, circling. He heard their hoarse, angry croaks.

Wat was motionless as the capercaillie had been on his mound. God save us! (he crossed himself) surely neither deer nor yet bear had sent these creatures up together? Trembling, he crouched low in the heather and felt for his axe. Mind, reader, this was in the time of monsters. The mists of creation still lay heavy on Scotland, and out of them came blood-eyed demons with black hides and killing teeth. Who did not know that there were beasts, the like of which no Christian man could look on unafraid, prowling the dark places of the world? O, this was the time when trolls and worse still lurked the forest, when strange silent men left their beds at midnight to bay at the full moon, when wise and fearsome old women could witch lovers into the arms of girls and sickness into the udders of the cattle as whim and interest took them. Had not Mungo, the village priest, once in Wat's own childhood flung a crucifix at a devil that perched on the altar rail mocking his devotions, and then seen the fiend shoot up through the roof with a yelp and a flash of blue flame? There were those who had seen it (forbye the priest, who told no lies) and Wat as a wee boy had helped repair the roof. The edges of the jagged hole, he minded, had been burned black.

At first Wat did not hear the hoofs, for the earth was soft with spring and deeply covered with needles. It was the scurry of hares he first noticed—half a dozen of them bounding down the path he had just left, then disappearing left and right into the undergrowth. Wat flattened himself in the heather. Riders in the forest! Two men—neither monsters nor demons, though ugly enough—rode into sight on big horses. Long spears lay across their pommels. He heard the jangle of their bits.

In the village Wat's tale lost nothing in the telling. How many were there? O, hundreds, he said. Huge great men, armed to the teeth: spears, shields, battleaxes, swords— he could not even begin to count their weaponry. Their leader wore a cloak of wolfskins, and by him rode a man holding a wolf's head aloft on a pole. To the Shirra he told the same story with greater moderation. How many? The trees had concealed them, confused him... Perhaps there were thirty, forty, who could tell? Yes, they had ridden close, scouts out to the fore, along the bear path. And the wolf's head—had he seen that? Yes, he was sure of that. A wolf's head on a pole.

The Shirra sat in the great chair of his hall; his emblem was the black raven, the corbie of the forest. Corbie and wolf were enemies. The wolfriders were the enemies of this strath, had been since his father's father first built the tower of dry stones and turf and crowned its summit with wooden battlements. In far off days, before his bearded men were seed-in-womb, the Shirra had fought by his father's side with a red dripping sword on red ground, and every pole of the great stockade that encircled village and tower had worn an enemy's head that same night. Makars still made songs of it, yon epic fight on the forest's lawn.

The Shirra sat in the great chair beside spear and shield; his three sons stood about him: black Somerled, fierce as a wild bull of many battles, coarse and brave; golden Donwald, straight as a war blade, hard as the iron of it; and young Fergus, whose eyes gleamed like candles when he heard their songs of glory. Wat ceased his speech and backed from the room. To his sons the Shirra turned.

"Aye. And what do you make of it then?" he said to the eldest.

"We will fight them," said black Somerled, his fists on sword-hilt and dagger. "And now is the time, before they can attack. They are massing in the woods for a surprise, perhaps tonight. Let's ride to fight them, there is more glory in it."

"Aye," said the Shirra. "And you?"

"We maun fight them," said tall Donwald, stroking his beard, "though forty is a great number. Better, I think, to meet them on the stockade with the folk behind us, than take our own men into the forest. Who kens but that may be the very thing they want us to do?"

"Aye," said the Shirra. "And you?"

"Is there to be any doubt?" cried young Fergus. "We ken the path they're on! Let's ride to their destruction before the hour is out!"

The Shirra said nothing.

"If they are stronger in numbers than oursels," said Somerled, "the forest will hide it from them. Fight them in the glen and we will lose that advantage."

"Open the gates of the stockade," said Donwald, "and fight them there. They can only pass it two at a time. We will kill them as they come."

"Folk would say we were feared and hid at home!" cried Fergus. "Let's out and fight them now!"

Still the Shirra was silent.

"They have shown the wolf's head," said Somerled, "in the place where no wolf maun go alive. Yon's a rank insult to us."

Donwald drew his breath.

"An insult it is," he said, "and they want to tempt us out with it."

"Father," pleaded young Fergus, "I've no yet fought my first battle!"

Nor had he kissed a girl: he was that young.

"This needs thought," said the Shirra.

The Shirra sat alone in the hall; his eyes were weak, his legs knotted and infirm. Years ago, before he had reached Fergus's beardless age, he had taken a man's head. Not long after, he had fathered his first bastard. But now he was old: behind him stood the Man With The Scythe and his cold breath was on his neck. Could he handle a sword as he had once done? He wondered. Suddenly it occurred to him that the wolfriders had waited for just this: they had bided their time until the day came when the warlord of the strath was a useless tired old man, and then they came in force, confident they would not be resisted.

He sent for Mungo the priest, renowned for bad poems and healing herbs.

"Shirra?" said Mungo, bowing very slightly from the neck.

The two old men looked at each other. One was a great red boar bristling steel grey hairs. One was gaunt and dry as a dead tree. One lived for war and the joy of war. The other lived for piety and the quiet chiming of evening bells. One had the strange gentleness and quietness of the gaelic soldier. The other prayed for bloody victory over the enemies of his true Christ. Alone in the hall were the two old men.

"You heard?" said the Shirra. "They're coming," he said, "just like they used to in the old days—by night, through the forest, down the bear paths."

"Aye," said Mungo, village-priest.

"Forty of them, maybe more," said the Shirra. "I have twenty men. We maun fight with them, but it's sore odds. We'll be needing your blessing, Father, and a taste of Our Lord's most pure and holy body if we are to get through this coming day."

"Aye, you will, and you will have it," said the priest, "but why do you no send down the strath to the Thane's castle and summon his riders?"

"No," said the Shirra.

"In another day," said the priest, "one day and no more, you could have twice as many men as you lead now, and with God's aid you could destroy these heathen bandits!"

"And have the folk say I was feared of them?" said the Shirra. "Say that the Tower of Corbies canna defend them, that their Shirra is a toothless old man who should be mumbling over his gruel in a corner? No, no!" he said, angrily slamming the table. "I'd rather my life's breath was out of my body this very instant than have folk say I'd hung back from a fight!"

"Yon is pride," said Mungo the priest, "and it is one of the seven woesome sins which make a devil's kingrik of this world."

"Ach, it is also common sense," said the Shirra, "for the Thane, whom I would willingly follow to war (and have done ere now, as well you ken), is in all honesty a robber near as bad as the riders of the forest, and once his thieving pack is burrowed snod in the glen we would have to fight another, bloodier battle to get them out of it."

"Then fight at the stockade gate," said the priest.

"No, no, never!" rasped the old warrior. "We *ride* to every fight, by God!—and to this fight I will ride at the head of my men, and we'll no skulk among the sties like a wheen of grunting pigs! No! A hundred reeking fields I've fought, and it's no to play the canny old wifie with this one. We ride!"

"We ride!" he cried, astride his warhorse.

His men cheered and shook their spears in the air.

*We ride!* thought each of them. Joyfully, the soldiers of the tower; with fear and trying not to show it, the peasant infantrymen who would march by the horses' flanks.

*We ride*, thought black Somerled—how many heads will be mine? Ah, though beasts maun die, friends maun die, and I maun die, the reputation we win, that shall surely live forever, he thought.

*We ride*, thought tall Donwald, and is my blade sharp enough? The beer was no of my choosing, but I'll drink the cup. And he closed his mouth on it.

*We ride!*—the words sang and danced in Fergus's young heart, and he was blinking tears of joy as he brandished his spear, for he was so young and brave, and the sun smiled so sweetly down on him.

Then the old priest raised the host, and the men crossed themselves, and the priest blessed them.

*In Nomine Patri*

"Dear God," said Somerled the wild bull, "give me necks to chop."

*In Nomine Filii*

"Dear God," said Donwald the bright sword, "give me worthy enemies to fight."

*In Nomine Spiritus Sancti*

"Dear God," said Fergus who was blushing, "make my father proud of me."

*Amen*

"Dear God," mumbled an infantryman, "bring me safely home."

"Amen," they all said.

Then they shouted again. The Shirra rode to the head of the little column (a great army it was to the folk of the glen) and the proud and noble stallion pranced and snorted and pawed the ground beneath him. They rode down the slope from the tower to the village, the Shirra leading, a fine scarlet cloak flowing over his chain armour, his grizzled head encased in steel. Behind him rode Somerled on a black with the corbie banner: the red pennon of the tower and the black flying raven sewn on it by the hands of fair women long under the hill. Next rode Donwald on a red with his keen eyes fixed on the menacing line of trees, his face steady and unsmiling, and the scarred shield was heavy on his back, and his free hand lay on the sword hilt. Next on a roan rode Fergus—and as he came to the first bothy of the village, Fergus threw back his head and began singing, for there lived a girl there who was his secret love. And this was the corbie song:

*A Scottish sword for the Scottish land!*
*O God of battles steel our hands!*
*Against the pagans we will ride*
*and cut them down on every side!*

Sixteen more riders, two by two, came in the wake of the words, and they sang it too; and on each rider's outer flank marched one of the men of the village, men who had just finished the spring ploughing, and here one had a bow, and there one had a scythe, another had a club in his hands, and another an axe, and all joined in the riders' chorus:

*O God of glorious rage,*
*be yours the honour of our age!*
*O God of golden love,*
*hear our words in your kingrik above!*

And as the aurora of shining spears and the sound of clanking iron passed through the stockade gate and crossed the burn and went on down through the dark dewy grasses of the glen, so the women and the children and the old ones of the village cheered and waved their hands after their departing menfolk, and the dogs barked and hens scurried out the path of the horses' hoofs; but some of the folk looked at each other silently and were afraid. And the girl for whom Fergus sang ran up the slope to the tower, and clambered up to the topmost wooden battlement, and stared with big eyes until she could see the men no longer, only the glint of weapons and the gleam of the red flag that led them in the noonday sun, and hear very faintly the thin sound of their song on the breeze, until finally the shimmering leaves of the forest closed over them and all was still.

# 3

## The Hunted

In the forest the birds rose above the treetops: the wren darted from the branches, the rose-coloured bullfinch fluttered above the bear path; the smoky eagle sought the coming dark clouds; the white swan clapped her wings on the loch as the rain began to fall.

It fell steadily for the rest of that day, and when the sun set over the misty forest it was still falling.

"I heard the fox bark over the meadow," said old Finella, the crone whom some called a witch.

"That is nothing," said Mungo the priest, "I heard it too."

"There was nothing good in its bark," said the old woman.

"I heard the wolf howl from the corrie," she said later.

"It is the way of wolves to howl," said Mungo.

"It wasna hare he was tearing," said the old woman.

That night Mungo had bad dreams. He remembered the time years and years ago when he had first come to the glen as a newly-tonsured young priest. Most of the folk alive then were dead now; Finella had been a handsome woman, and the Shirra a mere boy. Mungo had gone with the tower guards into the forest to fight riders from another strath. At Wolves' Crag the battle had been, and Mungo had hidden from it. Later he crossed the bloody glade to minister to the dead and dying, and the men lay there as the swords and axes had felled them, men and the splinters of men. He had been sick. The soldiers of the corbie tower had buried their own. The Shirra's father had ordered that the enemy be left to rot. They cut the throats of the wounded and rode away. Unknown to anybody, Mungo had spent weeks searching the forest by moonlight until he found the place again. He had a spade: he meant to give Christian burial to the fallen. There they lay, in the glade, surrounded by the crags, surrounded by the mighty trees of the forest and the eyes of the watching beasts. Mungo stood under a great pine and in the moonlight he saw the dead men. All of them had been torn by things other than mere weapons. Most had a face or an arm missing. In some of the helmets the heads were already no more than shimmering skulls in the night light. Mungo shuddered and crossed himself and prayed devoutly. To tear his eyes away from the horrible sight, he turned his face to the moon, which could be seen directly above the treetops, and sent his prayers towards it, addressing it as Our Lady. Then he suspected himself of idolatry and grew still more afraid. He saw a multitude of black wings against the silver sky and thought they were demons come to punish him. Then he realized that they were only bats. He took his spade in one hand and clambered down the crag.

(But the black wings weren't the wings of bats: they

were the souls of the dead. Now, in his uneasy sleep, he knew it.)

The glade was a small treeless hollow where wolves had their lair, a naked navel in the midst of the great dark body that was the forest. Two dozen men lay there, several horses besides, but for the most part they were indistinguishable. The creatures that had torn at them had pulled their bodies so that the bones of one interlocked with those of another, and together they shone like white veins in the dark covering of bracken and fallen leaves. Swallowing hard, for the heart of the forest has little air and the smell was of a charnel house, Mungo knelt transfixed with his arms together on his breast. Through the soft words which consigned the bodies to the ash and dust, he heard a panting and a snuffling around him. He finished his prayer. Above his head, against the blackness of the trees, the circling crag was ringed with fierce eyes. He looked at them dispassionately and included them in his blessing, but his hands were running icy sweat and he had to wipe them roughly on this cassock before setting to work. At first he tried to pull the bones and the remaining lumps of putrid flesh, the hair, the tangled muscle and entrail that he found there, apart into the recognizable forms of individual men, so each could have his own burial. But though he laboured at the task with the strength of one who believes salvation hangs trembling on its outcome, yet still he failed. Through the warm earth tree roots had come surging upwards to drink the hot blood that had been spilled there. Around legs and chests picked clean by the forest scavengers, these roots had wrapped themselves like tentacles, and like tentacles their hold was invincible. At last Mungo stopped. His shoulders were heaving with the effort. He stared down at what he called his failure, for he was still a very young man, and then he sat on a blue-gleaming boulder, put his head in his hands and wept. When he looked up, a huge wolf was staring at him...

(On his hard bed, Mungo shuddered and woke. "They are dead," he thought. He lay staring at the dark ceiling and not seeing it. The brave, fine smell of spring earth flooded his nostrils. "They are dead," he thought with certainty.)

In that glade, all those years and years ago, the young priest who had been born in a house by a desolate and treeless coast, had learned that the forest was a world in itself, a living creation that had its own understanding. He scooped up leaves and needles and earth on the edge of his spade. "Well, let the forest have them then," he said. He spread a shroud of russet and green over the killing-field. Dawn was nearing. From somewhere among the trees he heard a horse's whinny. He did not yet know the legends of Scotland; the name of Goban was unfamiliar to him. He thought the myths of the Gaeldom into which he had come were as absurd as those of the Israel he had never seen were painfully real. He caught the glint of a shimmering white hide amongst the trees...

"The moonlight plays some orra tricks."

He left the place without looking back. He heard the soft pad of feet over the glade, and the smell of creatures with pointed muzzles and sharp ears stayed with him until at cockcrow he crossed the burn to the stockade gate.

When the dawn came the rain was still falling and there was still no word from the men.

"Dinna fash," said Mungo village-priest to the folk who watched; but he thought—The old woman was right: heaven is weeping.

The burn was in spate; the clouds shot like arrows across the sky; the folk stood waiting.

Mungo knelt in the wooden kirk and prayed. Then he heard a voice.

"A rider! A rider in the glen!"

He ran outside.

A lone horseman was riding up the glen. In the distance they could see him. A terrible hush fell on the village. Folk stood by the stockade, by the burnside, on top of the tower. Children clung to the rooftops. Young ones wrung their hands, bit on their knuckles. The old and cloudy-eyed waited with patience. The rider moved slowly. They thought he was going to water his mount, for the roan wandered by the burnside, and over the howe of the bright water-grass it dallied. They recognized Fergus's horse. Had it been one of the troopers, one of the men from the village, they would have run to him then. The folk stared in silence.

Slowly the rider came on down the water margin. The beaver hid by the burnside, the stoat stared from the thicket. They could recognize Fergus now. His head was helmetless and rolled stupidly from side to side. They saw white wings fluttering around him. Nessa, the girl for whom he had sung, put her hands to her mouth. He was not one of them. Mungo, whose eyes were dim with age, was still wondering why the man rode so slowly.

"Why does he ride so slowly?" he said. "What ails the man? Can you see?"

On the other side of the burn beyond the stockade gate Fergus suddenly leaned over his horse's neck and fell heavily from the saddle. His empty sword-sheath splashed among the reeds and the running waters. One of the arrows that was drilled into him broke; the other two stood quivering above his chest, their feathers were white as wings. His blood was reddening the burn as the peaceful roan began to drink of it.

The folk looked at him silently and said nothing. Fergus moved his arms and groaned. They looked at him silently. His spurs tore at the waterbank. They said nothing.

Nessa began to sob.

Mungo village-priest hirpled to his side. The old man had broken the spell. Folk began to move. They carried

29

Fergus within the gate and closed it fast. They carried him to the kirk and laid him down in the cool and wood-smelling twilight of it. Lookouts mounted the battlements of the tower. Mungo knelt by the wounded man and washed his face with burnwater from the stone font. Fergus opened young eyes and looked at him wildly. He tried to say something, but Mungo could not hear it. Then the darkness came over him again.

In the room that was his own, separated from the rest of the kirk by a screen of hawthorn wood, Mungo was at his preparations. Ragged children came running to him from the forest with their arms full of its greenness.

"Father, what are you making there?"

He knew, this old man, that the earth was our mother, that from her womb we came in the nourishment of the sun's light. *Father sun*—in his prayers he said it—*sister moon, mother earth* . . . And shouldn't a mother nourish her children? He looked to the forest where the animals had no surgeon, and to the waters where the fish didn't know a healer's hands. He had walked all the path-ways with a wicker basket. There was not a growth that he didn't know, the meadow had no secrets from him. Sweet Jesus, he said, everything is possible to you. Holy Mary, he said, don't let this boy die out of time. For Fergus had an arrow near his heart. Before now word of this old man's prayers had caused discontent in the bishop's palace. More than once earnest clerics with pale sharp faces had been round sniffing for heresy. What do you *mean?* they asked. Why do you *say* this? What are we to *think?* There are prisons as well as comforts in the bishop's palace. Beware, or we will cage you there like a jackdaw and hear you whistle shrilly through your bars. And they stood there with cold silver crosses round their necks and called him a pagan through their thin bitter mouths.

The old man smiled patiently. Patiently he told them

his truth: *Mean*, *say*, *think*—what are they but clubs that beat and irons that bind? (They narrowed their mouths still more.) So I will think no more—sang lyrical grey-haired Mungo—for thought is aggravation; will creep to no more masters for they are shrewd thinkers on thrones of power; will promise no more heavenly rewards to enrich the exploiters of this world; but will return back down through the green door to the place of my beginning, where all stone commandments are broken, where all cold idols are thrown in the sea, where no cage stands, where no chains bind, in a land where there are no crosses; and I will be at one with the reeds and the foxglove, at one with the heather and the wild broom; I will sink into the earth and become the earth, this my flesh my body my blood will be; and the flowering hawthorn will know me in its roots, and the whaups will cry for me, and the white clouds will be my prayers, and I will be no more a servant of They Told Me To, but holy and wholly my own, and will in all things find the pure beginning, as it was in the beginning, when the wind first ruffled the earth's green hair...

But Mungo had only managed a few words of this before his tongue stumbled into silence.

Did they understand—a little ... perhaps?

*Nunquam!* they said. Heresy! they thought.

"Ach well," said Mungo, "I have the work to do." And he smiled.

The sharp-faced men from the palace shuddered and crossed themselves and muttered darkly.

Mungo, working among his beakers, grinding roots and leaves with a wooden pestle, was looking for a cure.

A wee girl came and stood by his side. Her eyes were bright as the sparrow's, her cheeks brown as rowan berries. She was perhaps ten years old. Her feet were bare; she couldn't have had a proper bath since she was baptised. Mungo glanced down at her.

"Aye then, wee yin."

The seventy years between them meant nothing. They understood each other perfectly.

"Is the man going to die?" she peeped, her face so solemn.

A murmur of voices came to them from the body of the kirk. The old man's eyes traced the sound.

"Maybe. It's in God's hands; but I maun do my best."

And he mixed the draught that cures. Powder of sanicle leaves, poultice of cowbane, cool ointment of the elder flower, butter-bur from the waterside, boiled comfrey root, juice of the daisy, woundwort and foxglove. All the goodness of the forest, all the glories of the field. Powder beneath his pestle. They went together into the kirk.

"Why do they hate me?" whispered Fergus.

They came to him lying on the earthen floor by the ragged altar rail. Most of the village was standing around him or poking their heads in through the door. Nessa was standing in the midst of them. Last year they had brought in a crofter that a boar had torn, and they had lain him on the floor just there, and the women had wept, and the men had first been graven with concern, and had then begun reproaching each other, as is the way of things; but the folk who looked on Fergus had closed their hearts to him. A strange, callous curiousity held them to the suffering body, no love lighted the aisle of the kirk—unless it were Nessa's, and she kept it silent. No one knelt to staunch Fergus's wounds. It was a thicket of heavy, indifferent bodies that shuffled out of the way of the old priest as he came from behind the screen with a steaming bowl in his hands, and the little girl trotting beside him.

*Why*, asked Fergus, *why?*

He lay looking up at the roof of the kirk. His eyes were full of fear. He didn't want to look at the folk. Fear and hatred were dancing round his delirium. Never in his life had he been so scared. Not the pain of the arrows in his flesh, not the horrible things he had seen just before they ripped into him—these could be explained. The sullen hostility of the folk around him—that could not. For one chilling moment he had thought that they were going to kill him, ritually tear his body to pieces, as they bundled him roughly through the stockade gate.

The girl, Nessa, never came near him.

*Why, father?—Dinna let them kill me.*

Mungo wiped the blood from the boy's branded face. Gently he drew the white-feathered arrows from his racked body; slowly the painful tale from his tormented mind...

They had ridden down the glen behind the Shirra, the men of the tower, and the red and black corbie flag that Somerled held had fluttered boldly before them in the mid-day light. And everything was so grand, the sky so clear and shining blue, the air so fresh, that Fergus sang over and over again the departing song about the Scottish sword and the Scottish land, and the sixteen troopers riding behind him sang it too, and the village men marching on either side of the horses joined in the chorus, and Fergus was so full of the joy of life that the idea that something unjust and terrible might happen never even entered his head, no, not even when Donwald turned in his saddle and angrily told him to shut up. Behind them the troopers of the tower were laughing and swapping jokes with the plodding village infantry, and they were seeing to their blades and their bowstrings and testing the grip of their spears. And everything was fine. They were off to beat a rabble of pagan bandits—for Fergus never doubted that the wolfriders were pagan bandits, or that they were going to beat them —and they would be back within a day or two for the sort of victory celebration that would be talked about years later when folk sat by their fires and minded the olden days.

Ah.

On the verge of the forest the Shirra stopped the columm and called for silence. He stood upright in the saddle with his head cocked like an old dog. At that moment a flight of crows passed overhead cawing sepulchrally. Involuntarily the men followed them with their eyes.

"That's no canny," said a voice.

Donwald rode up to the Shirra's side. Fergus heard the word "omen." These were superstitious times. The Shirra shook his head. Donwald returned, his face was hard and set. The column entered the forest.

Two scouts rode ahead and the riders and the village men filed after them down the bear path. Elm and alder folded over them. The sky-ocean dwindled to a trickling burn of distant blue above their heads. The forest world was in gloaming. Soon all was silence except the clank of their arms, the tramp of horses' hoofs. Without deliberate thought they listened for the sounds of the forest. Branches creaked above them, and they looked up. In a strange filtering sunlight, the catkins of a path-side hazel glowed blood-red. A man touched them gingerly, but it was only the light on their leaves. He grinned, but unease was gnawing at them. Troopers flexed the swords in their sheaths, villagers tightened their grip on scythe and sickle, pitchfork and axe. They heard the drumming of a wood-pecker, the yelp of an unseen fox as their shields brushed the undergrowth. They heard the song of a blackcap. For some reason it made Fergus feel sad. There was a song about a hero called Finn who had ridden to battle and died fighting. Fergus's mother had been wont to sing it over him when he was a bairn in cradle. Any moment, thought Fergus, he could be going the same gait as Finn, and he hadn't done enough with his life yet for anyone to want to make a song about him. The blackcap's song ended in harsh scoldings. Branches stirred around them. Needles and leaves whispered underfoot. The men were restless. Black Somerled wedged the banner pole between

34

his leg and his horse's flank, and stropped the blade of his blue-faced axe. Fair Donwald drew his sword, kissed the cross-hilt of it, and tested the point on his tongue.

Onward they rode.

Onward the Shirra led his men.

Onward the corbie host behind the red flag of the tower of ravens.

Where were the scouts?

Donwald edged ahead. Out of the corner of his eye he saw the grass was trampled and bloody; he saw a dead hand lying under the bracken. He let out a high-pitched whistle—alarm—and brought his horse round in a canter, slashing as he did so deep into a bank of ferns. A cold scream came from the torn stalks.

They had ridden into an ambush.

The Shirra drew his sword and cut down the bandit who sprang out to dirk him. Somerled swung his axe. It smashed through helmet and skull, and a man's brains trickled between his broken teeth as he sank groundwards. Suddenly the trees were spurting arrows at them. The first rider crashed from the saddle. Strange men were about them, thrusting with spears from the undergrowth, bending bows from the branches, riding down the path on them, howling like banshees. The world was all a red scream. Fergus rammed his spear into a man's throat— yanked it free—took an arrow on his shield and stabbed up at the archer astride a leaning pine—the man fell dangling with his stomach slit and his bowels running over his face.

"*Faol! Faol!*" shouted the bandits: *Wolf! Wolf!*

Who died first of the brothers? Fergus, grimacing through his own pain, asked and failed to answer, clenched his wet fists and didn't know.

He had seen Donwald's horse go down, and fair

Donwald lay with one leg crushed and a dead man to each hand, killing a tall bandit who had come out to cut his throat. Donwald's teeth were in the man's neck and the man was choking, dirking Donwald as he lay on him, dying there in each other's blood. Black Somerled leaned against a trunk. The weight of two spears was pulling him down. He was tearing the corbie flag with his teeth, and swinging his axe single-handed. Flecks of blood and flesh flew through the air.

Two arrows had already failed to reach Fergus: the first to do so took him below the shoulder-blade where the chain-mail was weak. He broke his spear on a rider's shield, felt a sword blow that tore the armoured shirt from his chest. Then that rider was gone: a villager whose name he forgot had cut him down with a scythe. He heard his father's voice shouting the warcry of the tower. The Shirra was fighting on horseback, half a dozen wolfriders about him, no more than two of his own men by his side. Fergus spurred his horse forward, trampling a wounded man who cried horribly. The second arrow took him when the Shirra fell. Fergus dropped his shield and clung with his mouth and fingers to his horse's mane. Another wounded man raised himself and Fergus hacked him across the head and arms with his sword. There were screams and blood all about. A panic of riderless horses clotted the path. The Shirra's great warhorse broke past him. The creature had been speared in the head. He nestled against the other horses and his blood stained their flanks. The last of the corbie troopers and a mounted bandit fell together. The triumphant wolf's-head danced on its pole. A third arrow took Fergus and the sword slid from his hand. The Shirra was standing in a whemmle of bodies. A flock of arrows perched on his mail shirt and his head was gashed with an axe. None of the village men was left in sight. The bandits in the trees began jeering. "Pax vobiscum!" they cried, waving their weapons and drawing their fingers *sliccck* across their throats. The Shirra slashed at one of them, and the man fell. Then an arrow took him in the face. He staggered. For the last time he shouted the warcry of the tower:

*Chlanna nan con thigibh a so's gheibh sibh feoil!*
which in the old language means: "Sons of the hounds, come here and get flesh!" Then he fell. The bandits closed in to butcher him. Alone of them all, clinging to his horse, Fergus escaped.

## 4

## Red Hawthorn

So that was it then. That was the story Fergus told as he lay on the ground beneath Christ's altar in the little kirk. The men were all dead. The eyes of the womenfolk shone with the welling of their pain. Fergus's voice cracked and whispered into silence.

They did not hope, for there was no hope. They did not search, for there was nothing to be searched for. The Shirra had taken the young men from the village and left the old and the infirm, the halt and the weakly. He had taken them bright as the flowers of the morning. Now the women knew that they and their men would never meet anymore in the strath of this world.

Old Finella's grand-nephew, her only kin, was dead with the others, the seedline was extinct. She had seen it, she said, she knew it was coming. It was in the bark of the fox, in the howl of the wolf. Now ravens were gnawing his head. She held withered hands to a cold hearth.

The other women reacted as age and suffering made them. One wailed and flung herself on the ground. Another sat keening, rocking on her ankles. A third stared glaikitly at the dark line of trees.

The men who remained wandered grim-faced from bothy to bothy. They had decided they would wait until daylight and then go into the forest to bring back the dead. Until then they had nothing to do. They didn't speak to the women, who were anyway beyond their words.

Bairns wailed with their mothers. Older children stood dumbly watching their elders with frightened eyes.

Where are you Coll, Roy, Torcall? Where are you Calum, who used to make the smithy ring with joy and laughter at your stories? Where are you Ranald, who brought the silver salmon home from the loch?

Dead, all dead.


This had happened often before; the story of Scotland was a web of love and hate, of great heart and also great cruelty.

Life for the folk of the glens was a fine rich thing, but sometimes the Troubles came. Then the harvest would fail, rat-hunger would tear into pained bellies, and the beasts would be killed that their owners might live out the winter—in fear, for when the spring came again there would be no cows to give milk and cheese, no oxen to pull the ploughs, and then what would they do? Or it might be that black rats would come with death behind their yellow teeth, and folk would stagger and fall vomiting on the hard earth, and lie crying for help as others shunned them, then twitch a little and be still. Or stranger-men would ride into the strath in a clanking of horse hoofs and armour; long their lances would be, waving like the wheat, with iron ears glinting in the cold sunlight; and they would burn what could be burned, and take what could be taken, and rape any women they could find between six and sixty, and kill any man who gainsaid them. And the priest would kneel among the blackened foundations of his kirk and pray, "O God, how long will You avert Your face?"—but no answer would come. Finella, the oldest one, could mind the time when these things had happened to this very village.

Knowing they were weak in all but numbers, the peasant and fisher folk fought back with the viciousness of the weak. Lone riders would be taken and slaughtered with sickles. Heroes of the sagas would lie gasping with pitch-fork prongs rammed into their stomachs, and small dark nameless men who smelt of goats and cow dung would perch on their chests and calmly slit their throats.

Then the Troubles would come back. They were an invading army. Their scouts rode to the ridge above the village and mocked down: "Hey gowks! put clean straw on your beds—we're going to sleep with your wives tonight!" Hard men with cruel eyes, they were, packs of them like the wolves.

And so to guard themselves against these wolves, the folk of the village brought in the ravens. The tower went up and a warlord was appointed to man it. He brought in men that poverty had driven from the land, men who did nothing except fight—who would now fight for the glen and the village of it. Yet the folk of the village looked at the tower, and at the food and drink which went in to it, and at the red banner waving over it, and at the in-evitable arrogance of those they had raised up to defend them, and a slow resentment began to fester deep inside them, a suspicion of these iron men and all they were, a dark joy in their misfortunes, a readiness to blame them for any disaster.

That resentment was a taut string, a thread of steel; it was the weed in the garden, the filth at the bottom of the clearest pool. It was there, in every one of them.

Where are you Sim, Niall, Tormod? Where are you

Donall? Where are you Frang? Where are you Mata? Where are you?

There is a red hawthorn on the ridge of tears. They say it is red with shame for the bloody cruelty of men. They say it is red with the blood of innocents spilled on it. They say the pure of heart can hear it sing. I think few have heard it sing.

That night there was a meeting of village folk in the smithy. Calum the smith had killed a rider with a scythe (perhaps it was he who had saved young Fergus's life); other riders had closed in and killed him. Now the forge was one cold lump of iron. Siubhan, his wife, had been delivered a few days before the men had gone. Mungo had performed the service of baptism on the head of little Eoin. In the glowing peat light Siubhan sat with her sister and her mother round the cradle. They sang.

Siubhan: *Lally, lally, sleep my baby,*
*lally, lally, sleep my dear.*
*Your coat is of many colours,*
*lally, lally, sleep my dear.*
*I made it of the skins of martens,*
*lally, lally, sleep my love.*
*Your father is a mighty warrior,*
*a hunter with a spear and club.*
*There is no man who is bolder,*
*lally, lally, sleep my dove.*

Sister: *In the mountains he hunts the wild boar,*
*in the hills the stag and the grouse.*
*He takes the fish from the falls of the Inver,*
*lally, lally, sleep little mouse.*

Mother: *No man is braver, no man is bolder,*
*no man is stronger with sword and with spear.*
*When you are a man you will be a great*
*hunter—*

> *lally, lally, sleep my dear,*
>
> sang Siubhan.

Her fatherless bairn slept.

A low hum of voices rose in the haunting light. The surviving men of the village were all there. And what were they? Mungo, who was old and a priest; Tomas, who was old, was there too; and Manus, who was older, and blind, and walked with a stick; and Fearchar, who was fourteen and nearly a man, and to his disgust had not been taken on the march because he was an only son and his mother needed him, said the Shirra; and Wat the woodcutter, who was of the trees and the beasts and survived everything; and finally Rob, who grinned and dribbled and was a Gowk. These were all the men left of the village.

And the women?

Grief kept most away. Six remained.

The three by the cradle: widows (two of them), unwed; mother, sisters, baby; all the generations. A red fox was at that moment slashing the genitals of Calum, having already torn those of the fallen rider. And these, also widows: Sine, who was plain as a turnip and capable, mother of many; Seonaid, a soldier's woman and darkly beautiful; and Finella wrapped in shawls, Finella who was oldest of them all and to whom everyone deferred.

She had come when the cradle was filled, the old one who saw in every birth and death. Then there had been joy and gladness in the smithy, loud laughter, hearty talk. She had sat in a corner and looked into the flames. Her old face was sharp as a bird's, her silver hair hung lanky about her ears. When she rubbed her hands they whispered together like withered leaves. "Wheesht," folk would say, "the old yin's *seeing*."

Between her and the priest were decades of damn near to war.

Outside in the darkness the village was quietening.

Usually it would be quiet and still and full of sleeping souls by now, but not many slept tonight. A few old women who had outgrown grief, perhaps they found peaceful sleep who needed it least.

There is a red hawthorn on the ridge of tears...

From one of the further bothies came the sound of keening.

"Who will that be?" said Una. They listened.

"It'll be Nessa," said another.

"No. Why should it be?"

The voice rose to a wail, then sank away. Seonaid sniffed loudly.

"Och, for God's sake, dinna *you* start again," said Una. Seonaid had been keening earlier and had torn her raven black hair. There was a smear of blood at her temple.

"Why no?" said Seonaid in a hollow voice. "What did you do when your man died? You grat and grat as I mind."

"At least I was a wife," said Una, "no a whore."

Seonaid screamed and flashed her nails.

"Enough of that!" said the priest.

"Women!" grumbled Tomas. Blind Manus sat with his chin on the handle of his stick and shook his head.

"Enough," said Mungo again. "The dead are with the Lord. It's the living we maun think about."

"What is there to think about?" cried Seonaid. "It's murdered we're all going to be, and yous ken it too, when they bloody wolves come down the glen!"

"That is no the way for a Christian to talk," said Mungo sternly. He looked round a circle of expectant faces. What do they want of me? he thought. "We ken that the Good Lord would no abandon us, black as things look. He has His reasons, never forget it. If the men are dead, then mind that they are only dead to us, but for themsels they are on the road to paradise—God be praised!—to the place where everything is fine and grand and there is no more war and suffering, so we shall pray for their souls to

43

speed them on their way there. That is the first thing we maun do."

They all nodded, willing to believe what the old man said—all save Finella, who snorted through her nose and muttered something to herself. Mungo ignored her. He looked round the circle of eyes, and a fear nagged him —the fear that perhaps in the end he too did not belong here. Aye, he thought, it's a war chief they want, a fighter! In the time of darkness a druid would have led them into battle. Pale piety they will laugh at.

"The second thing," he said, "is this: wolf and corbie, tower and bandit, are partners in a terrible dance, and we are the floor they dance on. Who is to rule the strath and have dominion over the folk? Until yesterday, the wolf was down and the corbie was up, the Shirra was our guard on middle-earth, his men were our shield, and the wolves stayed in the forest. Now the men are all dead, and the day of the wolf is on us. What are we to do? Our souls are the Lord's, but our bodies are worldly flesh and mortal clay: work bends them, disease wastes them, they bleed to the spears."

Again they all nodded; yes, they understood that: bodies bleed cruelly when spears are thrust in them.

"And we are women," said Sine, the plain one. "A village of women."

She's afraid of rape, thought Mungo.

"Aye, you women have another weight to bear," he said. "These bandits are full of fleshly lusts, and we maun think how a body polluted by their fornications will fare at heaven's gate. The Lord is full of mercy and forgiveness, but the more forgiveness He has got to use, the more scunnered He will be with us, and that is something we should all be thinking about, because I for one would not want to put too much of a strain on His patience, infinite as it is. So I put it to you. I dinna want to force any of you. Do we stay and wait for what they will do to us, or

44

do we up and go to some other place? There it is. We have no other choice that I can see."

There, he thought, that has spelt it out for you. They were still looking at him. What will women do? he wondered, being chaste. What will they want to do? The bandits are men, after all. Perhaps they will just lie down underneath them as contently as under their own menfolk. Their men are dead, and what use is a dead man to a woman, after all?

"Perhaps we should go to the Thane," said Sine, "and ask for his men to come and protect us."

"The Thane!" said Seonaid. "As though he would listen!"

"We havena the time anyway," said Wat, who had sidled round until he was behind young Sorcha. He laid a hand on her shoulder. (Una watched him, missing nothing.) "They'll spend the night licking their wounds," he said, "and be here the morn. The morn's morn we'll all be dead. The thing to do the night is make for the forest. There are plenty of places I ken of where I could hide you."

"The Thane—" said Sine.

"Ach, the Thane," said Wat. "The Thane can get stuffed! Bloody man. You all ken how much trust we can put on the Thane. Do you think it matters to him if another village goes up in flames? Dinna look to see his men till this time next year, and the worms will have had a grand feed out of you all by then if you dinna do as I say and clear off the night."

"No wolves the morn," said Rob, the Gowk. "No worry—no wolves. *Faol.*" And he howled like a wolf.

"Wolves like to eat," said Sine, when Rob's howl had lapsed into foolish giggles.

"They'll wait for the harvest—of course!" said Mungo. Last year's crop had been bad in the other glens. "Even wolves come out of the forest when they're hungry. It took Rob to tell us that. Bless you, brother Rob."

Rob wriggled like an eel in his embarrassment.

(And in his forest camp the leader of the wolfriders, who had lost half his men in the battle, was indeed saying to his principal lieutenant, "Ride in the morn and we'll find they've buggered off. Wait till the harvest's in, then we'll hit them—take them all unawares, like," he said, and spat.)

"But when the harvest comes, is our problem any the less?" said Wat.

"We've bought a pickle of time—no more than that," said another.

Young Fearchar was standing by the wall, his eyes going from face to face. At last he found his opening. "Fight!" he cried. "Fight them! We can make ourselves spears out of the pine wood. We can dig a trench outwith the stockade for their cuddies to fall in. We can kill them on the ground!"

Fight?

Mungo looked at him and sucked his few remaining teeth.

"*Fight?*" said Tomas, shifting in his seat. "Will you just look at us now. Aye, what a row of bonny fighters! Fight, is it? Jesus—saving your presence, Father—that's the daftest thing I've ever heard, and I've heard a lot of daft things in my time too. Laddie, laddie, do you no comprehend that we're farmers, no soldiers? Forbye most of us being women. How many of the womenfolk could handle a spear? How many of the menfolk could either, eh? Damn a one! They wolf-men, they've lived on blood, they've worked with spears and swords and that lifelong, and are we to fight them? It's massacred we'll be if we try it."

"There are none of you fighters," said Seonaid contemptuously. "If my man was alive now—But *you*, look at you! Pah!"

The men hung their heads.

"You hear that?" said Siubhan to her baby. "You hear what they are saying?"

"I think I could kill if I had to," murmured her sister,

46

gentle Sorcha, with the skin like milk. Her words hung heavily in the thick air of the peat smoke. Eoin whimpered a little in his cradle.

"And I have my axe," said Wat, and coughed. They all pondered this gravely. Rob, the Gowk, scratched his ear and looked perplexed.

"We canna fight," said Mungo eventually. "It is no for the likes of us to use the tools of death."

"Then what are we to do?" asked Sine.

"Leave the glen," said blind Manus over the clasped hands that still rested on the handle of his stick.

No, no, no, they all said.

"Listen," said the blind one, "I'm no thinking of the likes of Tomas and mysel. No even of the Father here —save your presence again, Father. We old yins are past with life now, and for my part I'm content to die here where I was born. But the young folk! Surely they have the right to a life that is no full of killing?"

Leave? said Sine. Leave? said Una. Leave? they thought.

"It's true that I want to have a baby someday," said Sorcha over her sister's cradle.

Wat grinned sheepishly and rubbed the hard brown nut of his head.

"Then it is your wish to leave?" said Mungo, in the voice of one who is fell weary.

They looked at each other.

"No," said Finella from the huddle of her shawls.

All this time she had been sitting listening to their clack, cherishing her own memories and her knowledge by the fireside. "No," she said now.

"You croak like a puddock, old yin," said Wat, who was nearest her.

"Ach, puddock yoursel," said the crone, rising slowly onto her creaking legs. "There is more sense to be had in a puddock than in yous that I've heard this night. You men!" she suddenly shrieked, shaking her fist under Mungo's nose. "Ach, you men! You make me sick so you do, you muckle bairns! For all the use of you, you should be put out to play in the woods. And you with your havers," she pointed a crooked finger at Manus who had opened an indignant mouth, "you're as bad as the worst, even if you're no the worst! I had my first man afore any of you were born, and ever since I've wanted to spit you out. Aye ready to fight when you dinna need to, and run when you do. Ach! Leave the glen is it? And go where? That is the first thing. Where? Down the strath, you say. And how long will it be afore we have to leave the strath? We dinna ken, you say, maybe never. But I ken, who am older than all of you. It will be the year after, or the year after that, for when you've run once, you will run again and then again, and in the end you will come to the grey cliffs on the wild sea, and then where? Are we to set sail in coracles? Try ploughing the waves and reaping the salt of them? You didna think of that, did you, you sumphs! And here is the second thing. There are a thousand villages in Scotland like this one, and a thousand towers like the corbie tower above us, and how many hundreds and thousands of old folk and bairns I canna think; and if this village falls so easily, then what will happen to the lave? Do you think the bad men will be content with one village? They're no as fushionless as yous lot, powers help you! They'll come for the harvest, and kill the old and the useless, and enjoy the young women, and slaughter the beasts for the winter, and make a smouldering desolation, and in spring they will ride on and leave all a ruin behind them. They are no a biding folk, men who are fighters. So they will ride to the next village, and there they will do the same. And north and south other caterans will hear of their successes. I am older than all of you, and before the oldest of you here was born, aye, I heard stories of the olden times when the northmen were loose on the land, and there was no law, and Scotland was one wasted killing ground, and the folk

lived on the knees in fear and trembling with a halter on
their necks; and what I would say is this," her voice rang
out. "That whatever the danger is, it is better for us to die
on our feet than live on our knees with our faces to the
clart, and it is better for women to take weapons and fight
with them than become the baubles and playthings of they
brutal men, and bring bairns into the world only to see
them grown up shamed and fearful and hating their own
mothers for the horror of it all. I have seen these things
happen, and I never want to see them more."

And Finella sat down and wrapped herself in her shawls.
There was a silence in the room.
The fire crackled and fell in.

*Lally, lally,*

crooned Siubhan in the gloaming of the
peat smoke,

*sleep my baby,*

she sang.

For little Eoin, should they fight?
Siubhan wanted no more fighting. But she also wanted
for Eoin, if not perfect Freedom (of which she had no
sense), then at least as much freedom as any child can
have east of the sun and west of the moon in this world of
ours. Sorcha wanted it for her unborn; Una for her two
daughters. Sine thought of her brood. Were they to be
bandit fodder? The thought made her indignant.

The men for their part were shamed by the old woman's
outburst. They sat there with the dying firelight flickering
on their cheeks, Tomas and Manus, Fearchar and Wat.
Rob looked at them with a worried, dithering expression.

"If we are to fight, then who would teach us?" asked
Mungo of the fire.

"We could look for a soldier to do it," said young
Fearchar eagerly.

"There are no wandering soldiers," said Wat. "Soldiers

are all in employ. Forbye, swine dinna have wings that I've heard of."

"We could aye look for a warrior in the forest," Fearchar hazarded.

The men looked at each other and said nothing.

Wat gave a snort. "The days of the heroes are over," he said.

## 5

## Forty-Six Scythes

When they buried their men in the yard behind the little kirk, the noontide sun was bathing the whole warm glen and the clouds were high and white. There was no sign of the wolfriders: war and banditry seemed so far away. Mungo recited the service of the dead. The newly washed bodies were lowered into the earth, soldier and villager together. The bandits had stripped them of their weapons. The Shirra was laid in last of them. There was no head on his body. Mungo made a small cross of twigs and placed it where the head should have been. The Shirra lay on his back, his feet pointing to the stockade. The whole village was assembled. Wat and Rob held young Fergus, weak and ghost-white as he was, between them. Mungo made the sign of the cross over each grave and sprinkled it with water. Then he and Tomas and Fearchar shovelled the earth over them.

Then the women stopped their keening and wiped their faces and went away, for there was work to be done, and the seasons do not wait on human grief anyway.

*Surrexit Dominus de sepulchro.*

As winter had turned to spring, so spring turned towards summer, and across the lie of the yellowing land the hares ran silently as shadows. Now the flowering white birch was scattering its seed on the ground, and the summer willow was a pasture thick with bees; now the alder turned its sticky leaves to the dry sun, and young stags foraged the sweet grass of the hill; now daylong was the twittering of swallows sweeping back from dark countries and the place of strange moons; now from the short approaching night came the hum of cockchafers flying through the warm dusk.

And from forest wall to green forest wall, the glen was all one shining carpet of summer. The burn sang and tumbled down from treeclad slopes, down through the sunlight and starlight on the meadows, and morning dew lay thick on its fringe of green watercress, and the high reeds turned softly in the gentle afternoon breeze and bent their heads over the clean, clear gravel bed below. Round the small pools at the water's edge tiny yellow and white star-shaped flowers were growing, and whirligig beetles spun like drops of quicksilver on the shimmering surface.

Alone of the village folk, Mungo felt some of this, because he was not a peasant as they were, and harvested no land beyond his garden by the burnside. And sometimes when he had finished there, and had no other business to attend to, it being evening and the vespers bell rung, he would wander away down to the loch in the lap of the blue mountains into which the burn flowed with all its music, and sit on a flat rock that was there, and watch the moonglade—the flowing silver track across the still surface of the waters—and think of the land he had come from in the distant years, and wonder how long it would be before the angels took him across the fiery clouds to his home.

*Fraank*—comes the cry of the heron.

*Fraank*. The bird waded out knee-deep into the water and stood there, motionless. After a while a kingfisher answered, *tiet-tiet-tiet*, and darted, a brilliant blue arrow in the last of the long light, towards the darker shore.

The ploughing had been done. Men now dead had carved furrows across the land. They had cut and stacked the sodden peats, and opened the draining ditches to the spring rains. On their own fields they had used the caschrom, the scyth-like hand plough that needed a strong arm and powerful shoulders, but that answered well on ground strewn with boulders because its short blade was subtle and could turn the turf all around the boulder's edge without breaking. On the Shirra's great field, the best field from which the boulders had been removed by the sweat and blood of their grandfathers, they had used the big ox-drawn plough that was kept treasured mightily in corbie tower. The field was the tower's, and fed the men of it and all their fine horses that were gone.

The women looked on the fields. It was fine, midsummer nearly it was, July treading on the shadow of June. The Shirra had taken their men between the ploughing and the haymaking, and the grass was now ready to be cut that would feed the beasts and warm the rough beds of winter. They looked on the grasslands that lay outside the stockade and beyond the ploughed fields, stretching round both sides of the village and right across the glen, up to the forest's edge. O, fields of it, seas of it, it seemed, moving as now in the quiet breeze that morning brought down on them from the mountain slopes. The wee girl who had helped Mungo in

53

the kirk came walking hand-in-hand with blind Manus. They went to the edge of the first field where it was marked with stones, and Manus sat down heavily on a drum-shaped section of log that stood there, and brought out a pipe. He tested it, blowing notes long and high and soft and low.

In those days, reader, a village like this was numbered in its scythes. It did not have such-and-such a number of people, nor some other number of households; it had so many working scythes, and that number was fixed immovably in the minds of the Thanes, and on the parchment scrolls of their clerks. The village of the glen had sixty-three scythes when all the men (save Manus) and the younger women worked them. Now forty-five scythes were at the edge of the field. Every woman of the village was there—and Fearchar and Tomas and Rob the Gowk. Wat was in the forest, scenting like a hunting dog. Although he did not normally take part in the mowing, Mungo hitched his cassock up around his knees and took a scythe in his hand. Forty-six scythes. Some of the women nudged each other, pointed at his spindly old shanks, and giggled.

Manus shook the water from his pipe and said something to the girl. She stood with her legs apart and her little fists resting on her hips. Mungo could not see properly, but he knew she was standing there looking at the furthest-away grass, breathing deeply, her flat boy's chest heaving with the effort. He smiled at her simply. The folk formed a line across the edge of the first field. At the end of the line a big young woman called Malai was to begin. She was standing waiting, the scythe pole lying across her full bosom, her right hand on the small projecting handle. The wee girl's voice started up in a high squeak, and Manus's pipe soared up to meet it:

*Willie, Willie, what makes you so sad?*

54

*And the sun shines over the valleys and all—*
*I lie sorely sick for the love of a maid,*
*Among the blue flowers and the yellow and all.*

And other voices joined in the last line, and as they did so, Malai swung her scythe right to left and the first row of silky grass fell with a rustle to the earth.

*O Willie, my son, I'll learn you a wile,*

piped the singer,

*And the sun shines over the valleys and all—*

answered Malai, in a hoarse voice, and the second row fell.

*How this pretty fair maid you may beguile,*
*Among the blue flowers and the yellow and all.*

The third row fell.

*You maun lie down just as you were dead,*

Sine, who was second in the line, joined in behind Malai, and to her left.

*And the sun shines over the valleys and all—*

A second scythe carved down the green.

*And take your winding sheet around your head,*

Sine drew back her scythe.

*Among the blue flowers and the yellow and all.*

And Sine cut again.

One by one, all the mowers joined, working in a diagonal so that they would not cut each other's legs. Mungo stood next to Siubhan who had her baby strapped on her back. Other weans lay outside the field wrapped in plaid. Several older children with sickles followed their mothers and cut down anything they missed. Two devoted little pests dogged Mungo's heels.

"How's the Father doing?" said Dot.

"Och, no *too* bad," said Carry-one.

"No *too* bad?" said Dot.

"Och, he's doing his best," said Carry-one.

"Doing his best?" said Dot. "We'd have our arses skelped for a best like yon!"

"Aye, it's no good," said Carry-one.

"No good?" said Dot. "It's bloody diabolical!"

"Peadair! Ringean!" shouted an outraged mother. "Will yous stop your damn blaspheming!"

"Och, Ma," said Dot, "he's making a right hash of it!"

There was muffled laughter along the line of women.

"Master Peadair," said Mungo with dignity, "when I baptised you these five years syne, if I'd kent what a thrawn wee bugger you'd turn out to be, I'd have dropped you in the basin. Show me what's wrong then."

"You're holding it too high up, Father," said Siubhan quietly.

"Hold it further out," said Peadair, "like that." The handle of the scythe was as high as the top of his head. He wrapped both arms round it and brought it down to his chin. "Like that," he said.

Mungo bowed. "Thank you, master Peadair; and if I have any more difficulty, I will no hesitate to ask you."

"Aye, any time, Father," said Peadair cheerfully.

"You see," he said to Ringean, "he's new to it, but give him time and he'll learn."

*Among the blue flowers and the yellow and all.*

By now all the scythes were working, and step by step in time with one another the forty-six mowers moved across the field, their blades sweeping right to left, and right to left, the experienced cutters swaying the whole of their upper bodies in time to their strokes. Mungo, who had begun badly by taking all the weight on his arms, began to do likewise, and then true enough he found the going easier, but still his shoulders ached, and at the base of his neck a hellish fire was growing that seemed fit to boil the bones out of his body. He stopped singing the daft song about how young Willie won his true love's affections by pretending to be dead, and began muttering his rosary through what teeth he had left, gey few and yellow and clenched to breaking point. His whole body felt wet under his cassock; the sweat was soaking his back, and running in rivulets, damn nearly, down his grimy thighs. "Lord have mercy," he said to himself, and keeked secretly at Siubhan. She was working easily, happily, swinging the scythe with precise movements, never losing her grip on it. Her arms were bare, white above the elbow, brown below; her hands were broad and hard and red.

> It's when she came to her true lover's bed,
> And the sun shines over the valleys and all—
> She lifted the sheet to look at the dead,

she sang. Beads of sweat stood on her bright, rosy face. Young Eoin, strapped to her back, was awake and gurgling at the sky. "My God, can she have forgotten her man already?" thought Mungo. They came at last to the end of the first row.

Mungo rested the scythe blade on the ground and leaned on its pole. Having stopped, he felt dizzy, then he straightened himself and the dizziness passed. He looked back across where they had come. A great swathe of cut grass, darker-seeming than the rest, ran the length of the field. He grinned at it. Aye then! We'll do it yet, he thought. Every fifth mower in the row had a whetstone. Una took his scythe and sharpened it, holding the blade over her knees. The last of the forty-six came to the end of the field. Manus tapped the water out of his pipe again, and he and the wee girl came across the grass to them.

57

"What will I sing now, Father?" she called, running ahead of the blind man.

"What will it be?" asked Mungo of the women, knowing no psalm would be to their taste at all. They decided on it—another song of love and witchery. Manus raised his pipe once more.

> *The lady sits in her door sewing,*
> *Aye as the gowans grow gay—*
> *She heard an elf-man his horn blowing,*
> *The first morning in May.*

And at the other end of the line a woman called Ealasaid swung her scythe. They mowed the second row deliberately and evenly as the little singer swayed behind them and clapped her hands.

"O God my help in ages past," grunted Mungo under his breath, his old body straining to the scythe.

> *Aye as the gowans grow gay!*

they sang.

"Help me reach the end at last"—these were not the words of the song

> *The first morning in May!*

They came to the end, and whetted the blades again. In the middle of the third row wee Eoin begain crying. Siubhan put down her scythe and knelt on the cut grass. "Go on, I'll catch you up," she said to Mungo, and to her sister, gentle Sorcha, who was on the other side. She opened her blouse. Her breast was very white, and the sun shone sparkling down on her as she fed Eoin and pinched his cheeks. God bless you both, said Mungo silently. She cut half a dozen quick easy strokes and regained her place beside him. She and her sister both smiled. The mowers cut a fourth row, and sat down to eat.

Women talked together. They said that the cutting

was going well, for all that there were hardly any men among them. Tomas and Manus were sitting together, legs out, two old heads nodding in the sun. Rob the Gowk was playing with some of the bairns. They were chasing him. The Gowk went leaping through the air with his great gangling shanks flying in all directions. He stood on the grass hopping from one thin leg to the other. "Fraank," he cried, heron-like. Some of the women laughed. Fearchar stood and looked at the forest, dangling the scythe blade in his hands.

The milk was warm from the udder. They dipped their bannocks in it.

When they began again, Mungo found himself beside old Finella. She was swinging her scythe as heftily as any of the younger women and humming tonelessly.

"Will we be finished here the day, do you think?" he asked.

Finella sniffed. "We should—aye," she said. "Men or no men. Maybe no quite so quick, no. Forty-six scythes are no sixty-three, no matter what you say about it. O, yon sweet sun!" she said, looking up and wrinkling her face at the sky. "There will be rain the night, though."

And the folk were singing across the field, and the women's voices were mellow red and orange and brown in the evening grass, and the girls' were blue and green, and the bairns' silver or sometimes grey, and Peadair and Ringean slept in a heap like puppies on a pile of shawls and twitched flies away from their noses with wee sleeping fists; and none of them thought about what they all knew, even the youngest—that none might ever see the fruits of this haymaking, that the coming harvest might be the last, for fire and destruction might fall on them any day out of a clear sky, and they and their work would be no more.

# 6

## The Telling

They had been in the fields since sunrise, and long before nightfall there was not a one, neither man nor woman nor child, who was not ready for sleep. Even blind Manus had a throat dry as autumn leaves, and his shoulders ached from the piping. Two good hours before dark, and with the sun glowing on the mountains behind them, they wiped and whetted their blades for the last time that day, and filed back within the gate, and lowered the beam across it. Mungo went a while to his devotions. Fearchar walked the round of the stockade to ease his stiffness, and noted the staves that were broken or missing. The Gowk went to sleep under a cart.

The first field was done. And beautiful Seonaid, who alone of the women was not used to such work and had found the going hardest of all, turned at her bothy door, and stood looking back into the long green shadows briefly before lying down and falling immediately, hungrily, asleep.

"Nothing moves," said Wat, whom the trees had given out at last.

"Nothing?"

"Nothing that shouldna," said Wat, taking his supper from Sorcha's hands. "They have faded like the shadows, so they have."

Mungo rested his chin on his knees and clasped his hands over his ankles. Una and Sorcha and Siubhan sat by him in the smith's house. Black Finella had retired to the cat in her hut apart. In the smithy they were too tired to eat, too tired to sleep—all save Eoin. They raked a peat for light. The wean whimpered in his dreamworld back in the cot.

"Maybe they winna come after all," said Una, who had sat down between Sorcha and Wat so they couldn't touch each other in the darkness.

"Hm," said the old priest. "And was there no sign at all, Wat?" he asked.

"Whiles a hoofprint," said the woodcutter, "that has been there for weeks maybe."

"Then they've ridden on and left us!" said Sorcha, stealing glances at Wat round her mother's body.

"Na," said Wat, his mouth full.

"Did you go to the Crag?" asked Mungo.

"Empty—nothing. No *faol*. Nothing but the wind," said Wat. "And the feeling," he added thoughtfully, "of eyes on me—but no of canny eyes."

There was a tapping in the night. Restless Fearchar had hit on a way to stop his sow lifting the pigsty door out of its bracket. He was nailing a scythe blade across the bottom of the door. In the smithy the folk talked for a while about the second field tomorrow, and how it would be harder, part of it being on a slope.

"I've felt the eyes too," said Una suddenly. "There are things that are no canny in yon place."

"What did you see, Ma?" asked Sorcha, whose appetite for such things was immense.

"It's no just the seeing," said Una. "It's the feeling in the place, even when nothing unco can be seen. I wouldna go in there at night, no willingly nor gladly either, no since yon time when I was a lassie, no yet married to your father (God rest him!), and no thinking of him more than any other."

"And what happened then, Ma?" asked Sorcha. The others listened.

"Well..." said Una.

"Well," she said, drawing her knees up, "you'll mind yon old kiln that stood ahint corbie tower before they dinged it down? Well, in my young day we lassies used to go there one by one at midnight when the new harvest moon was out, to find the name of our coming lovers. Aye! (She grinned over the one flame of the peat.) We would climb down inside the kiln-logie (the pit, you ken), which is a dark and dreich enough place at any time, but at midnight with the sickle moon glinting on the trees and the howlat hooting from them—brrrr! Well anyways, come my time that night, and all the folk were abed but me and two other lassies who were waiting by the gate and out of hearing, I climbed into the kiln, and sat atop the logie-wall, and looked right down to the narrowest place at the bottom of it where everything was dark; and I sat there in the stour and shivered and listened. My heart was in my mouth, I can tell you! I said a bit prayer. 'Blessed Virgin,' (I said) 'look after me and tell me who my man will be.' And then I took out the reel of blue yarn—which we needed for the purpose, you ken—and dropped the end of it down the logie, and then I said the words."

"What words, Ma?"—Sorcha, breathlessly.

"*Co e sud th'air ceann mo ropain,*" said Una. "'Who is

there at the end of my thread?"—that's what we had to say, while holding the other end of the line in our hands. Well, I asked the question of the darkness, and I sat there over the logie, near to falling in I was, and my ears up and flapping for an answer, for there was no a single sound from all the world in yon place. And then I heard a something—a scratching it was, like it was a rat maybe, only this was no rat—I canna say what it was—but this was no rat at all! Then I thought, 'It's no a scratching I'm hearing; it's more a tapping!'"

Young Sorcha slipped her hand into her sister's and edged closer to her.

"Tap-tapping," said Una, "like Fearchar's the now, only no a canny tapping. And I listened wondering what the tapping could mean."

"Most like some lads in the logie taking a scare out of you," said Wat.

Una nodded. "I thought so mysel at first," she said, "but then I listened a bit harder, and, no, there was something unco in that tapping, something that no man was making, and I sat there a while longer praying all I could, and chittering till my teeth were biting my tongue very nearly, and then I made to haul the thread up and couldna, there was something holding on the end of it—so I gave another great big pull at it, and then I heard this voice from down below laughing at me... So I dropped the yarn and ran and didna stop till I reached the gate, and there were the other two lassies standing waiting on me and giggling away. And one of them said, 'O aye, and who was that bonny-looking lad you were with then, Una?' And I said, 'There was no one.' And they giggled some more and said, 'Aye there was but; you can tell us.' And I said, 'But there was no one.' And they said, 'We saw him with our eyes. A great tall handsome man walked in behind you in the moonlight, and he was all in green.' ... Now what do you make of that?"

63

"O! And why was he tapping?" cried Sorcha.

"Dinna ken. Maybe he was trying to close the door on me and keep me there," said Una.

They all fell silent.

"And there is more than that," said Una. "There was something I saw. Years later. It was the winter before your father's death. I *saw* that."

Her daughters, Siubhan and Sorcha, froze motionless on a little gasp. Wat sat listening intently.

"Samhain-eve," said Una, "and freezing cold it was too. Other years I had gone there and seen nothing. It often happens like that. The Deil lulls you to rest—ken? Year after year you see nothing, and then you dinna come any more. But *they* come, the spirit folk. Aye, they do. Well, it was Samhain—yous two were sleeping—there wasna a fire showing anywhere, and I came round the back of the kirk, Father—round the back in the darkness and the starlight, and there was snow on the ground as I mind, and I stood there with my back to the kirk wall, hearing all the wee rustlings and cracklings of the night, and telling mysel, 'Yon's a howlat, woman, no a bogle; yon's the wind, no a banshee's wailing!' And the burn was crying past me and the forest soughing... Och! I was nearly feared to death, so I was, before an hour was up. Well... it would be past midnight, I think, and the noises had all slid away into silence. And then I saw them."

Siubhan swallowed audibly. Sorcha sat staring with enormous eyes. The sisters were holding each other as close as ever they could.

"You dinna mean—?" exclaimed Wat from his side of the fire. Mungo rubbed his hands over the peat.

"Aye, just that," said Una, nodding her grim satisfaction. "That's just the thing I saw, Wattie! There in the kirkyard coming down from the fields and over the burn without touching the water, they came, and bone white they were, and their eyes glaikit and gawping, some of them

64

thin and wasted, and some that torn and gashed with great hanging wounds in them. They were the folk of the village who were to die the coming year, and I kent and recognized them all. There was an old grandfather that folk had been expecting to die for ten years past—he was that wasted, fair like a skeleton he was already; but there was also young Eachunn who was fine and full of health, and I saw him so bloody because a bear tore him one day in the wood; and also Maldonuich, who broke his leg at the ploughing, and the blood in him poisoned and he died of it; and then Neilli, who had been with me that very day at the butter churn, and Neilli's wame was all red and dripping, for she died of the bairn in her; they all went past me into the kirk. And then himsel, my Deorsa, your father—God rest him!—he came too, limping and twisted as though his bones had all been broken. 'O Deorsa, my eyes,' I said, 'what has happened to you, my life?'"

"You spoke with it?" said Mungo severely. "Save us, woman! that was a terrible risk."

"Aye, I spoke to his wraith—himsel being home in bed—and it looked at me then and said, 'A fatal calf this is for me.' That was what it said, and that was all it said, and it passed into the kirk. I couldna understand what the thing meant. I ran home and woke Deorsa (for he was sleeping in bed right enough) and told him what I had seen—but no what I had heard—and at first he laughed, and then he scowled and had it that someone was playing jokes, but we went back together and looked at the snow, and no a footprint was on it. Well," Una sighed, looking into the peat, "he made out I was daft—you were no long born, Sorcha hen, and women have strange notions at such times—but I warned him against calves and having anything to do with calves, and he laughed at the idea that a calf could cause a man's death. Yet one did," said Una, "that same summer when they were driving the kye down, a calf bolted and ran away into the forest, and did my man no chase after it, though it was no business of his whether it ran or not? And Torcall, that is dead now, followed him hard on his heels, and he heard a scream from the trees, and he came to the clearing at the Crag there, and there was my Deorsa with a wolf at his throat, and he cried out to Torcall as he fell under the beast the very words I had heard by the kirkdoor."

Wat rubbed his throat unhappily. "O yon's a terrible business," he said. "And that was how it came about, was it? I mind seeing him when they brought him back, with his thrapple all ripped out. Och, terrible it was."

"Aye—and those the very words," Una continued, "the very same words. And yet he wouldna believe me when I told him. He wouldna do anything to avoid it."

"Nothing to do," said Mungo. "Death just comes, that's all. There is no avoiding it."

"But to *see* it like that," murmured Sorcha.

"I'm minded of the man in the land of Israel once," said the priest, "who thought he could avoid his end, and couldna, because he had the same sort of warning, and it was Death himsel that he saw. He was the servant of a master, and one day his master sent him down to the town of Jerusalem for to buy something—a sack of oats, or something like that—and there was a fair in Jerusalem that day, and a rammy of strange folk all milling about, and as he was walking along in the midst of them, who did the servant man see but Death his black sel stalking towards him, and Death saw him there and looked at him!"

"O dear Lord!" said Una.

"And the man turned round and ran like the clappers," said Mungo, "and didna stop till he reached his master again, and said, 'Master, master, I'm in an awful pickle! I've just seen Death walking the town, and Death recognized me! I'm sure He's come for me! Give me your horse so I can ride and be in Bethel the morn!' And the master

66

gave him his horse, and off the servant man rode. Now the master must have been a right brave childe, and he didna take kindly at all to Death walking round scaring folk, so he went down to the town of Jerusalem and there, sure enough, he saw Death in the crowd; so he went up to Death and seized him by the shoulder. 'Hey, you!' says the master. 'Wha, me?' says Death. 'Aye, you,' says the master. 'What's the big idea of scaring my servant witless? Out with it, man!' he says. And Death looked at him there and said, 'I'm sorry for scaring him, indeed. I didna mean to do it. It's just that I was surprised to see him here. You see, I have an appointment to meet him in Bethel the morn.' So you see, there is no running from it," said Mungo morosely. "None at all."

Mungo's voice ended, and there was a cold and awful stillness. Suddenly from outside came a sound, one of those sudden, inexplicable noises of the forest night. They all started.

"Dear Lord and all the Saints preserve us," whispered Sorcha, crossing herself hastily.

"Ach," said Siubhan then, "what unco tales you've both been telling us! It's no just bad in the spirit folk, but good as well."

"True," said Mungo, "but a mortal maun be careful of them all the same."

"Well," said Siubhan, "there was the *glaistig* in the dairy that Finella met. Mind? It was when she was churning the butter for the Shirra. She took a lick of it, and, my! (she said) it tasted fine! So she took a lick more, and did it no taste better? Och, he will never notice, thought Finella, so in the end she took nearly a quarter of the butter home with her, and ate most of it, and gave the lave to her cat (a different cat it was then —yon grey beast that she used to have). Well, the next day she decided she would take no more, but she was standing there by the churn, turning it and turning it, and the cream looked rich and thick as it had never looked before, and outside the clouds were squalling and the rain was spitting, and the cream was glowing in the churn, so she dipped the end of one finger in it and licked, and then dipped and licked again, and by night she had eaten a third of it nearly, and took away some in a bowl for the cat. Well, the next day she was feeling that warm inside and rich with stuff that she was saying, 'Ach away—they'll never notice!' and dipping her spoon in it quite the thing, when what should happen but the Shirra's steward (him that's dead now) should come through the door and say that the Thane's taxmen would be here the morn's morn and there is six stone of best butter needed to go with them to Thanehall in payment. And so Finella weighed the butter that she had churned, and there was one stone there and five missing, and what hope had she to churn five stone of butter by the morn? So she just sat down and grat and grat."

"You're never meaning to tell us that she ate five stone of butter?" said Wat.

"That's what she said."

"Away! I dinna believe it," said Wat.

"Well, that's what she said," Siubhan repeated.

"She was aye fond of it," said Una, "and there was the cat too, mind."

"Aye, there was the cat too. *Anyway*," said Siubhan, "she was just sitting there like I was saying, greeting and greeting—for how could any body produce five stone of butter overnight?—when all of a sudden, like, she hears this wee voice beside her. 'What are you greeting for, Finella?' the voice says. And Finella turns round and there sitting in a corner of the bothy is the semblance of a woman with a green shawl about her shoulders, and young she is, and bonny, but she hadna come through the door, nor had she ever been seen anywhere before. So Finella kent she was a *glaistig*. 'I'm greeting,' says

Finella then, 'because the Shirra is wanting six stone of best butter the morn, and there is only one ready for him.' 'Is that so?' said the *glaistig*, and began turning the butter churn.

"And she turned and she turned, and by cockcrow the Shirra's butter was there, all complete.

"Well, they loaded it onto the cuddies and sent it down the strath to Thanehall; but they were hardly out of the glen when four men came on them from the forest and killed the guards and took the load away with them to their own bothy somewheres deep in the trees. They kindled a fire and took their supper, and afterwards they sat round the hearth, spending the price they would get for the butter when they sold it. And they cracked about this, and they cracked about that; whiles one of them up and said, 'Aye lads! All we need now is four lassies to keep us warm, and we'd be happy as the king himsel!' And three of them laughed, thinking it a right fine wish to make, but the fourth was canny and said, 'Goodness be between me and that wish.'

"It was night then, and the fire dying, and the three men who had wished the wish went to sleep in a corner of the bothy, but the fourth, the canny one, sat where he was by the flame. Then shortly four lassies came in, and three of them went into the corner and lay down beside the three men who had wished, and the fourth came and stood before the man who was sitting at the fire. Now when the man saw this, he felt in his stomach that there was something unco about, so he drew his dirk and began whittling a piece of wood with it, and whenever she tried to come near him, he turned the dirk towards her and forced her to back away. She tried this and she tried that. Whiles she asked him for a piece of the butter, so he cut it and held it out on the point of his dirk, and told her to eat it from that if she wished. So she knelt in front of him and opened her mouth and asked him to feed her with it, like it were a spoon. But he kent fine that she merely wanted to grab hold of his dirk-hand, so he was careful. As soon as he saw her stretching for his arm, he turned the point on her and gave her a poke with it in the face to see if it would draw blood. And the lassie gave a yelp and jumped back, and stood there on the other side of the fire glowering at him.

"So they spent the rest of the night, until the cock crowed on the hill above. 'The white cock is calling us,' said the woman. 'You were lucky tonight, robber, but dinna think to be so lucky for ever.' That was all she said, and she louped for the door, and her three sisters went out behind her. The man waited till the sun was up, and then went over to his three friends in the corner—and what did he find but them cold and dead with their throats cut and every last drop of blood sucked out of their veins! The man kent then and for sure that the lassies were *glaistigs* so he took the cuddies loaded with butter down to Thanehall himsel and said that he had found them wandering on the way, and before another night fell he said confession to a priest, and went to become a monk at some cloister in the south—where this story comes from," said Siubhan, "through a travelling man who told it to Finella. So you see how the spirit folk can be good when they want to be, and protect the poor like us who need them."

No sooner had Siubhan finished than a high wailing sound came out of the forest, and some of the village dogs began barking. Wat got up and went outside. Sorcha, whose arm had never left her sister's all the while, hid her head in the folds of Siubhan's shawl.

"A wolf maybe," said Wat, coming back. "Unless it was Finella changed shape," he added.

"I've often thought," said Siubhan, "that the *glaistig* was maybe her cat."

"Like enough," Una nodded. "There's those with the power to change shapes: everyone kens that."

70

"And they say she was a fox once," Siubhan went on, "that a hunter chased and took her a clout on the leg with a stone, and the beast ran straight into her bothy, and when he came to the door and looked in, there was Finella with blood on her leg, and the cat glaring at him, all teeth."

"That's truth," said Wat. "I ken that for a fact."

They were all silent. Mungo poked at the fire with a twig.

"Perhaps the *glaistigs* will help us when the wolfriders come," whispered Sorcha out of her sister's shawl.

"Perhaps," said Mungo.

He was thinking, an idea that was strange and fearsome.

"Shapes and shapes," Wat was saying. "But there are *trees* that turn into men and walk, as I should ken who live among them."

"The *uruisg*," said Una.

"Aye, and I can tell you something about that," said Wat from beyond the fire, his tired face ghoul-like in the flame shadow.

They all looked at him.

"It was on a warm summer evening, as I mind," he said, "and there was a good drizzle hanging on the trees, when I went down the lochside to fish my supper from the waters of it. A couple of trout, I thought—a couple will do me nicely. Three, and I will eat like the Shirra himsel! So I sat with my heels on the rocks and my bum on a heather clump and cast out the tackle. Holy Mary! no sooner had the hook touched the water than a fish took it! I cast again, and again the same. Soon I was hauling in the trout so thickly I hadna time to hang them on a string, merely tossed them on the sweet grass and cast again, praising the Lord for rewarding me so. So anxious was I to let none of the goodness pass me that the night was fairly down before I noticed it, and the starlight was glinting on the water, right fine it looked, and I was sitting gazing at it so, when—splat!—another fish landed on the grass beside me, and who should I see there fishing at my side but a great *uruisg*, matching me trout for trout and throwing them down beside my own catch on the grass.

"I saw him with those eyes," said Wat. "Half man, half beast he was, with hair like the reeds, and teeth, and claws. There was no help for it at all, no use saying anything, for I kent well enough why he was there. We sat there side by side and kept on at the fishing, until the best part of the night was past.

"Then the *uruisg* cried, 'It's time to stop, Wattie man, time to stop and divide the fish.' 'No, no,' I says, 'it's no the time at all, no while they are taking so happily.' The *uruisg* said nothing more, but returned to his fishing. A good while later he cried again, 'Let's stop now, Wattie man, and divide the fish.' 'No, have patience,' I says, 'No just yet, no while they are taking so happily.' So the *uruisg* went back to the fishing again, but no willingly, for the day was fast approaching, and he had fishing of another sort to do before cockcrow. A wee while later he called on me a third time to stop, and I kent from his voice that I'd no win another delay. So I says to the creature, 'Will you gather the fish or divide them?' And he says to me, the *uruisg* does, 'I'll gather the fish, and you divide them, Wattie man.' So I says to him, 'Vexed I am to admit it, but I canna think how to divide them.' 'Ach,' says the *uruisg,* right scornful, 'it's easy enough, man! A trout for you, and a trout for me; a trout down, and a trout up; a trout here, and a trout there; and the last big trout for me.' Now I didna like this arrangement at all, for you see, I kent full well that yon last big trout the creature was reckoning on was none other than my own sweet sel, and that he wanted it before the day would come and he had to return back into the wood.

"So I had to keep the work unfinished until cockcrow,

and never did I long for that beast to crow so much! I went as slowly as I could, and saw to making a hash of the dividing. Whiles a fish would slip from my hands, whiles I'd lose the count and needs must start again; and all this time the *uruisg* stood there glowering at me; and when he saw the fish falling, he would stamp his feet and cry out, 'Winna you take care, you scunner? Winna you take care?' And when he saw that I had lost the count, he would shake me by the shoulders so that my teeth rattled and my bones were near to breaking under his claws. See," said Wat, pulling the shirt down from his shoulder, and there, true enough, were five blue welts on his white skin. "I was near to my mortal end," he said, after the others had all expressed their horror at his wounds, "but just then, just when the creature's patience with me had finally run out and he was raising a great fist to make an end of it, then did the red cock no wake just in time —O the bonny bird!—and crow on the knowe behind us, and straightaway the *uruisg* vanished out of sight."

"And did you ever go back again, Wattie?" asked Mungo, who had listened attentively to all this.

"Damn the fears," said Wat; "I'll never go night-fishing at yon lochside again!"

Mungo said nothing more, but resumed his poking at the fire.

"Surely, there's more things than us in the world," said Una. "That's the truth, and no mistake."

"And if you had jumped into the loch to swim away, Wattie, maybe the water-horse would have got you," Sorcha babbled in an unnaturally loud and trembling voice.

Siubhan wheeshed her gently.

"But everybody kens it," Sorcha protested. Yes, the stories she had heard had made her more and more excited, and now she wanted to tell her own tale too. Her eyes were bright and flickering as two candle flames.

"There was that lassie at Achantore," she said, "that

everybody kens of, her and what happened to her with the water-horse, and how she saw it, a great handsome beast grazing with the kye in the meadow, and on its back a saddle and bridle all glittering like the river—for silver it was, to be sure!—and she thought to hersel, this lassie, that this must be some great warhorse wandered off from some lord's stables, for it was the biggest blackest creature you ever did see, and what a fine thing it would be to ride on it, just the once; and she went across the field towards it, this lassie did, and the beast turned its muckle great head and looked at her, and—God!—the fire that was in his eyes! And she stood there so pished with dread she couldna move hand nor foot nor anything, and she couldna even think to cross hersel; syne the creature came towards her, the great beautiful beast, and the terror faded from his eye, until it was all a strange gentleness that she saw there, and he nuzzled himsel against her breast, and there was beauty on his head, and the look of his eyes was as a deer; and the lassie's fear vanished, and she stroked his shining head, and then one foot was in the stirrup—and she mounted," said Sorcha, "and the great horse whinnied to shake the very trees, and plunged like the lightning into the loch of the Spey, and she was heard of no more!"

"Phew!" said Wat. "It's bad enough sometimes to be on middle-earth hung between heaven and the fires of hell, without having to walk the shingle, lost between *uruisg* and water-horse. Why should such things be?"

"There's a lot of things abroad we hardly ken the beginnings of," said Mungo.

"They do say though," Una exclaimed, "that she *was* heard of again, yon lassie. They say that the place where the cuddie took her never froze, even when all the rest of the loch was thick solid ice and the very falls were frozen to the rock."

"They say that, do they?"

"Aye, they do. And they also say that folk could hear the lassie's voice in the winter when it was that cold and dreich, and the wind blew strong and the snow was drifting from the hilltops; they would hear her voice then from under the water crying, 'I am cold, O I am cold!' So the folk went and found an old wife who knew how to speak to ghosts, and she came and stood at the water's edge, and cried out, 'What ails you, lassie?' And the lassie told her that her soul wasna at rest, and wouldna be until seven masses were said for her. So the folk said the masses and her voice was heard no more on Speyside."

"And is she in heaven now, do you think?" asked Sorcha.

Mungo nodded. "Away from all her worries," he said, "in the place where everything is young and green and happy."

The women sighed.

"But is it true," asked Wat, "that some living folk get a glimpse of it—like the man who was taken by the *glaistig* folk inside their hill?"

"That is more than I would ken of," said Mungo. "They're orra folk, the People of Peace."

"Rob's mother was scared by a *glaistig* when she was carrying him in her wame," said Una. "A gowk he was born, and a gowk he's been ever since."

"Well, God above defend us from all such things," said Siubhan, and yawned.

Sorcha curled up against her sister's side with a corner of the shawl in her mouth and her eyes wide open.

"God defend us all," said Mungo.

They were silent.

Tales of a highland night...

Suddenly a gust of cold night air blew into the room. The peat fire glowed brightly for a moment, and then died down.

75

Two small eyes were regarding them from the door.

The wee girl stood there, ten years of her, her shift about her dirty knees.

She pummelled her nose. She looked at them with a shiny, sleepy face.

"I couldna sleep," she said.

"Wee yin!"—Mungo, tenderly.

"I was alone and that feared," she said.

"Is the mannie, Fergus, asleep?" the old priest asked, rising stiffly.

"He's having the horrors," she said. "Talking and screaming to himsel. I was feared."

Mungo put his fleshless arm about her. "No now?" he asked.

She nuzzled his shoulder. "No—no now," she said.

Her name was Mairi.

The old man and the little girl went kirkwards into the night together.

Inside the bothy the talk died away with the fire, and at length they slept, the four of them, Sorcha and Siubhan, Una and Wat. But Una kept between Wat and Sorcha, her daughter.

## 7

# *Mairi*

*Cockedoodledoo!*

Yes, and the many-coloured cock who had saved brown
Wat the woodsman from the bad and sparing *uruisg*, and
the canny furtive thief from the good and murdersome
*glaistig*, brings the sun up again obedient as ever to his
call, and the ghoulies flee for another good and Godly
summer day into netherworlds west of the treeline, and
the long-legged beasties crawl back out of nightmares and
into the creaking woodwork and ever-crumbling stone
walls, and the night grows slowly silent, as daybreak sails
back in glory all victorious to its green haven. Ah, the
frogs of the gloaming are hushed on the waterbank, the
steam of the kye rises over the warming fields, the
sounds of the forest fade into its secret inward places; and

"Back to your graves, you corpses!" cries the Evil One, as the breath of brief life vanishes from the dead and they crumble to dust and ashes once more before the first rays of dawn can touch them.

*Cockedoodledoo!*

So the heavenly rooster perched on the gable-end of the world will see each clump of heather glow like a burning bush on the faraway-stretching God-seeking land. And the fine horses of the sun come galloping: yellow they are, golden-yellow on the meadow (so the singers praise them) and purple on the mountains, and noble cloud-white too, and the colour of the all-blue ever-rushing sky; and their shining hoofs rustle and sink in the sea of long stirring grass; and so folk say, "The wind is galloping," and old ones say they have seen him, the naked boy who rides the wind's back and calls to the horses in not-to-be-spoken-of magical names.

*Cockedoodledoo!*

And in the place where she slept, under the bench, behind the hawthorn screen, Mairi stirred in her close-eyed world. What are you dreaming of, Mairi?

—O here's me gliding swan-free and daft in a green-lathered land of all lovely wildfruit and warm things, and a horse came up to me and said where are you going then lassie this earth singing morning he said, and I said if you please sir I'm going home to my Ma and Pa who are king and queen they are in a palace of gold on the other side of the mountains where the moon goes, and he said have you ever been in the mountains of the moon then, and I said no sir but I would like to see where the moon goes when he wants to sleep, and that's the land of Nod Father said that's east of Eden, and the horse said climb up climb up he said and he lifted me up on his back and we galloped free...

"Free!" she cried to the flea-ridden straw bed, to the

smoke-darkened wood vaulting above, to the midsummer dew-damp earthy floor.

...through the swaying forest, through the moon-burning night and the sun-cold day until we came to the land of the red rooster strutting on the gable wall, and the rooster talked to me and he said look lassie I'm God's chapman he said spreading out his feathers, and you can have your heart's desire of me, and I said please sir to stay up for the midnight fires and a gaberlunzie ribbon to tie up my hair with, that's all I want for now—

And she turned on the ribbon edge of sleep as the rooster strutting in neither dream nor heaven but within yards of her ten years old head cleared his throat to bell, clock and siren in the next haymaking day.

*Cockedoodledoo!*

And Mairi opened her eyes wide and looked at the ceiling, saw—a cloud keeking down the smoke-hole—jumped out of bed, rubbed the feech from her eyes, near swallowed her fist in a yawn, dipped two fingers in a clay pannikin of yesterday's burn water—cleanliness is next to Godliness—and wiped once, cautiously, over the eyes and behind each ear. Brrrr. She pulled the blouse over her head, grabbed hold the milking bucket and ran. Outside, the Gowk was stretching.

"Aye, Robbie!"

"Aye, Mairi!"

Nice lassie, thought the Gowk, one who never teased him, never, even when the others were throwing stones.

"Aye, there, Mairi!" cried Una at her door. Wat was long away. Mairi collected the bucket from the smithy door and ran with it too.

"Aye!" "Aye!" from Nessa and Malai, Seonaid and Sine, and a gaggle of Sine's bairns already at the tumble in the clart.

In the field waiting for her, Dapple the cow that once was the Shirra's, now owned by kirk and smithy both.

79

The Father's bucket first... Yawning, she grabbed at the udder, dirty-faced Mairi with a mouth like flowers and morning in her eyes; and there was fresh dew on the ground all around her, dark footprints on the bright meadow where Nessa sat nearby, wistfully holding the penis-like udder of a beast next in line and giving it little tender jerks. Una's bucket now... Seonaid was humming boldly, Nessa snivelling again, daft bitch. And the whole sleeping village awake now as she clattered back up the one street. Old Tomas out early, grumpy as usual. At the smithy, Una's bucket—no a drop spilled (how's that!)—then homeward like the hammers of hell. And the village awaiting destruction was breakfasting on porridge and bannock and thinking of the day's work ahead, and—och will it no soon be night again?—and—sweet Jesus my back's killing me!—and—slap some docken on it, there's nothing like the docken leaf for a screaming back—and Tomas swearing blue fire at the red rooster: I'll run you into the pot, my lad!—and the dull clunk of iron as the first scythe was dragged out and shouldered for the morning field.

"Father," cried Mairi by the hawthorn screen door, breakfast at the ready. And cried to silence.

"Father!"

She scratched at the wood.

"FA-THUR!"

No answer. Opened it. Looked. Nothing. The priest's room was empty. Uncrumpled straw on the pallet. Untouched new candle that she put yesterday on his table. She glanced at the wall crucifix, the wooden dangling painted Jesus, the shell basin with its holy water. Nothing broke the silence of that room.

Mairi backed out slowly and let the screen close behind her, an expression of puzzlement on her small face. Recollect: last night he had come home with her—yes; he had gone to tend Fergus in the kirk. To the kirk, a door away—but only Fergus was there, asleep in his place on the floor by the altar in the sweet rotten smell of his own wounds. Well! Mairi laid the food on the altar, mumbled her thanks to heaven, tended to the man on the earth. Fergus, have you seen the Father? (Between sips, mopping his dribbles.) Fergus whimpered slightly and shook his head. No, not this daylight. Where is he then?

She sought him. At that forenoon's cutting her song was inattentive. When they stopped to eat, she searched for him all through the village and up and down the glen to the very shadow of the forest, speiring at everyone she met, fearing that in some sudden feebleness of age a cunning stroke or fall had maybe toppled him all unawares into a hidden place where he now lay helpless, out of sight and out of hearing perhaps, waiting plaintive on her coming. She searched, but when against expectation she did not find him, she returned dejected. The women cheered her with words, said the Father had probably gone, priestlike, to some secluded spot in the forest to pray for their salvation, said he would return with Wat in the evening like as not; but they too frowned at the line of trees, and, when they thought she was not looking, they glanced at each other and shook their heads.

Why had he gone without a word? Why?

Blind Manus took up his pipe once more. Sine gave the first stroke, and forty-two women and Tomas and Fearchar followed in the wake of her. Mairi was not excused her part of the work—which was her singing over the swishing scythes—nor did she seek to be. In the hay must come if the beasts were to survive the winter, and no one, neither woman nor man, even be he God's own priest, was more important than that. For survive they would. The women had determined it. They were going to hide the beasts deep in the forest under bairns' guard; then, though they themselves would doubtless be raped, and the bothy roofs burned, and the younger ones maybe abducted and the elders killed, something would yet remain for those who came back. Their reason and their few men told them there would be no survivors. The ache in their bellies said there would.

And so they cut the long grass to the little girl's trembling song. Then, when the last scythe stayed its motion and the women turned to look over that second day's field, she ran. She did not wait for Wat's return from the hunting with a dozen hares swaying in his belt and a hind high over his shoulders, or see him shake his brown head, or hear the "no" his mouth gave shape to. She was already searching in every ditch and cutting, in every fold of the howe, beneath every growth of bracken, behind every whinrig bush, and her voice and those of the other bairns, of Peadair and Ringean, Sesi and Bride, Sim and Anna and Lucais and Ceit, sounded over the land like the cries of the wandering birds.

Where was he?

She returned alone in the gloaming to the kirk where a frail wee boy called Ruadh, who was good for nothing else, had been left to watch Fergus that day long. Ruadh was a sleeping bundle behind the door. Mairi smacked him awake and sent him greeting home. Businesslike, she rubbed her hands and saw to Fergus's supper, then changed the dressings on his chest. The wounded man followed her with his timid eyes and mumbled his thanks to her and the Father and the Blessed Virgin On High for saving his tortured dying body. Seeing the weariness that was on him now the screaming had stopped, Mairi knew he was dying. O, she wished the Father was back! Then Fergus smiled at her weakly, and held up one feeble hand, and it stroked her hair once before it dropped numbly to the floor. Fergus closed his eyes and he was unconscious once more. Heaving mightily, Mairi pulled out the foul straw from under him and replaced it with clean. Then she bathed his face and looked at him—so young, so old to her. "Poor soul," she said.

While Fergus slept in a nightmare of glory, Mairi knelt and gabbled her prayers to the foot of her cot.

"Wirfather whart in heaven, Hallowed bethy name, Thykinduncome, Thywill be done, Onearth astis in heaven. Givussisday our daily bread, And forgive us our debts as we forgive our debtors, And, er, liver us from evil frever and frever, Amen."

She climbed in. There was still a grey smear of light in the sky above the smokehole. She lay awake and thought; and sometime or other she fell asleep, but could not remember when.

She had lived with the old man ever since he had found her.

And when was that?

Mairi could not have answered. Her memories of that time were fragments of colour flickering in the void. She had questioned the Father about it ever since. Ten years ago Mungo had stood at the threescore and ten year summit of his alloted span. Ten years ago Mairi was a whimpering thing wrapped in a shawl.

"Was I, Father?"

"Aye, so you were, wee yin."

Ten years ago the tough old man had hirpled infirmly with a stick, his back bent forward stooping, his thin face gleaming with holy malice. He hated the human race, he cursed it. He felt he had plenty of reason to, and perhaps he had. He loved the perfection that was Jesus, and loathed the imperfections with which he was surrounded. Folk came to him shuddering. He ministered to their ill bodies with gentle hands, but with harsh and searing words over them, and they preferred the tolerant cures of the witch-wife Finella. Even the soldiers of the tower treated him with respect and forbore their swearing in his presence. He loved animals and the green cloak of the world and walked alone in the wild with his stick and turned his scowl on anyone who dared come near him.

One warm summer evening those ten years syne, Mungo, having walked further than usual into the forest pursuing some particularly rare and healing moss, chose upon the whim of the moment to return home by a stranger path that led him through the echoing green shadows of the inner wood. And he walked there, where none seemingly had walked since creation day, for it was deep inside the virgin forest and even Wat, who went everywhere, seldom came as far as this. Now the old man waded through the rustling waves of bracken in the places where the sunlight reached, and through thick powder of years and years of fallen leaves and needles covering roots where the sun never penetrated, and he bent under the low-sweeping branches and the twigs that plucked his sparse grey hair, and the dust rose and made him sneeze. He could hear no sound but himself in the warm silence of the forest.

The old priest was on his guard, as always, for this was the pagan place and who knew what ghastly thing might lurk there, or where Hell might have one of its too many mouths. Left, right, like a stalking bird he glanced, with his heafty stick and his bag of mosses.

Listen.

There was a singing in the silence—yes—a singing of water, and he came out of a sudden from the green fold of bark and bracken and leaf-sky, to a glen, and above that glen the sky was a narrow blue river, islanded with evening cloud it was, and down through it ran the trickle of the mountain burn that sang and sang in its stones. Mungo stopped and rested on his stick and listened. Some late geese bugled overhead, paddle-footing northwards. He raised his feeble eyes to them. "I'm

84

seventy," he thought. "I've lived my alloted span of God's earth." Unlike the geese, he had no companions. Within his heart the loneliness of it screamed out like a gull on a wasted headland. And then he smiled to himself at his daftness, and looked again at the water, the dusty silver water under the dull blue heaven by the darkening wood, and he rejoiced in his very solitude, that he could think and feel these things uninterrupted by the cackle of humanity.

Listen!

It was a very wee burn, scarcely more than a bright thread of water stitching the ground amongst the heather roots, and Mungo knelt stiffly by its side, and pulling the brown sleeves up to his elbows, he let the cleanness of it scour his clarty moss-raking hands. Ah. The cold pebbles beneath were bonny to the touch, and, feeling them, the old man did a strange thing—he picked one up that shone like white crystal, and, shaking the years off him like so much water, did he not then up and throw it with all his force and a wee laddie's laugh into the nearest furze on the glenside, and sit on his heels smiling happily as it walloped in and vanished among a rippling of bracken stems?

Listen!

A cry came up—listen!—a cry came up out of the depths—listen!—it was the cry of a beast, the cry of a bird—listen!—it was... Mungo scrambled to his feet, fear, anger chasing each other through his eyes.

*Uruisg!*

There are many creatures in the world, and the red skin does not make the apple—*uruisg!*—the creature that was human but not human, that was manly but made out of the earth and trees, that was the angel of the forest but fallen often—*uruisg!*—the creature that as a Christian he disbelieved in, but that as a man he feared nevertheless in the stillness, in the darkness, in the sudden inhumanity of what he was surrounded with. *Uruisg!*--that was the strength and cruelty and killing power of the very fiend he fought...the creature now calling him?

"*Uruisg,* you spawn of Satan, come no near me!" threatened Mungo, raising and brandishing his stick at the moving stems a watersong away.

The cry gave way to a soft whimpering. Mungo lowered his stick. The violent fear left the old man's eyes. A voice from his past was calling to him, "Mungo," it was saying, womanly, "Mungo." He couldn't mind the voice, or whose it was, but it was there. It was a voice from a garden, strange and beautiful. Something touched the old man. He crossed the burn at a stride, it was narrow enough, and plucked the crier from the bank of undergrowth. It was a shawl, homely and rough, and in the midst a tiny puckered face was greeting. Widdershins went the old man's fear. The stout clubbing stick dropped unnoticed to the earth and lay there on a tangle of heather. Its dust may lie there under the purple to this day for all I know. A wean? he thought, a wean in the forest? In the place of his own belonging, mothers had cherished their children. Here—and though he preached against it, yet it was done—desperate parents were known to abandon unwanted mouths for the wild beasts to devour them. He glanced around for signs. The long light was closing over the trees. Somewhere a woodpecker was drumming, and the still air was mothy with wings; a single hoof had printed water on a flat rock nearby that dried and vanished even as he saw it; under the small overhang of reeds the water was one black gurgle.

A hunting fox circled past him; a churring nightjar flew over his head; a bat went flackering down the burnside, a water rat carved the ripples of a pool. The stars came out like village lights, one by one.

Slowly, slowly the night spread across the fallen sky; slowly the evening sun set over the shoulder of the distant mountain; slowly the fiery clouds swam into the dim sea of dusk and vanished there. Mungo looked at the wean. What do I ken about children? he thought, and grunted his disgust. One more mouth in the village to feed, he thought, as he rearranged the shawl about the little limbs. If anyone thinks I'm going to fash mysel with this brat, they're sore mistaken! he thought, hearing the soft breath, seeing the wee clenched fists. There's no reason in this world why I should bother with you! he thought with finality.

"So what will I call you then?" he said to the bundle as he tramped off down the glen with her in his arms.

And so it was that, like the saint of the old days, Mungo had struck at the stony heart of him, and the hard skin cracked and a well of pure, clear water bubbled out over the barren ground, and—Glory Be To God!—the old man fell from grace into humanity, and the angels sang for him upon the further shore.

In darkness he entered the village. The sentry atop corbie tower was pacing against the summer moon. A dog barked once in his sleep as Mungo walked, limpless, to the door of Finella, the one person who wouldn't laugh at him or think him queer, for neither the saints nor angels that worked miracles on the kirk's behalf had told him how a squalling bairn should be changed and fed. Yet a miracle this was, said Mungo, and called her by Our Lady's name, Mairi.

Together they watched her grow. Finella snorted at the knee-bending prayers the priest taught her; Mungo was piously outraged at the witch-woman's charms and curses. One day he went into Finella's bothy to find the old woman telling Mairi never to harm a spider, creepy though the beast was, for sister spider was the wonder-worker and luck-bringer.

> *If you wish to live and thrive*
> *let a spider run alive,*

she chanted.

"Havers," said Mungo "Everybody kens that it is because a spider wove his thread across the cave where the Holy Family was hiding in Egypt, and that saved them from they Egyptian heathens who searched no further, seeing the web intact."

"And if you drop a fork," said Finella to Mairi, "you will have a woman visit you; and if you drop a knife, you will have a man; and if you drop a spoon," she said, dropping her wooden porridge spoon at Mungo's feet, "your next visitor will be a dithering old gowk."

Mairi's silver laughter spun whole webs about them.

Another day Finella came into the kirk and found the old priest instructing Mairi in altar-lore. The cross where Christ had died was the promise of resurrection, he was saying, and the hope and glory of the future world; and that was why the cross protected, and even the thunder and the lightning could not harm the home where the cross was.

> *No common gallows was yon tree*
> *where Jesus won our victory,*

he hymned.

"Blethers," said Finella. "Everybody kens that it is because yon cross of your's is made of oak, and that the oak is the tree of the Hammer-man that makes the thunder in the mountains and sends it down on the folk when they scunner him."

"And if you take an acorn," said Mungo to Mairi, "and rub your ears with it, the wax will fall out; and if you take a hazel twig and throw it at a witch," he said, removing the twig he had been chewing from his teeth and tossing it at Finella, "the donnert old bitch will vanish—poof!"

Mairi choked.

So several years passed. Then, when Mairi had taken communion, and was combing her own hair, and had words in her mouth and a song in her soul, he told her a story one night as she lay in bed in the room in the kirk behind the hawthorn screen. Once upon a time, said Mungo...

"Was it in the Beginning?"

"Well," said the old man, thoughtfully rubbing his chin, "in the Beginning, if you think about it, there wasna really an awful lot of anything; but it must have been *near* the Beginning, because there were creatures in the forest the like of which there are none now—muckle great beasts there were with three heads that had four eyes apiece, and a great red tousle mop standing up on end with six pairs of golden horns keeking out of it that they cleaned and sharpened against the iron trunks of Nowhere Wood, which, as I telt you before, is the darkest and furthest and dreichest and drubliest part of Anywhere Forest."

"Ooohoo," said Mairi, and she drew her knees up, and though she knew it was just a story, yet she liked it, for she was in a warm bed and it was a cold night and Mungo was beside her, and it was grand.

"Aye," said Mungo, "and it was freezing and there were ici-*cic*-les hanging from every twig, and every wee leaf was frozen hard as a blade, and the very bears were wearing big hairy brogues to keep their toes from falling off. Now there was a wee lassie called Mairi," he said, poking the tip of Mairi's nose with his finger, "and she was lost right in the middle of Anywhere Forest. She was so lost that she wandered into Nowhere Wood and there she became even loster. And, O it was cold! The grass was crunching, and the air was turned to haar, and there were hungry wolves howling all around, and the moon was frozen to the sky and couldna even wrap a cloud around itsel; and Mairi was that cold and lost and lonely, she sat down and burrowed hersel like a wee squirrel into a pile of leaves, and then looked up at the moon and said—"

"Hail Mary full of grace," said Mairi's nose, which was all of her that was showing from under the bedclothes.

"Aye, that's what she said, and she closed her eyes and waited for the wolves to come and eat her. Now, after her eyes had been closed a wee while, she suddenly heard a thumping, walloping sound round about her. What's yon? thought Mairi. So she stuck her head out of the leaves and looked, but she couldna see anything. Maybe it's dreaming I was, said Mairi, and she was just about to go back to sleep when—thump! wallop!—there it was again. And then she began to feel that things were moving round her. *Moooving,*" said Mungo darkly, "and cracking, and crunching, and groaning, and creaking; and at last Mairi was frightened into speech, and she asked aloud, 'Who's making that awful racket?' And a voice, a sort of rumbling, crashing, red voice, said, 'It's only us tree trunks coming round you to keep off the cold wind, Mairi.' And the lassie said, 'O Holy Mother,' because she was feared of being swallowed up by the trees.

"And then she heard another sound, a sort of sighing and a whispering and a rustling sound in the air above her, and an acorn fell and dunked her one on the head; so she looked up, rubbing her pow, and she asked, 'Who's making that awful racket up there?' And a voice, but a gentler, kinder, silvery sort of voice, said, 'It's only us branches bending over you to keep off the cold rain, Mairi.' And she said, 'O Holy—but please dinna dunk me to death with acorns first.'

"And then she heard a third sound, and it was a twanging and a snapping sound underneath her, like lots of threads were being pulled apart at the same time, and then she felt the ground heave and some earth popped up and hit her on the nose; so she rubbed the clart off and looked down and asked the earth, 'Who's making that awful racket down there?' And a happy-sounding, chuckling, chestnutty voice said, 'It's only the heather coming up to warm your bed, Mairi.' And she said, 'O Mother—but please dinna batter me to death with dods of clart first.'

"And then there was a great quietness, and the rain and the wind and the howling wolves and the roaring beasts all stopped. And Mairi listened to it, and at last she asked, 'Who's there in the silence?' And the loveliest voice in the world said to her, 'It's the Holy Mother who has herded the trees and the branches and the heather all together to warm you, and the Archangel Michael who is standing with a fiery sword to guard you, and everything is well, Mairi.' And Mairi asked nothing else because at last she felt safe and happy."

Mairi was asleep, and seeing it Mungo smiled, and blew out the flickering taper by the bed, and kissed her eyes, and went through to his own place, to his own world, to the writ and thoughts which are unknown. Yet the chaste old man knew her in the secret places of his heart.

And folk saw that he smiled more, that his words were gentler, and the lines of righteous anger softened on his brow. He walked without a stick and sang even as he went about his medical preparations. Mairi plied him with her wicker basket. They walked together in the afternoon woodland seeking herbs and lichen. Finella chopped broth carrot and leek with her and muttered mysteriously over simmering pots; a bearded hard tower soldier made her dolls out of wood and rag; and Mairi sang with it all, and the folk who heard her were lightened by the hearing. She sang in the house like a doo, like a linnet over the sunny field, like a whaup on the windy meadow. The migrating birds knew her, the swallow and the martin of the rooftops. The lame of the world came to her till she shared her room with a foxcub, a crippled wood-pigeon, and a hedgehog. Folk looked at her, and their eyes shone.

And, when Mungo stood before the altar, under the shadow of the cross, in the wood-smelling village kirk—and, though gentled, still clutched the altar, and said: We are damned, We are deceived; said: Lord save us, Lord have mercy on us; said it with his tongue flickering blue fire like Arcturus—he would suddenly look up in the midst of it all to hear her say patiently, "Aye, Father, but the broth is ready ben for your supper."

This was the man of whom Mairi was thinking that night as she lay in bed between sleep and waking, counting the stars that passed over the smokehole through the summer lift.

## 8

# The Foxcub
## and Those He Met on the Way

The next day, the third of the haymaking, old Finella was also missing from the line of mowers. Her bothy was empty; the supper bowl hung cold from the ingle-hook; even her cat was gone without a trace.

Dear God, said the women. They wondered. Had they gone together to work magic on the bandit leader? The men thought possibly bandit raiders had taken them, though they didn't know how any strangers could have entered the village undetected. The children thought that they had sailed off together in an eggshell to the far-away castle where the king lived on top of a golden mountain, and that they would soon return at the head of an army. "I swear," said young Fearchar, "it was none but hersel I saw last night with her cat and all flying over the moon on her broomstick," and he laughed, looking around. None of the others laughed with him. Wat scowled at the forest line and said that By God's Blood And Bones he would search it, he would, but you could lose the heavenly host itsel, just about, in its vastness. That the missing two had perhaps run to save their own skins occurred to no one.

And it rained. It had been raining during the night; it drizzled now. No, not yet quite drizzled, for no visible rain seemed to fall at all. Rather, there was a moist tingling in the air, and a smoky dullness over the sun that darkened all the colours of the summer field. The rain was rumouring itself in the fresh morning, the long grass of the hayfields nodded heavily, and the trees whispered darkly as it moved amongst them. The surface of the burn prickled with its midge-drops, the kye wore coats of shining dew, and the scythes of the womenfolk lined up again across the field glinted as they swung in the shimmering damp.

They were cutting the third field, which was more strenuous than the others because on it they had to use their scythes uphill; but then, wet grass, provided it is. not too wet, is easier to cut than dry, and it fell heavy and green and fragrant over the blades, and the women waded through it with wet seeds sticking to their naked legs while blind Manus piped and Mairi sang—and sang, with her eyes on the treeline from which he did not come.

*O Father!*

Summer was nearly at its peak with a promise of white cloud and blue sky, but they decided to start loading, for, after all, showers can come from the clearest sky and a sprinkling of small white clouds often betokens rain. Pity the mown field left under a downpour! For the stalks will rot at the bottom for want of air and drainage, and the hay will be bad, and the beasts that eat of it sicken. So while some of the women worked on that third field, others, the weaker ones and the children, began loading the last two days' cutting onto their cart, and Rob the Gowk drove the plodding ox over the burn to the village. Then they gathered to eat their bannocks. Mairi sat with her hands on her lap and would say nothing.

"Will you wear my ribbon, Mairi?" said beautiful Seonaid. She brought out the green ribbon her dead soldier had given her, and tied it round the wee girl's hair. Seonaid's perfect breasts rubbed against Mairi's thin shoulder. "There!" she said.

All the women admired Mairi. Una put her arms round her and hugged her, motherly—but Mairi was a lump of wood. Fearchar came swaggering, said she needn't fear for he would be her brother, manly—but Mairi was a clod of earth. Blind Manus called over to her, asking would she sing for the folk whose work was resuming?—but Mairi's mouth was a cleft rock.

Mairi said nothing. Without looking away, she began to cry. Slowly, slowly the tears ran down her freckled cheeks. The women looked at each other hopelessly.

It was mild as Mairi walked home that night; the fine weather clouds had melted away, and the star called Vega, that folk knew as Telyn Arthur—Arthur's Harp—was a glimmering faint fire behind the darkness. One light showed in the kirk where Ruadh sat with Fergus. The boy slunk away from her. Mairi didn't look at him. She cleaned and changed Fergus again, and tried to feed him. He hadn't eaten that day. She dipped a piece of bannock in milk and put it between his teeth. It lay unnoticed in his mouth. After a while she took it out. Fergus blinked at her, his breath a rusty scraping. She told him the Father had just gone out and would be back soon. She told him that the no-pain he was feeling meant he would soon be better. She told him Nessa, who had not come near even once, was sitting there by his side—there, Fergus. Fergus's eyelids flickered a little. She raised his head into her lap and put her arms about it.

95

*'O well's me of my gay goshawk,*
*That he can speak and flee!*
*He'll carry a letter to my love,*
*Bring back another to me.'*

*'O how can I your true love ken,*
*Or how can I her know?*
*When from her mouth I never heard couth,*
*Nor with my eyes her saw.'*

*'O well shall you my true love ken,*
*As soon as you her see!*
*For of all the flowers in fair Scotland*
*The fairest flower is she.'* . . .

And Fergus slept, and she laid his head down and covered him and went into her room.

It smelt of fox. A pair of bright eyes regarded her there, the smell clouding her room like the peat smoke. He was *sionnach*, the russet dog. She had found him that same spring while foraging with the Father, only survivor he was of a litter that some predator had butchered, and he was blind and helpless and less than ten days old. When they found him he was giving little whimpering noises and nudging the dead body of his mother, and Mairi, who also had no mother, lifted him up and looked into the blind eyes. *Tha mi fuar* (I'm cold), said the cub—or so Mairi thought he said, for she was only ten after all, and it was a raw spring day true enough, and a fox cub will not appear outside the warm breeding den until after his fourth week. Mungo hadn't heard the voice, but Mairi the forest child had, and so she called him *Faidh*—which is to say, Prophet. They took him home in the basket, and Mungo washed him in water in the kirk, and exempted him from the curse which peasants put on the clan of the red robber. And true enough, Faidh showed no interest in the village chickens. ("But time will

96

come," grumbled Wat the woodsman, giving the beast a scowl.)

And Faidh grew. His face changed, as the faces of fox cubs do, from the flat-eared round-faced four-week-old, to the long muzzle and pointed ears of the ten-week dog. His eyes were alert. He snapped at everyone except Mairi. By day he followed his nose into the forest. At night he usually slept by her cot. Sometimes he stayed out all night, and Mairi worried. She tried to teach him words. *Ith gu leor*—eat well—she said; *gabh deoch*—drink. Faidh looked at her wonderingly. "Well, and have you no got him kneeling to his prayers yet?" asked Mungo, coming in. Mairi ignored him. *"Is fhasa a bhi bruidhinn na a bhi deanadh"* (It is easier to speak than to do), she said to the fox. Mungo laughed and pulled her ear.

Faidh was the forest—like her. He was its creature in all things, born with its evergreen branches above, and the white winds rushing over the wild howe of the sky.

The fox looked at her now. She took him in her arms. The red face nudged her elbow. She whispered in his ear.

No book can record the words she said, but as she slept the fox cub trotted out into the night.

Faidh crossed the kirkyard, passed through the palings of the stockade, and came to the burn beyond the village. He scrambled down its steep side, jumped three feet onto a large mossy boulder round which the water divided, then jumped two feet more onto a narrow platform of gravel and root at the bottom of the opposite bank.

A moving fox goes at a quick jerky trot with complicated zigzags, head held low and muzzle thrust out, sniffing the multicoloured world of scent for prey and danger, rooting for slugs and beetles, pawing over anything which might be edible, and always, for all its meanderings, it will move in the same general direction—into the wind. Faidh galloped down the glen with his tail down and ears up. There was a gentle breeze strolling over the mown grass, and he kept his nose into it, entering the forest at a long diagonal approach.

We folk, living through our eyes, are afraid of darkness, for our hearing is so inadequate, our sense of smell so slight: these ears and noses of ours are no more than shut, curtained windows through which only the faintest murmur of the outside world can ever come. Consequently, lying in our warm beds on a winter's night, we will say that all the beasts of the forest are safe in their caves and nests and burrows, but it is not so. For many, our night is their day. There are flowers which open at night and drink the darkness like water. There are insects which fly at night and populate the minds of the superstitious with whispering ghosts. There are bright eyes that shine at night, and which probably brought demons into the world as they were seen by trembling saints at vigil in the dark. In those days there were also the powerful killers of the forest, the bears and wolves—especially the wolves—for whom darkness was an invisible shield, a decisive ally in any combat with man; so man said that the dark was evil, and black was hell. And how many stories of hauntings and banshees, I wonder, began when out of the trees came a pale staring spectre that swooped and screamed hideously, and was after all only a hunting white owl?

Through the dark forest Faidh pursued his way, sniffing here and sniffing there—on the trail of badger and hare, wolf and beaver, once even a wild boar—but not on the trail that he sought. At last, about moonset, he saw a pale little light glowing dimly in a patch of reeds. Faidh gingerly brought his muzzle in closer. A glow-worm was sitting feasting in the mouth of a snail shell at the end of a tall stalk.

"Hullo there, sister," said Faidh. Glow-worms don't speak vulpine, but there is a primitive common language in the forest, usually of alarm, which most creatures share.

The glow-worm licked the remnants of snail dinner from her jaws and blinked her light at him.

"Hullo there to you too, red face," she cackled (glow-worm speech is rather like that of old women gossiping in a shop). "Now your reverence wouldna be thinking of eating me with all this putrid snail-gut in my insides, eh? Heh, heh," and the glow-worm laughed wickedly.

Faidh shook his head.

"What, no even a wee bit nibble? Heh, heh, heh," said the glow-worm chuckling again.

"Na, no thank you," said Faidh politely. "But there's something else, like. Would you have seen a *duine* (man) hereabouts? It's a *duine's* scent that I'm after."

"And why's that?" asked the glow-worm.

"Well, I want to eat him," said the cunning fox, "because he is a magician that will put spells on foxes so they never catch a hare again, and put spells on glow-worms so that they boke themsels up at the very thought of snails."

"Whaaat!" screamed the glow-worm, and her light flashed flames all down the stalk, "me lose my favourite food?"

"That's about the height of it," said Faidh, "unless I can collar the bugger first. Have you seen him at all?"

"O, I've seen him all right," said the glow-worm bitterly. "Two nights and two days syne, crashing about like a boar he was, talking to himsel, bloody heidbanger. Started talking to the trees. Nearly flattened a grasshopper. 'Sod off!' shouts the grasshopper. 'O what beautiful music,' says the loon, cupping his ear with a daft-like smile on his gob. Ach, if I'd only kent what he was up to, I'd have hatched my eggs in his ear and drunk out his brains, so I would!"

"Aye, they're orra folk, they *duines*," said Faidh. "And which gait was he going, would you say?"

"There!" answered the glow-worm, and spat a stream of snail juice in the direction.

"To the wolves," murmured Faidh, his heart sinking. The glow-worm sniggered.

"Aye, *faol*," she said. "Maybe you've lost your meal after all, red chops. I think he was a bit over muckle for you anyway. Heh, heh, heh!"

Faidh snapped at her, but she was too quick and darted back into the shell. Faidh held the shell between his teeth for a moment. Caterpillars, he thought, slugs, grasshoppers, beetles of most sorts—but this sleazy thing? Snails' brains, he thought. He dropped the shell. It landed on a patch of grass, mouth up, and he could see the bright glow inside it. *Heh, heh, heh!* came the glow-worm's voice.

"Dirty wee shit," muttered Faidh to himself, trotting off through the trees. "Two nights and two days. The trail's stone cold. And the wolves forbye. Ah well."

Daybreak. The trees rose up and splintered the sun. Faidh trotted on, sniffing. He'd picked up Wat's traces once or twice, but knew it was the wrong trail. He asked every creature he came across that flew or ran or swam, and that wasn't too afraid of fox, or too agile for him to catch. *Duine?* he asked. Some had seen a *duine*, and some hadn't. Some recognized this *duine* by his smell and knew he was harmless. Most forest creatures in those days were yet to learn fear of the *duine* race, for there were not many of the *duine* then in Scotland, and few had cut their way into the forest for pastureland and timber. Even the boar and deer thought of the two-legged kind as just another predator, a nuisance in their lives, and not as the blood-enemy that plotted their destruction. So Faidh snuffled through that first day, his nose close to the earth, and always his path led him, however circuitously, in the direction of Wolves' Crag, the place where least he wanted to go.

Another night came, cloudless, and patches of the huge white light shone on the forest floor. Faidh had killed a fat woodcock, and slept a little, and was now standing on top of a fallen mossy trunk, panning the glade. An owl fluttered onto the branch above.

"Hunting, red nose?" he said.

Faidh poked his nose upwards. The owl was out of reach.

"None of your folk, brother," said Faidh—for a grown fox will kill an owl, given the chance, whereas only men and wolves and eagles have the power to kill a fox. "None of your folk," Faidh repeated. "Why no come down," he added, cocking his head, "so we can have a blether, eh?"

"*Kee-wick*," screeched the owl. "Does the red dog think I'm daft?"

Faidh sighed, and the two carnivores grinned at each other.

Well, they talked about this and they talked about that, and Faidh scratched himself, and the howlat shat out a pellet from his supper—feathers, fur and bone. Faidh sniffed it suspiciously.

"Would you have eaten a *duine's* eyes today," he said, "or the hair from a *duine's* head?"

The owl snorted. "Just stay with the woodmice, laddie," he said. "More your size, like."

"I was just wondering," said the cunning fox. "I lost my Mammy to a hunting *duine*, you see."

"There was a *duine* here two nights ago," said the owl, "but he wasna hunting."

"No?"

"Na. There was no saying what he was doing, but it wasna that. Him hunting!" the owl snorted again. "Yon creature couldna catch a cold. Between the two of us," he said confidentially, "he was daft, real gyte. I've seen it afore, ken? Long time back there was a whole flight of *duine* in the forest hunting each other, but the thing I still canna understand is that the stronger lot picked up their own dead and took them off to eat them, but left their prey just lying there for the rest of us. Daft, that."

Faidh agreed.

The owl continued, "I was looking at it from my branch. One of the *duine* prey hid himsel in a hollow trunk, and after the others had gone he clambered out. But he was lost—ochone, the poor soul—and he wandered round and round howling away and talking to the air, syne he just sat down and began pouring pine needles over his head, and a wolf got him. I got the leftovers," said the owl, fondly stroking his hard black beak.

Faidh had swallowed hard at the mention of wolf. Now he coughed to clear his throat. "Ahem, aye, yes," he said, "about that other daft *duine* now, the one you saw they two nights back—could you tell me which way he went? Maybe I might have the luck this time."

"You dinna want to follow him, son," said the howlat, squinting down at Faidh.

"Aye, I do," said the fox, staring back up at him.

"Awreet then," said the owl, and gave Faidh the directions—straight into the middle of wolf territory. O bloody hell, thought Faidh.

"Much beholden to you, brother," he said breezily.

"Well I'll be damned," said the owl. "And are you really going then, red mop?"

"*Cha 'n eil an corr 'g am dhith*," replied the little fox heroically, which means "there's nothing I want better" —which was a lie in any language.

"Well—!" screeched the owl. "I think I'll tag along, and when they wolves bite your napper off, I'll keek under and see what you've been using for brains all this time."

And before Faidh could say anything, the owl swooped off. The little fox heard his raucous laughter hooting through the night.

Faidh travelled onward during the dark hours. He was now so far in under the towering forest roof that, given a fox's night vision, the difference between night and day, between the worlds of moon and sun, no longer existed, and what in the blue sky above was the light of the brightest noonday, was down here no more than a pale green drizzle filtering slowly among the vast swart masses of the forest.

It was about the middle of his second day in the forest, and Faidh had made himself a bedding place under a tangle of tree roots on a slope upwind of the obvious path and with an escape route at the back. He lay curled up with his tail over his nose and his eyes nearly shut. Anyone who saw him would probably think he was dead, but in fact he was just dozing warily. All his instincts told him that the part of the forest he was in now was unsafe for foxes—for adult dogs, let alone a big cub like himself who, in the normal run of things, would still be playing games outside his parents' earth. There was a feel of wolf around the bases of the trees. Faidh had never seen a wolf, but, before his newborn eyes had opened, there had been the smell of the creature and the feel of the strange muzzle that had come snuffling over him after his mother's terrible scream had broken. These things triggered his fear. He lay motionless and invisible under the thick roots.

All of a sudden his nose began to twitch and he opened his eyes. Some distance away a young hind was coming through the trees. Faidh eyed her from his lair. Aye-aye lassie, he thought, if you were a wee bit week's old calf, I'd be taking a bite out of you mysel; but as it is (he added), you're too sodding big. And the little fox stared longingly as the red deer cantered up the slope, and then stopped and began casually browsing on a clump of nearby fern.

He was looking at the deer and thinking of all the good dinners he could have if he were three times bigger, or if she were that much smaller, when suddenly there was a movement, a very very slight movement, behind a tree at the bottom of the slope. The deer's back was turned to it and there was nothing to hear, but Faidh's eyes were on the spot immediately. An animal movement—yes, he was sure it had been. He cupped his ears forward and stared, completely immobile. There was still no sound, and no scent came to him. The deer cropped the scanty undergrowth contentedly. Then Faidh saw it: a shadow just slightly darker than the other shadows began moving on the other side of the old pine. As he watched, it detached itself from the black trunk and crept forward, just as Faidh himself would do, slowly and cautiously with its stomach almost touching the ground. The little fox saw the sharp pointed ears and the hungry cold black eyes of a dog much more powerful than himself. The fur bristled on his back. For the first time in his life Faidh knew he was looking at a wolf.

*Faol!*

Now the grey dog is not a monster: it is flesh and blood, instincts and appetite, affectionate to its own and brave; but to any animal that is its natural prey, the wolf is the strongest and most fearsome of enemies. As its power haunted the nightmares of human children too weak to use manly weapons against it, so it also lived in the fears of deer and fox, and most other creatures too, as the terrible horror dog, more cunning than the wild boar, faster than the bear, against whom instant flight was the only, uncertain, defence.

The wolf crept up slowly behind the unwitting deer, getting itself near enough for a quick spring, and then—

Without knowing why he did it, Faidh broke cover and jumped out in front of the hind.

"Wolf! wolf!" he barked. "Run—hide—*falaich*—quick!"

The deer started, saw at a glance that the fox wasn't big enough to attack her—and then caught the smell of wolf. With a little cry of terror she sprang forward and scrambled up the tangled brittle undergrowth of the slope even as the wolf lunged at her, all long wet teeth and cruel burning eyes.

This wasn't the deer's territory at all. She was too far into the forest, the trees were too close for her long elegant legs to work properly and take her away from the knife-edge of danger. As she pulled herself up the slope a low branch swished her back and her front hoofs stumbled over the roots that had hidden Faidh. The wolf grinned and tightened his muscles for a final spring.

At that moment the little fox popped up in front of him. "Hullo there," Faidh said cheerily.

What the—? The big wolf skidded to a stop.

"So how's it going then?" said Faidh, giving the wolf a friendly shove with his front leg. "I wouldna bother with yon deer: bugger's no ready yet."

"Whitra fuck you talking about?" said the wolf.

"I'm just saying," persisted Faidh, his ears cocked to the sound of the deer's hoofs, "that she's over peelie wallie to bother about—all bone and that, ken? Now if you want my advice," he heltered on (the deer escaping all the time), "sonny boy here kens a thing or two about they long-legged wallopers. There's hinds and hinds, Jim, and I mean you've just got to learn—"

A branch crashed behind them and the deer was out of sight. The wolf's head jerked up. In the stories, wolves are always being outwitted by foxes, and he resented it.

"Yon deer's my dinner," he hissed, and his muscles tightened again.

"Aw but Jimmy, that's just a load of crap," said Faidh. "Now if you listen to the man who really kens—"

"Geroutra fucking road!" shouted the wolf.

"—he'd tell you yous lot of grey fleabags dinna ken your arses from a hole in the—"

"I'll get you for that, you fucking wee bastard!" the wolf yelled, and launched himself on Faidh.

But Faidh wasn't there. Faidh was already going like the clappers away from the wolf—away from the deer as well. The wolf forgot all about the hind and chased the red tail, snarling and snapping as he went. Faidh was wolf-fast, but he was also smaller and more agile. If I can keep this up, he thought, I'll leave the bastard standing, but if I come a cropper anywhere... He didn't think about what would happen then. The wolf's teeth were gnashing the air a few bounds behind his rump. Run for it, Faidh lad, said the little fox to himself. You're running for your life now.

The wolf was running for Faidh's life too. He knew the fox was nimbler, but then this fox was no more than a big cub, while he was a hefty adult wolf with cubs of his own and the strength of much hunting in his shoulders. You'll tire before I do, sonny Jim, he thought, and then I'll skin you. I'll bite your balls off. I'll have your guts. Red dog and grey crashed throught the forest.

Faidh galloped between trunks of pine, birch and alder, through long grass and over the bracken, a flying shadow in the place of shadows; but the wolf's legs were longer.

Faidh galloped as a fox who minds that first and greatest Fox, father of all foxes, the dog of the great stallion Goban beneath whom the grasses did not bend nor did the heather rustle; but the wolf's shoulders were still the more powerful.

Faidh galloped until the pain in his legs was one terrible burning, the breath came red and rusty to his throat, and the very ground seemed to heave under him and try to suck him in; yet, yet the wolf was there at his back: Faidh had gained half a dozen strides, no more, and the wolf's breath was deeper and his stride did not tire.

Then bang right in front of them suddenly there it was, the gorge that scarred several miles across the forest floor—in some places deeper, in some places a mere hollow, where an ancient burn had long ago ceased to run; and the walls of the gorge were made of black rocks, creviced here and there and tousled with the purple heather and patches of harsh dry grass. At this particular point, as the wolf had known from the start, it was deep and sheer and too broad for the exhausted fox to leap.

Faidh came to a halt at the cliff edge and looked despairingly at the killing drop, and then at the opposite wall where there did not seem to be a foothold for a squirrel or a sparrow, far less a fox.

"Awreet sonny," said the wolf's voice behind him. Faidh looked over his shoulder. The wolf was strolling towards him wearing an amiable grin. "Awreet you dirty wee red fucker. You gone all silent? What's wrong with you, eh? What's wrong with the dirty wee fuckface?"

"I thought you might be losing your breath," said Faidh hoarsely. "I wouldna want to take advantage of a blootered old bum like you."

"Aw, that's right nice," said the wolf, getting close to Faidh. "That's real considerate, sonny. And so's this, you fucking cunt!"—and the wolf's huge teeth tore at Faidh's throat.

But again Faidh had seen it coming. With the last of his strength the little fox flung himself off the edge of the gorge and flew away with his jaws open and his teeth in the air. Some feet below, on the same side, an ash sapling grew out of a cleft. Faidh landed on it, thump, and held on desperately. He felt the lithe wood bending beneath him. Don't break, he said to himself, please don't break. The slender ash bent and bent—but it held. He pulled himself along it with his teeth and claws, and the wood bent more and more until it was pointing to a small ledge on the opposite wall. It bent and creaked—but still it held. Then, near the very end, Faidh leapt once more and touched his forepaws to the ledge, scrabbled to haul his back legs up, and then clambered to the top and stood there panting. The wolf was still standing on the other side staring at him, but Faidh no longer cared. He lay down with his chin on his paws and his whole body heaving. The wolf looked down at the sapling, looked at the fox, then looked down at the sapling again. He lowered one paw over the edge and groped for a while before thinking better of it and contenting himself with giving voice to every obscenity he could think of. But the little fox wasn't bothered. I did it! he was thinking. I did it! I beat the grey dog! And to this day folk call the spot where Faidh jumped the gorge *Creag an t-Sionnaich*, the Rock of the Fox.

After a while the wolf grew tired of his temper, and as he was still hungry he turned and louped off back the way they had come. Faidh lay quiet, listening and sniffing intently in case the wolf decided to circle round and cross the gorge somewhere else. There was no sound of him, however, so after some wee while had passed Faidh got to his feet and stretched himself gingerly.

"Hey," said a timid voice from behind the nearest tree. Faidh spun round. It was the young deer. "Has he gone?" she asked.

Faidh swaggered over.

"Who? Aw, *him?*" he said. "O aye, they grey dogs are all wind. Nothing to it. Bunch of chancing bastards. Just stand up to them, and they canna take it."

"That was magic," murmured the hind.

"No problems," said Faidh.

"I was that feared," said the hind. "I got lost a couple of days back. Went off the wrong way. See this place, it's a fucking maze."

"Bloody murder," Faidh agreed.

"I wouldna have got out it yet, 'cept a *duine* pointed me the direction."

"Well he did a grand job of it," said Faidh. "Was he a decrepit old creature with a grey wispy beard acting all daft, like?"

"Never! He was that handsome an old gentleman, with a grey pow, dead distinguished, and he was acting like, like he was saintly—ken?"

"Aye, that'll be him," said Faidh. "Ken where he is?"

"Said he was heading towards Wolves' Crag," answered the deer. "Ken where that is?"

"O aye."

"Said it wouldna be good for me, but."

"Dead clever brutes, they *duines*," said Faidh.

The deer didn't smile.

"He was kind," she said quietly. "It's a pity all you killers take it for daftness. He laid his hand on my nose, dead gentle, and spoke to me."

"And did you understand him?" asked Faidh.

"No," admitted the red deer. "But he sounded so gentle."

"Well, if I was you," said Faidh, "I'd clear off, I would, and no stop for anything. They fucking wolves are no very gentle."

"I was just hungry," said the deer.

"Sod it, lassie, so are the wolves."

"You're right, I'm off. But mind about the Crag."

"Ach, dinna say it; I'm trying to forget."

"I mean, you're sure you ken how to get there?" asked the deer over her shoulder as she trotted briskly away.

"Easy," said the little fox. "Just follow the wolf reek. You canna go wrong."

Faidh reached the Crag that same evening. He had gone full belt up the side of the gorge, right through the land where every bush was dripping the smell of grey wolf hair. More than once paws not his own had thudded amongst the trees, and the *faol* howl had broken out behind him. But he outran any pursuit, and at last reached his destination.

Wolves' Crag—the navel of the forest.

He smelt it first, then saw it, the thin thread of smoke curling upwards above the treetops in the mild twilit air. He heard the brief sound of *duine* voices. In the branches above, a stanechacker began scolding him:

> *Stane chack!*
> *Deevil tak!*
> *They who harry my nest*
> *Will never rest,*
> *Will meet the pest!*
> *Deil brak their long back*
> *Who my eggs would*
> *Tak, tak!*

Faidh pressed forward to the edge of the trees. The Crag was high, but not steep. Its ice-rocks fell down in jagged steps into the bowl of the glade. Behind the summit of the rocks a fringe of tall and ancient pines formed an unbroken wall, while at their feet were the dark holes of the wolf lairs. Faidh sensed the watching circle, the forest birds high in the branches—red crossbills and coal tits, goldcrests and woodpeckers. *Kee-wick* screeched an owl, "So you still have your head, do you then, red tail?" A squirrel and a tree-creeper hugged the same trunk, staring fascinated at something below; and pressing his nose in between the lowest branch and a grass-capped rock, the little fox followed their eyes downwards.

There was a fire in the hollow, a scarlet twinkle of light in the darkness and a loud echoing crackle of twigs and dry roots. Some distance away, at the bottom of the cliff, Faidh could see the eyes of the watching wolves. He heard the *duine* voices again and peered into the darkness trying to make out Mungo, and wondering who the others could be that had come to such a strange place and kept such an audience so enraptured. The moon rose over the forest and slowly its light spilled down among the trees, silvering the further wall of rock and painting the pinetops on it in sharp black silhouette. Then, as there were few clouds, one beam stole directly down into the glade, lifting its feet among the thickly tangled heather and bracken and old roots of the bottom and closing on the fire until its wee red flicker was swallowed in the greater light of the white planet. And then Faidh saw them, two brooding unknown figures by the smoke pall, while beside them on the ground lay what at first he thought was a fallen trunk, and what he then recognized as the biggest *duine* he had ever seen...

Mairi woke before the waking hour. The sky was yet night, the crowing of the cock was still a way off. She looked about, wondering what it was that had disturbed her. The woodpigeon whose wing had been broken was scuffling on the beam above her head. She took the creature on her hand and stroked the hard blue crown and green neck. "What's wrong?" she murmured. "What's wrong with you, my mannie?" The bird swivelled his head uneasily, gave one *coo* by way of morning, and said nothing more. She held some grain to him in the palm of her hand. He refused the food.

She went outside. Dawn was one thin pale wave on the eastern trees. She looked at it indifferently and knuckled the sleep from her eyes. She heard a familiar movement in the grass of the kirkyard: her hedgehog coming home to his nest under the bed. She stroked his snout with one finger. "Been milking the cow then?" she said. "Old Una'll make you into a hedgehog pie if you're no careful." She walked to the stockade. "Where's our Faidh?" she asked, leaning against it. "And where's the Father gone?" The question hung over the darkness of the strath.

And dawn was a silver boat from a distant country. Dawn was a white rider cresting the black shore.

Soon it was light enough for her to see the morning mist rising off the ground and vanishing at man's height.

The burn was completely hidden by it; the first trees that became visible seemed to have no trunks, but sat legless on the hillside with their lower branches making waves in the smoke. Mairi sniffed the air. Summer mists that rise in low ground and soon vanish are a promise of fair weather. For the last haymaking day: for the stacking and the drying of it against the winter.

A second ripple of dawn rose and washed over the sombre treeline. The furthest acre of the sky began to sparkle.

"It's the bright wee bird you are the day," said Wat the woodsman behind her, yawning luxuriously. He had his axe on his shoulder, ready for the day's work.

Mairi turned to him. "Take me with you, Wattie," she said.

Wat's mouth froze, but he composed a poor smile for her. "Aw lassie," he said sadly. "Lassie, lassie," he repeated. And he was going to say, What's the use of it?—but on the first word he stopped, and stood staring over her head. Mairi spun round. She heard the high-pitched yap of a young fox.

"Faidh!"

Wat's hand clamped down on her shoulder and anchored her to the spot. She squirmed.

"Wattie," she pleaded. "You're hurting me. Let me go, Wattie."

Wat neither spoke nor looked at her. He was staring straight ahead with something like panic in his eyes.

On the other side of the glen, where the mist was rising into the trees, a man was walking towards the village. A flowering yellow elder bush stood there at the spot he had just passed, head and shoulders above the mist. Wat knew the bush well, knew its height exactly, and knew that, unless he were marching on stilts, the man he was looking at must be at least ten feet tall.

# 9

## *How the Old Man Met an Angel and What He Said*

That night those nights ago, when Mungo had left the
bothy with Mairi, he walked quickly to the kirk where
Fergus lay dying. The young man was delirious, shouting
commands and warnings and flailing the air with his fists.
Mungo sat with him till the fit passed. Mairi sat by his
side. They both looked at the tormented body on the bed,
and sighed and said nothing. Mairi took the old priest's
hand. He felt her smooth fingers warm in his wrinkled
old skin. What would the bandits do to her? He ever
thought of his childless past with regret. Now he looked
to the likely future with fear.

Fergus groaned till his face went slack and cold and
he fainted.

Poor boy, thought Mungo, mopping the sodden face.

Poor Mairi. Poor women in the bothies. Poor bairns. Poor me. Poor everyone. Ach!

The futility of a pitying life choked him.

Fergus was quiet at last. Now his faint would become a sleep.

"Away to your bed, lassie," said Mungo. "I'll take the air a wee."

He stood in the door of the kirk. Mairi's sounds scratched away to nothingness. Just like a wee mouse in the wall. Mairi my heart, he said, you never will ken how much I love you.

He walked slowly back through the village in the direction of the tower. He was eighty years old. Those long years dragged at him. He hadn't slept. It didn't matter.

What mattered?

*Nothing*, hissed a despairing voice inside him.

What mattered but?

There is no mansion that has not death as its foundation.

Mungo prayed. His prayer was, as ever, a fantasy of justice beyond this place where there was none. Yet how many prayers had he said in his life?

*O what good are prayers? We must act!*

How?

He looked up. The night sky was a dark silver; the full harvest moon was spreading its wings over the sleeping land. O the beautiful cruelty of the world! Mungo entered the tower of the ravens. It was desolate, the gates unguarded. No, a soul remained. Old Luath the wolfhound padded there looking for his dead master. Mungo ruffled the old dog's head. There were no torches. He climbed the stairs knowing where each step was. Here was the guardroom. Here the men ate and made merry. Here was the great hall where the Shirra sat, so full of life, so red, so rich in blood he was. Where was he now? Where were any of them? Grey moonlight filtered through the arrowslits. Soon it would be a place of cobwebs and bats.

He came out into the open sky at the top of the tower and sat among the stars.

O Scotland, Scotland! Poor dream of glory! The peat fire by night, and blood labour by day. Sweet Jesus have mercy on you. No one else ever will.

There is not a human sound from the village. The men are dead, and the women sleep.

Aye, Mungo had looked at these women. They had all been so strong and capable that day at the scything, and he had allowed himself to think that, yes, they could take swords and spears in their hands and fight off the bandits when they came; but then, listening to their talk that same night of *glaistig* and *uruisg* and witchcraft and wonder, he knew that they would never do it. For what, in the end, were they, and all their love and witchery, against a horde of armed men? O they were ready to be killed defending the young of their nests, no doubt, but could they kill? Certainly not without a lead. Possibly not at all. Could he, for that matter? He put his head in his hands. "O God, what am I thinking of?" he cried. "*Kill!*—and am I no a priest of the Lamb of Love? God, tell me what to do!"

And his voice echoed,

| | |
|---|---|
| *There is no mansion* | *Tell me* |
| *that has not death* | *what* |
| *as its foundation* | *to do!* |

Night. The trees are creaking, the branches are singing to themselves, an age-old melody. A swanwhite stallion is galloping through the midnight forest; his hoofs are muffled in the silence of the soft earth; by the neck of him the breath is beating the cold air like two great wings. He has no rider. No man can ride him since the valleys yawned; no saddle has lain on his stately back since the mountains first shuddered and heaved themselves skywards. Beneath the branches of the ancient forest he gallops, and stories grow in the wake of his hoofbeats. He is the spirit of Scotland, they say; he is the genius of her dead heroes; he is the soul, pagan soul, of their lost cause.

And what am I? thought the Christian man. A foreigner in my own country!

"How's this, man—greeting?" said a voice, for indeed Mungo was weeping.

"O dinna think they're tears of grief," said Mungo gruffly. "I love this little acre God has given us, and I love every one of the damned cantankerous scunners who lives on it. And it is because I love it all that I am greeting."

And he wiped his eyes and turned to face the voice. There was no one there.

He drew a breath—but it didn't really surprise him. He often seemed to imagine things these days, and surely this was a haunted place. He turned wearily and climbed down. Talking to mysel. Ah well. He walked back the way he had come. Not a soul stirred, not even Luath. Inside their walls the folk of the village slept. Mairi was mumbling gently on her pillow behind the hawthorn screen. He held the little light of a reed candle over her and smiled pensively. Went into the next room and straightened Fergus's blanket, felt his brow, sat down by the bedside once more. Surely, surely the morning cock would not be long in his crowing? He would stay up till the daylight. Mungo took out his rosary, held it in his hands for a few minutes, said nothing, then began to pace up and down the room.

"Where are you going, Mungo?" said the voice.

*Where are you going, Mungo?* said the walls. *Where are you going?* said the roofbeams, where the words hung, and faded.

Mungo looked about. He saw no one.

"Age," he said. "I'm going gyte."

He pinched out the candle. Again he settled himself down on the stool. The stool was hard as iron and his old bones hurt him. He remembered how he had actually welcomed discomfort, once, when he had been a young priest kneeling for hours (or so it seemed) at his various devotions with a happy spirit. That wasna yesterday, laddie. He grunted and shifted his weight from one buttock to the other. He could hear his skeleton creak as the bones moved inside him. O dear God, he groaned, my soul's slid into my backside. He closed his eyes.

"What are you doing, Mungo?" said the voice.

*What are you doing, Mungo?* said the walls. *What are you doing?* said the roofbeams.

Mungo's eyes were wide open. Beyond Fergus's bed, in the blackness of the further wall, he saw a point of light. It grew bigger. At first he thought the kirk was on fire; but there was no smoke and no crackling—and what would burn in a clay wall? But the light grew and there was neither sound nor smell, and Mungo swallowed deeply and crossed himself and closed his eyes like a wee boy.

"Mungo," said the voice.

When he looked again, the light was covering the whole wall like a great patch of golden mist, and in the centre of it was a small perfect figure, so small he thought at firest it was a yellow cat, but which he then saw was more manlike, and it had transparent wings that reached to the ground. Mungo crossed himself again.

"In God's name, who is that disturbing the night?" he said in a reverent voice, for—of course—he knew that he was in the presence of an angel.

"You ken well what I am," said the angel simply.

Mungo went down stiffly onto his knees.

"You will ken also that the voice of Our Lord speaks through my lips," said the angel.

Mungo acknowledged that he did so.

"You are in great distress," said the angel.

"We are that," said Mungo. And as the angel was silent, he added, "There are evil men gathering to destroy us; men who lust for gold and filthy things."

"The Lord kens," said the angel, "and therefore I am sent to help you."

"What are we to do?"

"Listen: you can neither fight nor run, but the Lord will work a miracle for you."

"Alas, we are no worthy of it."

"Listen," said the angel. "You will go into the forest, into the very heart of it, to the place that you ken of, and there you will make a Soldier—aye, one whose purpose will be to fight for you and defend you in the evil days that are to come."

"A Soldier?" gasped Mungo. "But how?"

"You will make him out of the bark of a tree," said the angel, "and out of the earth of the glade, and out of the fire of the wood, and out of the water of the mountain; and you will put this cross about his neck, and he will be your own Soldier." And the angel took a small golden cross from his own throat and gave it into Mungo's hands. "And you will never say the forest is pagan," said the angel, reading what was in Mungo's mind, "for the same God created all things under the heavens, and He created hell and the devils that are in it."

"Forgive me, I am an ignorant man," said Mungo, trembling.

"Before long you will rise to heaven," said the angel, and something like a smile was on his face. "But remember—the Soldier must only be used for good. Use him for anything less than that, and you will destroy yoursel for ever."

*For ever*, said the walls. *For ever*, said the roofbeams. And the light slowly faded, became a point, and vanished altogether.

Mungo was alone in the black room. He felt numb.
"Perhaps it's dreaming I was." He clenched his fist,
and—there it was. Cold and hard and very real: the cross
the angel had given him. On his knees still, the old man
gave up a prayer of thanksgiving for the miracle of that
night. Then he got to his feet. I must go into the forest,
to the very heart and navel of it.

He knew the place that the angel meant.

Wolves' Crag.

Saints preserve us! Why to that heathenish place?

Then he minded on the angel's words and was bitterly
ashamed. Am I the man who is to ape the power of God
and embark on my own creation? But may Your will be
done, he said.

He walked out into the night.

# 10

# *The Tale*
# *of the Unextinguished Moon*

A tale told in the bothies, a tale of the long nights of winter—but one that was never told in the hearing of any priest.

Once upon a time the Moon fell into the earth. This was after the mountains had been created, and the seas, and the straths, and the forests, but there were no men or women. This, the folk in the bothies said, was how men and women had come into the world.

It was the Bog King who caused it. When the straths were made, many wee glens were made with them, and the water from the mountain burns got trapped in some of these glens and became stagnant, and the earth there became soft, and the two blended together, water and earth, and so the bogs were made, and the black Bog King sat at the bottom under the reeds and the mud and the sticky green slime, and ruled it all, and the bogs became full of ghoulies and bogles and dead things and horrors that crept in the night. Then all walking creatures learned to fear the bogs, because whenever a fawn or a boar, a badger or a cuddie, or even the harmless little hedgehog entered them in dark moonless nights, the bogles would rise up wailing out of their holes, and the wisp lights would flicker, and the slimy hands of all the dead horrors beneath the mud would grasp at the poor creature's legs, and pull it screaming piteously down into the terrible death that waited, grinning, in the Bog King's court.

Now the Sun was distant and wouldn't stir himself for the sake of animal-kind, but when the Moon heard of all the evil that was going on in bogland whenever her back was turned, she decided to go down herself and see what could be done. So she covered her shining body with a dark cloak, and pulled a black hood over her gleaming hair, and entered the bogland, stepping easily from tussock to tussock by the light of her white feet; and whenever the ghoulies and bogles came wailing and gnashing at her, or the horrors and the dead things rose and scrabbled at her with their cold fingers, she threw back her hood, and the light of her beautiful face flooded the whole countryside, and the dead things fled shrieking away.

(Mungo, crossing the burn, feet scuffing the wet stones, fingers scrabbling for a hold among the tufts and the waterpurpie, running, walking, running again with the gait of a hunted man.)

But it was a huge bog, and the squelching mud seemed to stretch away for ever and ever, and at length the Moon began to weary of picking her way across it. So she sat down to rest on the trunk of an old tree that was lying fallen and half-submerged in the ooze. She sat back thankfully and rested her feet on one branch, and laid her head on another. Then the tree began to move! Aaah—but it wasn't a tree at all! No, it was the Bog King himself lying basking there like a hippopotamus in the slime, and the two branches were his arms. He grabbed her feet in one hand and threw the other round her neck and, struggle though she might, the Moon couldn't get free. Then the Bog King drew her down, down into the clart, down under the peat and under the very roots of the reeds, down into his own dark kingdom, and a black bubble or two burst on the surface, and the Moon was gone.

I need hardly tell you how great was the rejoicing among the bogles when they realized that their hated enemy was gone, and that every night would now be a black night with only the faintest starfire from heaven to watch their evil doings. They jumped and skirled and screeched with joy, they made the very branches of the forest dirl and ding with their clamour. They grew bolder in their forays from the bog; they crept by night over the moorland tearing and butchering any living creature they met; and the owls and the eagles and the ravens perched higher and higher on the branches for safety, and the squirrels and badgers burrowed deeper, and the deer and boars, the otters and beavers, even the smallest beasties, the very beetles, glow-worms and spiders, retreated further and further yet from the marches of bogland, and darkness and death were on the face of the world.

Then Goban the creator stamped his hoof, and the trees —the real trees of Scotland—began to talk and move. In the wind their leaves whistled to each other; in the still their bodies creaked and groaned tree-language. Where is the Moon? they asked. They swivelled their heads, turning from side to side. Where is she? They sent out their leaves in the days the world would later know as autumn. Find her! they said to the leaves, and the leaves went fluttering and whistling across the straths. The birds took to the air, the burrowers took to the earth, the fish plummeted the lochbeds: they all sought her. But the Moon was nowhere to be found.

(And Mungo, clambering the learigs, entering the forest as the first bird awakens, senses rather than sees the disturbed hunters in the bracken that rustles and scrapes noisily under the hem of his cassock, Mungo desperate with mission.)

Beside the bog grew a small hawthorn tree. She was so close to the bog and so small that the bogland folk had forgotten all about her. Well, the hawthorn held her wheesht until all the other trees had had their say. Then she piped up, "Ahem, folks, I think that maybe I might just ken where our Moon is," though she had to repeat herself several times before they all heard her. Where? said the rowan, Where? said the birch, Where? said the yew and the pine, the fir and the alder, Where? rumbled the old oak last of all. And so the hawthorn told them how she had seen the Bog King pull the Moon down below the surface. When they heard this, the trees marched in a great mass—yes, the entire forest moved —down the mountain slopes and along the straths until they had surrounded the bog on all sides. Then they sank their roots down under the reeds and into the slime and mud until they found the hall of the Bog King, and began knocking on his roof. At first it was a gentle tap, then louder, then louder still, until it sounded as though the thunder had sunk under the earth in pursuit of the vanished Moon, so loud did that hammering sound.

And that is exactly what the Bog King thought it was.

"Who's that banging on my roof?" he called, and the pine answered, "Me, *Guithais*, with the thunder in my roots wanting our Moon." "Away to hell," said the Bog King, and laughed.

"Who's that thumping in my loft?" he shouted next,

and the alder replied, "Me *Fearn*, with the thunder in my roots wanting our Moon." "Ach away and boil your heid," grumbled the Bog King.

"Who's that skirling down my lum?" he growled a while later, and the oak said, "Me, *Darach*, with the thunder in my roots wanting our Moon."

And then the Bog King, fearing that the roof and walls were going to fall in about his lugs, broke the twining chains which held the Moon, and the trees saw the strange beautiful face of the lost Moon rising up through the foul waters of the bog, and a moment later she was shining down on them again from heaven, and all the bogles and ghoulies and dead things fled shrieking away. But from that day to this the Moon's face is pitted with dark shadows whenever she remembers her stay in the Bog King's hall.

(Mungo, resting against a trunk, raises his face as the cock crows in the invisible village and thinks of Mairi sleeping. And asks himself, "Is there any sin I would no commit to save her life?" And there is none. And he smiles, knowing it.)

Now the Moon had twin bairns by the Bog King, and the laddie's name was Nechtan, and the lassie's was Mongfinn, and they were gey bonny to look on, but as they were made in part of the cold black mud of the bog, they could not fly up to heaven with their mother. So they stayed here on middle-earth, in this world of ours, and whiles they would look up to heaven to see their mother's shining face, and whiles they would look down below into their father's darkness; and they were the first humans, because they were tall and slender and supple as young trees, but their roots were not anchored so deep in the earth, nor were their heads held so high to heaven; and they had legs like the deer, and eyes like the hawk, and a throat like the songbird's, and an appetite like the wolf, and pride like the eagle, and cunning like the fox.

That was how man and woman first came into the world, they said in the evening in the peat-fire light.

Well, grass grows, water flows, folk lust, and one day Mongfinn was heavy with her brother's child. A boy it was; but, looking at the squalling wee thing with the pride and joy that all parents have felt since, Mongfinn and Nechtan had a sort of premonition that things were not as they should be. And as there was this shadow lying over them which they couldn't understand or explain in any way, that is what they called the bairn—Shadow—because he had come between them like a shadow in the night.

(And Mungo smells the morning in the forest, the sweet summer morning, and finds himself among the blue and yellow flowers that are slowly opening to the first sun, and Ah! he sighs suddenly, cheerfully, breathing the morning, and his fears take bat wings and fly off with the vanishing night.)

The mountains were still moving in those days, the thunder giants still rolled boulders for sport, and cast great slabs of warm rock at each other across yawning ravines. One bright forenoon when the rainbow was standing high among the clouds and the water was dripping from the heather flowers, a hundred and more firs fell to their knees and bowed themselves like young novices, and when the earth closed again it closed around their topmost branches, and all below was gone back into the earth once more, tree and leaf, squirrel and nest, and Mongfinn and her Nechtan who walked no more in the light of the world.

What became of the son? Human, he had the appetite of a wolf, and the wolf-folk found him, hunting. Strangely enough, they didn't kill him, because they thought he was a wolf, so they raised him as one of their own, a young wolf cub. Shadow grew strong and forest-wise and stealthy. He killed for food, and he killed for pleasure too; but then sometimes a feyness would come on him, though it never came on his four-legged kindred, and he would take a scunner to himself and his bloody hands and his dripping jaws; and then he would wander away into the solitude, away from blood and the stink of blood, and talk gently to the trees and beasts, and whiles he would press his face into the soft moss round the tree roots and weep. Then the forest folk looked at him and wondered.

All except the corbie. The corbie is a wise bird, and understood things better left unspoken. One day, as Shadow walked disconsolately beneath the branches, the black corbie perched above his head and spoke to him. "Shadow, Shadow, what makes you so sad?" And Shadow answered her, "O, it's all alone I am, sister, and no one to share the burden of life with me." So the corbie spoke to him again and told him to go to a certain birch tree, and to take the tree and to make from it a woman of the white wood, and Shadow did so; and because her body was white as the heartwood of the tree, and because her hair was fair as the shoots of it, he called her Bas-Barra-Geal, which is Princess Bright Palm; and from their loving line the folk of Scotland and of all the world are descended.

(And the warm sun glowed in the green overhead, and down into every glade and clearing it spilled the cascade of its golden apples. On such a day, thought Mungo, I ken the life that is immortal. And reassured by the miracle with which he was surrounded, the old man pushed on to work his own bit miracle for the folk, there in the forest's depth.)

## 11

## *Uruisg*

Waiting. Waiting.

The trees bent over him. We are waiting. Brother pine stood at the edge of the rocks, his long legs were thick and scaly, reddish-brown to black, his chest was bright red-yellow, and a hundred feet high in the air he nodded his broad short head. Sister birch by his side shook her white tresses, and a fall of early seeds drifted over the Crag's lip and settled on the ages-deep cones and bracken and needles and tangled roots of the glade, and the lime bed below where bones human and bestial fermented in the earth dew.

Waiting.

The tree folk stared at him. Yes, we too are waiting, brother. The blackcap kept his scold and instead warbled shortly *hee-ti-weeto-weeto* and was still. As briefly a redstart answered *tick-tick-ptui*, and around the rocks the warning went out, but it was a summons to gather and watch rather than to flee. Squirrel heads appeared—here!—there!—out of tree holes at midmost height, and a leaf—a second—a shower of dusty moss fell as a branch was lightened of the scamperer's paws. Mungo looked up. *Se-se-se* said a goldcrest, *se-se-tzit.*

Waiting.

Wolf-eyes were regarding him—and he them—without fear. A young male wolf padded up to him and sniffed dog-like at his cassock. *Pruk!* cried a corbie from the high pine wall. "You are all here then, children," said Mungo. "Now I maun begin it."

He touched the earth and the earth quivered. From the carpet of cones and needles that lay about his feet he pulled out the arm of a fallen alder and looked at it.

*You will make him out of the bark of a tree.*

Well... I dinna ken about thon.

Mungo held the branch at arm's length. "Come forth, Soldier, and be a man," he commanded.

He counted One, Two, Three—and nothing happened. He counted first seven, then twelve, and nothing happened. He said the Paternoster, in Latin, then in Gaelic, and still nothing happened. He stuck the branch upright in the ground and tried again. Nothing happened. He sat on his hunkers and scratched his head. Then he minded that it was the *bark* and not the body of the tree from which life was to come, and clambered to his feet again. There were as many trees in the forest as drops in the sea, nor had he minded, so taken was he with the event of the night before, to bring an axe for cutting the bark with. But he had a little gardener's knife in his girdle, and with that he scrambled up the rocks and cut a fair-sized sheet of bark from a pine tree standing at the top of them. He laid the bark on the ground. "Come forth, Soldier, and be a man."

Nothing.

"Aye, I just kent it sounded too easy," grumbled Mungo.

All the rest of that day Mungo laboured devotedly at his miracle, yet his miracle resolutely refused to happen. *Earth!* He made a small crumbly doll-like figure out of a few handfuls of topsoil and grass roots, and he muttered over it a while, feeling rather daft, and when it failed to move for all his mutterings and incantations, he cast the thing aside angrily and it broke. *Fire!*—But how could anything be made of fire? Still, he used the bark, rubbing at it industriously with a stick until the point began to blacken and a little trail of smoke rose upward; and when at last his strip of bark was alight, he held it up and drew cross-shapes in the air and called the Soldier to come to him, even as the three miraculous Jews had come out of the burning fiery furnace in yon pagan place Babylon. It glowed and it sparkled and smoked, and then there was nothing left but a sweet smell, and the ashes of it black in his dry withered hand. *Water!* He turned to the earth again and dug into it like a dog, finding many bones certainly, but also water beneath them, for the whole area was soft and green. Then he fashioned a larger figure, scooping the water out in his palms until the whole was one compact mass of mud. It lay staring up at him, a great carcass. *Wind!* Man is born of the wind. When the wind blows out of his mouth, he lives; when it ceases, he knows death. Mungo tried to breathe life into his creation. As he knelt by the muddy pool he had dug, spitting the wet earth out of his teeth, he wondered: perhaps the Lord's affronted with my playings? But every man who fathers a child plays God, and every woman who holds creation inside her plays God, and how many baptisms had Mungo sanctified in his time, every last one of them a mind-defying miracle?

"Och, why give a man the lock without the key to fit it?" He felt that he had all the parts of the secret, but how these parts fitted together and what moved them then—these were things he did not know. He asked his God to help him. He prayed, O he prayed; but in the end there was nothing to be heard except the sound of his own praying. So he stopped his Latin, for it came to him that the words were going outside the forest that should not. I have the tree, the earth, the fire, the water, the very breath, but I have not the man! He sighed and sat himself down looking despondently at his hands. From one of the great trees overhead a bat took flight.

It was the time of dusk deepening into dark on that first night when little Mairi was lying awake wondering where he was; and all the folk of the village were lying wearied with the haymaking, and Una and Siubhan and Sorcha were closing their tired minds to wide-awake thoughts about the future fear, and Wat and Fearchar were open-eyed in their separate beds thinking about the coming butchery, and old Thomas and Manus were happily not thinking at all, and Pedair and Ringean and all the bairns had long been in the land of Nod, and Nessa was sniffing, and beautiful Seonaid was rubbing her rich wasted body; and then the rain began to fall.

And Flittermouse the bat flew with it through the forest giving the shrill little cry that folk who heard it—and, hearing it, crossed themselves—understood as *Gu la bais!*, "till the day of death!" In their language they called him *Badharan dubh*, the dark wanderer. For the bat had once been very beautiful. Ah yes, in days when the world was young and guile unknown, he had been blue as the kingfisher and white as the swan, with eyes so big and lovely-bright that they had been a flashing fire darting between the trunks of the perfect land, even as Flittermouse darted now in the owls' time. So beautiful was the bat then, that on the day of Crucifixion he mocked our Young Hero's agony, and while the robin was trying to pull out the nails and soaking his little breast red with the precious blood, the bat had circled, mocking, "See how lovely I am! See how swift I am!" And Christ turned his tortured eyes and looked at him, and the beautiful blue and white drained away like water from a pool, and he became blind and black and whirled away helplessly until he met the rising of the night and there he drowned for evermore. That is why he now wanders the darkness like a ghost and cries in his thin wee voice: "See how blind I am! See how ugly I am!" *Gu la bais.* And singers cried him *Dealan dubh badhalaiche choille*—the little black wandering flame of the woods.

Not a light showed in the village as Flittermouse passed his soft squeal over the roofs, and the only sound was the steady patter of summer rain on the thatch, the louder singing of it on the swelling waters of the burn, its rustle in the still uncut fields. Flittermouse found the roof he wanted and slithered neatly through the smokehole.

Black Finella sat in the darkness unsleeping. In truth, she was so old that, like Mungo, she hardly slept at all. Night after night she sat in her one chair, her chapped lips moving, her dim eyes staring ahead, thinking of everything or nothing—who knows?—and her cat sat curled there nose in tail beside her feet. Only for the last hour before dawn, maybe, would the old woman lie down under her shawls. Flittermouse fluttered onto a rafter and perched there. The cat looked up, one open green eye. Beneath the hanging iron cauldron the fire was a lingering haze of smoke.

"*Gu la bais,*" said Flittermouse quietly.

Unheard sounds hung in the air. Strange, unheard voices assailed the little bat. Flittermouse felt unsafe and unhappy. His head darted around and around. There was nothing living in the black night room except for the old woman and the one green-eyed cat, the beetles in the wall, the spider beyond the hearth, the worms turning like fate beneath the earthen floor. Part of the daub and

131

wattle wall slid silently away from its bracing wooden posts. Flittermouse gasped—bat squeak. This happened every night. Finella didn't move, and the cat, impervious through long experience, made out he had heard nothing.

The mild, fresh, very black outside air entered the very black and stuffy room with a smell of... soup.

Hairst bree—the harvest pot: neck of lamb, chopped
(the sound of the chopping of it)
The pattering feet of a sister long dead coming with a pitcher full of water, and her own mother there at the wooden platter preparing the vegetables: 4 turnips
(chop)
6 carrots, young
(chop chop)
6 spring onions with green
(chop chop chop)
a bowlful of broad beans
*Ella!*
Herself, the shawl-wrapped bundle that she was long ages ago behind the cowl of years in yon little white house with the red roof by a blue water among green green hills; and her mother telling her, older now, such braw tales of rivers that sang like girls, of great trees that shouted like warriors, of the glorious songs of the land where creatures were, any one of whom might be a wizarded prince or princess (for there was a power in the land, her mother had said, a power that was there by grace for all folk, the very pulse of the living earth that beat and thrust up its green shoots into glory, onto the chopping board, into scullery soup); her mother with the boulder-heavy womb of a wean that never was to be born.

(And Manus and Tomas too, unsleeping that same night, heard the whinnying visions gallop past the bothy door; and Pedair and Ringean, lost in puppy sleep, deep in the warm folds of it, caught glimpses of adventuring swords and fire flashing on the boy-made mountains; and Seonaid and Nessa turned with a thought of black beards and strong sinewy arms—

Soldier...)

And in her memory too, the devastation, now as always, of that day the riders came, of the day after her father had marched off, unwillingly and in fear, to die bloody in another's war, and then the coming of that war, of the men high on the ridge above the little house, on the shoulder of that greenest of hills, riding down whooping—*Faol!*—their weapons flashing head-high amidst flowing plumes, so beautiful is the panoply of war; and there the priest of a Christian village, the priest decked in mistletoe, holding out his pink palms, and his soft lips crying "Brothers!", aye, For The Love Of Christ he cried, "Brothers!", and they butchered him like a feeble lamb, the long swords that rose glinting (in the rainlight, she minded), and he fell crying them his Latin that they neither knew nor cared about—*fratri*, *fratri*—and the high tide of blood was about her feet as she ran to the place where the men were heaving on her mother's straddled womb; and one laughed at her ("Ye're over wee for us, lassie!") and cuffed her aside with his sword-hilt (the scar on her old head now aching with the memory). And she ran from it, bare-legged and near to naked, through the laughter of red jaws in the black beard, through the smell of the burning as her little house clothed itself in flame, as the white walls blackened and fell inward, as her pet wood-pigeon rose through the smokehole screaming with wings of fire, her Beauty, trying to outfly the flames that outflew everything and were everywhere.

(And gentle virgin Sorcha moaning in her sleep, kicking out her limbs, "Yes! No! No!" screaming as her dream lover turns to nightmare and roguishly rapes her on the floor of her burned dwelling.

"Sister, sister!" cries Siubhan shaking her. "Wake up! Bad dream! That's all, hen, that's all!"

Soldier...)

And in the smouldering afternoon, when the vicious burning had finally faded to shadows and pale flickerings in the falling rain, Finella returned to the place where her heart had been. Sword-fall, echo, and silence; the world ended on a bitten scream; a world lost while she was yet a child. O blue water among the green hills! O little white house with the red roof! When we are young, such cruelty. When we are old, the usual memory that such cruelty never was. But for her, the truthful memory.

When she came back to the village, when the violated women who survived were picking themselves up, when the silence was that is beyond tears...they saw the horse with the dead rider standing by that one remaining wall, drenched both by the rain, skin slippery with rain and blood. And the raped women walked slowly into the ruins, and picked up what they could: charred sickle, hot and broken scythe, here a flail, there a piece of broken post; and slowly, deliberately, without fear or hatred, they wrote the story of their manyfold rape on the body of the dead rider, till there was nothing left of him but a few shreds of raw flesh, and the soil turning red where his life's blood had trodden it.

Soldier...

And in the smoky air said Flittermouse, "*Gu la bais. Gu la bais*"—Till the day of death!

Never again could Finella sleep without hearing cries as she lay in bed. And in the candles burning on a Christian altar she saw the flaming wings of her woodpigeon called

Beauty, smelt the terrible burning of her harmless flesh. And when Mungo, also hag-haunted, knelt in his kirk that was made out of forest pines and prayed, "Son of Man, save this village; Son of Man, save your flock," Finella was different: she longed once more to sink her sickle into the hateful flesh of the evil ones, and nail their guts dripping to the stockade gate.

The memory and the vision faded; the village quietened; the sound of the thundering hoofs and the wolf yell, the screaming and the burning, sank back into pools of silence till summoned again; night closed once more over the strath, the sleepers sighed and were still; humanity was safe while only the owls hunted abroad. Finella opened her eyes. Cat, laird of the fireplace, stood up and stretched and yawned. The old woman scratched his wise head and looked up at Flittermouse.

"Aweel then, my hinny," she said, "and what's the old fool doing?"

And the bat answered: *Gu la bais.*


For Mungo in the morning, Mungo in the blaze of noon, Mungo in the evening light, Mungo striding, seeing stars in revelation, still did not know how to accomplish the godly task set to him. He sat on a tussock deep in the glade and threw wee stones on the ground. The beasts of the green world circled the strange *duine*. The beavers, boars and wild pigs that were in Scotland in those days nuzzled about his legs, and, yes, the glow-worms shone in the undergrowth, and the owls swooped overhead, and a little deer, wolf-hunted, was sent ben with a saintly blessing while the wolves hung back and listened to his sad *duine* words.

> *Strath of the winding waters, pools and waving reeds, how can I bear to leave you, even in the days of my age?*
> *How fine is your oak, there, with the thunder on his head*

*how brave your pine that strides the mountain-
side; how lovely the soft birch, smoother than girls'
skin, cool as gravestones, cool as the evening mirk.*

*Deer, little antlered one, deer, little belling one, I hear
you lowing in the sheen of morning; fox, red-faced
hunter, wolf, free dog of the wild, your bark is on
the evening wind.*

*Eagles, sons of the cold cliffs, hawks, daughters of the roar-
ing gale, swift, swift is the wind in your pinions;
loudly, loudly the northland calls to the children of
the sky.*

*I hear a strain of music in the forest. The stag shakes
the green dew from his antlers. Salmon are
crowding the secret places under the hill. The cry of
the bittern is on the winter loch.*

*Over my strath, God has thatched a roof of stars. Sky-
fruit of the moon, silver berries of the night tree,
they shine like frost needles on a black pine, icicles
hanging from the rafters of heaven.*

*If the hopes of humankind were ears of corn, still they
could not fill this valley in its beauty of the harvest-
time. If the sorrows of humankind were autumn leaves,
the loch would yet carry them all to the further shore.*

*I have only one desire, and may God forgive it. Strath of
the winding waters, pools and waving reeds, let me
never leave you, even in the days of my age,*

sang Mungo.

Suddenly a bat fluttered about his head, a dark cat
cried from the still. "Is it yoursel?" said Black Finella,
hirpling towards him out of the gloaming. The cat ran
beside her. The bright eyes of the glade drew back.

"Aye, it is that," said the old priest suspiciously.

Finella cast a look at the tangled floor and saw evidence
of the old man's work. "You'll have managed the white
magic then," she said. "Or is it my help you're needing?"

"There is no magic save how you got here, you old rickle of bones," said Mungo. "I was praying in the wilderness as behoves a godly man, and you would do well to pray likewise, if it's in you."

Finella gave a toothless cackle, bat and cat together echoing the squall of it. In the dark the sight and sound were most alarming.

"By God, I believe you are the very witch they say!" said Mungo, jumping up.

"Ach, hold you wheesht," said the crone. "I ken something of your reason for being here. It's the *uruisg* you'll be after. I saw it in your eyes yon night, listening to that wheen of lassies' blethers. You're here to charm the *uruisg* with your words—is that no it?"

Mungo said nothing, but glowered at her.

"No," said Finella. "No." She turned over a bark shaving with her toe and saw the earth within it. "Aye, so that's it," she murmured. In such a voice she spoke whenever she saw another wean delivered safely to the world. Mungo snorted his indignation down his nose. "What wood are you using?" she asked.

"Wood, woman? The wood I found."

"What wood, but?"

Mungo gestured. "How do I ken, you daft—? There! The wood on the trees."

"But no the ash?"

"Eh? Ash? Well—"

"It's the ash you maun use," she said with finality.

The ash. *Uinnse*, they call it.

Why?

The story was sufficiently well known to the old pair standing there in the glade as night slid slowly into morning, for it tells of the beginning of things and how the world ash tree holds heaven in its upper branches with its roots in the earth below and its green leaves overhanging all the worlds of the universe, the place of fire, and the place of cold, the realm of the frost giants, the realm of the dwarfs, and the abode of eagles; for in the beginning, the One Who Was hanged himself on that tree to discover the secret runic wisdom, and that tree was his first mount; and when his heels knocked on the trunk, a slab of wood broke and fell in, and from a hollow within the tree shot a huge white swan that whirled up into the air in high spirals. Now the Evil Thing that was in the world in those days took the form of a great black raven, pursued the swan, and, sinking his talons in the soft downy chest, tore the white one apart. Out from the swan leaped a blood-red wolf and galloped off across the ridge of the world. The Evil Thing became a vast shaggy bear, took the wolf one swipe from his paw, and knocked the red muzzle clean away. From out of the wolf galloped a stallion, swanwhite and wolf-fast, with the strength of all creation in his flanks: Goban, horse of the terrible one. And the Evil Thing is still chasing him to this day.

"Yet I dinna see why the elder or the honeysuckle shouldna do, to say nothing of the rowan," Mungo grumbled.

"We maun use ash wood, and none other," said Finella. "The abode of the good spirit."

And so they used ash wood. This was during the second day (the third of the haymaking back in the strath), and a wet mist came and hung over the land, and the trees climbed upward into the grey smoke and lost their summits in its vapour. What are we doing? thought Mungo, and answered himself: *God's will*; and commanded his doubting self not to doubt it, no, not to doubt it for the slightest moment, else their faith might not be strong enough to accomplish the awful task.

Forenoon mounted and passed. The sun travelled westward to the land of ghosts. They worked on. Midmost in the afternoon they stopped and ate. Ate in silence, looking sideways at each other while they chewed, their bodies blurring in the greeny mist. And then Finella said, looking at Mungo,

"When I was a bairn, ken, I dreamt I would meet with a bonny young lord and wed him."

To which Mungo answered,

"And when I was a bairn, did I no dream of meeting the bonny young lady and all?"

Two wizened mouths cracked and grinned.

They made him of earth and wrapped him in ash bark, their *uruisg*, and by the time night was coming on again they had finished, and a huge manlike figure lay on the ground before them. Mungo lit a fire of dry juniper twigs. A strange awe gripped them when they saw what they had done: a feeling that possibly, just possibly, they had done that which is not canny, that which no human should aspire to do, even if guided by a good spirit. Even if guided by God.

Finella whispered to her companion, "How...? The last thing... I dinna ken how to do it."

And Mungo whispered back, "An angel inspired me and he has given me this." And he drew the little golden cross from his bosom.

Still lay the forest; not a sound, not the breath of one, cracked the silent ache of that moment. The pines, the tall black brothers, were still as statues; even the quivering aspen tree ceased its motion, and it seemed that the rushing night itself paused westlins on the crimson rim of evening as Mungo took the cross and hung it on its thin golden wire round the neck of their creation.

"*Uruisg*, folk's *uruisg*," said Finella. "Keep our enemies out of the strath."

And Mungo said, "Come forth, Soldier, and be a man."

And it happened.

By the light of the juniper fire the giant began to move.

He was huge, this Soldier. There was at least ten feet of him, and his shoulders were broad as the ox's, his head massive as a bull's, his arms were two strong branches, and each hand was vast as the anvil in Calum's smithy.

He opened his lids, and there where Mungo had made two socket-like hollows with the balls of his thumbs, were two deep eyes that looked at the old couple in the firelight.

He drew up one leg, and there where Finella had fashioned a knee out of knotted bark, the joint bent upwards and powerful muscles were seen to move down calf and up thigh in a sudden shimmer of shadow.

He began to raise himself on his elbow.

"Wait," said Mungo.

The giant stopped. He had a wide-open bewildered face, like that of a beast being herded to the slaughterhouse almost.

"You are no human," said Mungo, fighting his own fear of this wanchancy thing they had made. "You will have no name. You exist for one purpose only, and no for any other at all. You will obey my voice, and no any other voice. No demon or wraith or evil spirit must enter you. You are Soldier. That is all you are, all you ever will be; and when your purpose is done, you will return to earth again. Do you understand that?"

And in a deep sepulchral voice the Soldier answered, "*Yes.*"

Mungo and Finella nodded their heads at that and smiled to each other. Mungo muttered a blessing in the name of the Father and the Son and the Holy Ghost, and took a palmful of water and sprinkled it on the Soldier, while Finella murmured to herself and passed a mistletoe sprig over his head.

> *Stane chack!*
> *Deevil tak!*

cried a stanechacker in the overhanging trees, *keewick* screeched an owl. The forest began to move once more with the sound of a great mouth that has held its breath and can now breathe again. The night rose up and poured across the sky. A young fox barked on the Crag.

"I ken yon voice," said Mungo.

It was little red Faidh who came scampering down the rocks towards him like a puppy to his missing master.

And the moon, the reapers' moon, rose over the forest and spilled its light down among the trees. It fell on the Soldier's face and he blinked fearfully at it.

Standing by his creation Mungo gave a great shout, and the owl that swooped across the forest's roof, and the wild duck that flew seawards to the river's mouth, and the corbie that fled screaming over the loch in the rain and the summer's night all cried to the world, "They've done it!"
THEY'VE DONE IT!

And so with new hope rising in their hearts, the priest and the witch-woman, Mungo and Finella, walked back to the village in the first glint of morning, and the great Soldier walked by them with a steady tread, and red Faidh ran barking, and Finella's dark cat trotted by her ankles, and Flittermouse the bat fluttered above them all making his shrill wee squeals ring over the curling mist.

# Interlude

## *That Same Night*

Miles away, inland, in the western mountains that same night, the bandit leader raised his head. "Ach, only a bat," he grunted as the small shadow sped across the moon. His men were sleeping under plaid. The leader lay awake looking at the stars. There was no mist. The weather was fine. It would be a good day.

The camp was on the shelf of a mountain slope. A horse track led to it and from it, sentries on each door. They were beyond the forest. Trees flowed through the glen below like a wooden stream, but here was only the heather and the windblown grass, and a camp that no enemy could surprise.

The leader was never short of riders at his back. They respected him; they would happily follow him, cruel as he was. He never lost a fight, never turned his back on one; never abandoned one of his men, never forgave an enemy; he could find cover on a moor where the hares felt naked, could feed and reward his followers in the harshest land. He could do all this. He was nobody's fool.

The leader stared at the sky. It had been a summer of harsh cries and glinting death blades. His band had been hired by one thane to fight a neighbouring thane, two valleys at war; and he had fought that bitter war for them. He had prolonged it until both valleys were exhausted, then burned and sacked one and raised the thane's head—his original paymaster, incidentally—above the ashes of its toppled tower. He now had the other at his mercy. And he had no mercy. •

His men loved him for having no mercy, for his many betrayals, for the foolish guests he had murdered under trust, for the weak oaths he had broken. Yes. They were a part of his hardness. He rode alone as befits a leader. And they, as they rode stirrup to stirrup behind his wolf's-head totem, made brave talk about his prowess, until even those who died obeying his orders did so boldly, with a joke in their mouths.

Day was on the mountainside. The black wolf's-head on its pole stood out against the lightening sky. Where next to go for a killing? Today's valley was already dead. His men knew it. In a few hours they would be dicing for the women. The leader was bored. He was sated with slaughter. There was something that eluded him. He lay awake trying to think what it was. He had no real religion but plenty of superstitions, and this uncanny feeling upset him. Life was one debauchery of smoke and burning, and *himself* there in the blood and torn dwellings of it, *himself* cutting through the crying and the rapine and the children sprawled like broken dolls, *himself* riding from campfire to campfire in the smell of horses and leather and male sweat and last night's embers crackling in the thin rain, and at the end of it all, still, the undeniable indefinable joy of tossing his reins over a bush and saying, "Here I will make my camp tonight. Here I will lay me down to rest." And sleeping by his horse in the gloaming.

It occurred to him then that his life was one riding on a long red road from a place that was coldness and anger and hunger and hate in the chill and ever-blowing sea wind of his own past. He had made a song about it, all fierce agony. His men sang it as they rode to another burning. He had been known to spare an old grandmother clutching an infant child.

A horse snorted and jerked her head. The two sentries rubbed their eyes with morning dew. Soon they would mount and ride, their straining horses would crest the ridge, and they would descend on the helpless valley like the sails of death.

The leader stretched and yawned. That's how it would be. And then... At the back of his mind was that other valley where they would be gathering the harvest soon. His men had wondered why they hadn't taken it after they massacred its men in yon bonny ambush. But the leader knew. Let the gowks feel secure in their valley! Let them think we have gone for ever! After the harvest the wolf-riders would come and they would winter in that fat valley with its bulging granaries, and all that was there would be theirs, and in the spring they would ride on.

Then... And then...

The camp was quiet. The sky was lighter. No one was stirring yet. The sentries were out of sight. *Faol, faol*, said the words of their song, *let me grow the jaws of a wolf and the skin of a wolf and forget the terrible loneliness of being a man.*

The early morning fear was on the valiant and mercilesss leader of the wolfskin band.

# 12

## *Midsummer Fires*

"God in heaven defend us!" hissed Wat the woodcutter, grasping his axe. Some of the women bolted indoors and stayed there. Una and Sine reappeared, ready for battle, each with a sickle in her hand. The sickles were trembling like ears of wheat. Young Fearchar brought out a short bow and, after several fumbled attempts, fastened an arrow to its string. Blind Manus sat at his threshold and asked everyone what was happening.

"Folk, dinna fash yoursels!" Mungo cried, striding forward with both arms out before him. "This is no monster, but the tree-man a good angel from heaven instructed me to make; and we've made it together," he said, motioning to Finella. "This is our Soldier, this is, and if they bandits are half as feared of him as you are, we'll have no more to fear from them, ever." For indeed he was talking to a row of blank walls.

Feigh! what a stramash there was, what a dauding and a dinning! As the Soldier came to the stockade gate and, the gate being shut, lifted it out of the ground as easy as plucking a flower and walked inside, even Wat took to his heels; Una's and Sine's sickles clattered to the ground behind their vanishing skirts; Fearchar, finding himself locked out, skinned up onto a roof and clung there with his legs wrapped round the gable-end; and the oxen bellowed, and the hens squawked, and the dogs ran barking with their tails between their legs, and generally the din was terrible. The Soldier stood in the midst of it all, and what a strange uncomprehending look there was on his face! And there too, behind a pair of enormous eyes that were near swallowing the freckles on her face, was little Mairi with Faidh the fox nuzzling about her knees. "I'm n-no feared, Father, I'm no f-feared," she said to Mungo, though her eyes were tied to the huge earthen face of the Soldier.

Rob the Gowk, who had just woken up, came out yawning and bade the giant *Aye, grand day* without a care in the world, being a gowk. Blind Manus, whom no one had yet told what was happening, folded his arms in a huff and began to whistle the tune of "Fair Janet sat in her bonny bower."

> *Sewing her silken seam,*

piped Mairi. She gulped hard and loud,

> *And wished to be in Carterhaugh*
> *Among the leaves so green.*

"That's the stuff, wee yin, sing!" Thus Finella, chuckling.

Slowly doors opened, and here and there heads appeared. A gaggle of bairns stood about the Soldier staring up at him open-mouthed, even as fieldmice might sit staring at a scarecrow towering hugely overhead.

So Mungo brought the Soldier to the village on the last day of the grass-cutting.

The reaping season, however, left no time to stand and gawp, and the folk—those whose world was, after all, just their own homely village, and the strath around, and beyond that mere passing rumour from unseen realms—soon accepted the existence of the great unhuman Soldier as another manifestation of the fearsome ways of their One awful true God; and though they took good care to steer safe of his long shadow, yet, for all that, he was no more strange to them than the *uruisg* of the forest or the *angel* of the kirk—in whom they all believed most heartily—nor saw they anything odd in this Earth, which gave them the terrible miracle of life itself, now yielding up a fighter for earth's people from out its own hidden bowels.

So within the hour they had fairly recovered themselves from their fear, and on their old priest's assurance, most solemnly given, that the Holy Spirit was with them and that God's will bound the Soldier to them in bonds of gleaming gold that nothing evil could ever break, they nodded, and said Aye, but it was damn uncanny so it was, and they had never seen such an orra great hulking creature, no, and never wished to again, but that if the Father said this giant brute of his would not go crashing about the bothies and making a mess of them and causing a sore disturbance to the kye, well then, they said, they supposed they were happy enough to go to the fields and God's will be done. Mungo smiled like a daftie and blessed them and assured them again and again that all was safe, but still it was not until he had ordered the Soldier into the kirk, and the giant had boomed out "Yes" in a voice that made them all jump half a foot backwards, and then stooped his great form nearly in two to pass the threshold into the cool shadows of the place, that they decided that, Well, the Almighty being happy to accommodate the creature in *His* house, they were happy to go fieldwards and get on with their work. And so they did, though many a doubting neck was turned in all the claik and blether of it back to the village half expecting to see the great treeskin running there amuck with the belfry of the kirk hanging in ruins about his mighty lugs.

Haytime. They finished the cutting of the grass as the pollen was falling, and though the proverb says "haymake is heartbreak," and says so truly, this season all was well in the strath and the world was kind to them; the honey-faced year smiled into its midsummer dimples, and the days went singing by like linnets in the lift. Only young Fergus, wounded to the bone, lay dying in the midst of it all. But he was only one, and a towersman, and the village passed him by.

They worked eagerly, singing. Twenty forks heaved among the cuttings of the field while Sine steadied the unwilling ox and Rob giggled on the carter's seat. Then, when the cart was loaded, Rob kicked the beast once and off they went, rumbling and grinding over the howe, the huge grass heap green and fragrant swaying like some lumbering creature on its creaky wooden legs, while the Gowk, with more sense than ever given credit for, manoeuvred the solid oaken wheels carefully around the many holes and broken crests of long dried mud as Sorcha and Nessa walked ahead, lifting any dangerous stones out of the path, and a bevy of bairns followed behind picking up any spillage, while Pedair and Ringean always cornered the easiest job, lying together on the top to steady the grass on its journey and making themselves king and warlord of their own green trembling castle there in the bright summer sky. And over the meadowland the Gowk steered his load with a thump and a wallop on the rickety cart that had for years past been threatening to disintegrate and never did, and down they went in procession to the gate where, within the stockade, the lave of the village folk were assembling the drying fence.

Every autumn they dismantled the fence and stored it in the barn together with the forks and other weapons of harvest. Now, while some worked in the fields at the loading, others scoured the littered stake-holes then brought out the long stakes and hammered them in at intervals of some nine feet, measured toe to heel. Next they tied five lines of rope between the stakes, the lowest being a full foot, no less, off the ground, the second a foot above that, the others being similarly distanced. That done, the women began filling the fence. They took the grass in big handfuls, as much as they could hold, shook it until the stalks were all lying roughly parallel, then laid it carefully over the lowest line, not too thickly, else there would be no ventilation, and not too thinly either, for the dried stalks, being so much lighter now, might blow away. Then they did the same with the second, third and fourth lines, adding more to each. When they came to the fifth and topmost line, which was at shoulder height, they fastened another length of rope immediately above it to hold the grass down, joining the two ropes at regular intervals with ties of rush or twisted stalks. The upper layer of grass was always the thickest and acted as a protective thatch in case of rain.

However, once the mist had cleared, the weather stayed dry, and a gentle breeze blew down the glen, enough to keep the midges away, but not enough to disorder the grass on the lines. On the first day the women filled half of the fence in this fashion, and on the second day the other half was filled likewise. When the third day came, the first filling of grass was judged to be dry enough for stacking, so while those in the fields forked more loads of green onto the Gowk's cart, those in the village stripped down the first half of the fence and moved the grass, now dry and light and minus two thirds of its bulk, onto a couple of wooden sledges and pulled it to the smaller of the barns, where it was shaken out again and spread on a rack until thoroughly dry. It was then stacked for good, though there was always someone there with a long fork to test it and prevent it from heating and catching fire. This job was constant until the winter came, as was the haymaking itself: on and on through July and August, September and October, anyone who could be spared from the coming harvest worked on the grassland, and cart after cart went down to the fences. But June hay is the best.

That afternoon of midsummer's eve, which is the eve of St John the Baptist, folk took time away from the business of the grass to stack the midsummer fire, and they sang in doing it, the Gowk's cart labouring with all manner of wood and shavings to the bonfire site; and in his small room in the kirk dying Fergus heard them and did not understand what their gaiety meant.

But then he did not really hear it, because he was dreaming. He was dreaming that he was in the room he was really in, but everything was fine with him, and he was wondering why he was here and not in the corbie tower with its smell of fancy women and soldiers and horses, in the midst of which his home was. And even when the boy was nestled for a while in the crook of Mungo's arm, and the dry old voice muttered various pious things over him, and wee Mairi's freckled hands came gently and laved his face, he still wondered why he was there, so kirkish, and where was the shouting of the troopers and the snorting of his father's horses as the Shirra rode off to the hunt.

And so he looked at Mungo and at little Mairi and did not understand who they were.

Then that afternoon came—and outside it was bright and the sun was shining and the world was all a peaceful glow of summer and the women sang—and Fergus turned in bed and no one was with him, the room in the kirk was a cube of emptiness and silence in the midst of it all. Then the door opened and his father came into the room, such a big proud bearded man, and his mother, who was so kind and so beautiful and whom he had loved so very much, and his brothers tall as trees, black Somerled and fair Donwald. And young Fergus rose from his bed then, and went out to where their horses were waiting, and they mounted (his father had a corbie on his wrist) and rode all together once more as they had done in the days that were, and the blue breeze took them rivering through the ocean of corn, the stalks of it bending and waving like girl dancers at the hips, and his father sang out that they were going to their home in the place of the wild winds that suck seas dry and unlock the wombs of forests, and Fergus laughed, soldier-boy, and spurred his great trumpeting stallion onwards; and under the brown feet of the unkenning reapers and the Gowk's churning cartwheels, the strath heaved with the passing of his springtime blood, and it was the end of all his brave hopes and dreams and loves and fears, for they rode their fine white horses down to the silent sea, and the waters of oblivion closed over them, and all things were finished.

So Fergus lay still at last and became a piece of death, and his name went sighing into the cold earth. But the women were singing as they worked, so no one knew, till Mairi came in with the supper bowl, that in their midst a human life had ended.


During that same afternoon they were building the solstice bonfire on a knowe of the learig that climbed up yonder into the forest. They raised it on a patchwork of flat stones that had lain there time out of mind, criss-crossing them with wood, then covering it all with peats and heather faggots until a tall beehive mound was standing on that grassy hillock, easily twice the height of young Fearchar who was the tallest one left in the village. Then, when the vespers time was long passed, and the night of the year's shortest night, which was a mere northern gloaming between two yellow days, was coming on them at last, all the folk assembled on the rig: Una and her daughters, virgin Sorcha and motherly Siubhan; beautiful Seonaid and tearful Nessa; Sine with all her bairns; Malai and Ealasaid, queens of scythe and cutting field; and all the other women; and the surviving men: brown rough Wat; beardless Fearchar; blind grey Manus with grey Tomas supporting him; and the Gowk, Rob, silent for once. Mungo and Finella stood there too, the Christian and the Pagan in joint reverence. Mairi, who had spilled tears for Fergus, had dried them now and had put Seonaid's green ribbon in her hair to be with a batch of wee ones like her, and whoever could have guessed she had been girning that afternoon? for they were all twittering like a flock of sparrows.

But the adults stood mostly silent. They were remembering the last time they had lit the the solstice fires here (the spot was blackened around the stones) and the brave men—all their men—who were dead since then. And Wat looked long at the dark mound with his calloused fists on his hips, and Fearchar did his best to imitate him.

Then when the sun was flickering down into the western mountains, Mungo gave them the blessing. He had his little basket on his arm full of the herb which, because it is in full bloom at this season, they call St John's Wort, and as they handed the little yellow flowers to the folk, he and Finella intoned solemnly,

> St John's Wort, St John's Wort,
> My envy whoever holds you.
> I will pluck you with my right hand,

*I will preserve you with my left hand.*
*Whoever finds you in the pasture*
*Shall never be without kye.*

For the plant was magical. The folk would take it home
and hang it above their doors together with birch sprigs,
and next the smoke-holes of their roofs, and by the barns,
and the mill, and round the stockade, as a charm against
storm and evil spirits.

When they had done this, the sun's final glimpse was
fading from them, so Mungo sent Mairi down the slope to
the kirk ("And no to be feared of the poor dead man who
is lying there—or of the Other."), and Mairi ran, her
knobbly knees pumping beneath her smock, with a
long-stemmed heather faggot in one hand, and the little
yellow lucky flower in the other (lest bogles jump on her),
and she entered the kirk, and bobbed to the altar, and
glanced a second long at Fergus, and a second longer at
*the Other*, then lit the faggot at the altar light and ran and
leaped the burn and scrambled back up the slope to the
waiting crowd with Faidh jumping and barking at her
heels and the flame streaming above her head. Mungo
took the torch and thrust it deep into the base of the pile.

Immediately the fire roared up the women began throwing flowers across it: not the St John's flower—no, they
kept that safe for their protection against the bad things—
but the white yarrow and the yellow stonecrop, the fern
and the elderberry. They did this in memory of their
dead husbands and sweethearts saying, "This is for you,
Calum. This is for you, Torcall. For you, Ranald, for
you, Frang..." Then they took a wooden wheel with straw
twisted about it, set it on fire, and rolled it down the
slope into the burn. It crashed onto the burn rocks and
lay there, hissing and spluttering, its flames diminishing
into the dark and invisible crying of the water. They
did this because the sun would be diminishing also as the

nights began to lengthen, and because they hoped that with the wheel their ill-luck would run away from them.

While this was happening, Wat the woodcutter had left the crowd and gone to the fringe of the forest. He climbed a certain tree that he knew of there and stared hard. Along the strath he could see other fires burning in the dark. Villages that would not help them. Friends who had forgotten their name. He cursed them all and came back.

Then the folk took burning torches from the pile and walked with them down to the cornfields. The fields were all a golden sea, fine they looked in the firelight as the folk snaked around them, making a sunwise circuit of all the fields, fifty glimmering points of flame held aloft.

Manus, who was blind, stayed sitting by the bonfire. Tomas stayed with him. "The whole glen's aglow with fiery haloes," said Tomas. Manus could feel the heat of the burning flickering on his withered cheek. He nodded his head.

Sine's bairns were singing and dancing. The youngest ones could not understand why the grown-ups were so dour.

"Leave them to it," said Una to Sine. "I dinna think we'll be spared to celebrate the harvest this year."

They took their torches round each field, and round the stockade, imitating the course of the sun. This was to bless the corn and hold off the rain, and to bless the kye and make them thrive, and prevent those in calf from casting their calves, and to make those not yet in calf fertile.

Sometime in the course of that night Una missed Sorcha, her younger daughter. Wat was missing too.

"Leave them," said Siubhan, her elder. "Who kens what will happen to any of us." And Siubhan nursed her baby, Eoin, in her arms and cooed pet names over him. Una looked at her daughter and wept unseen tears in the dark.

At last, as the bonfire was dying, the custom was for the unmarried young men to jump through it. Fearchar hesitated, and then jumped. There were no others. Then the unwed girls each dug a half-burned peat out of the fire and carried it home. In the morning of St John's day they would break the peats across and there the colour of the fibrous stuff still holding the two parts would show them the colour of their future husbands' hair. What could their mothers say? They said nothing.

In the morning Mungo took what was left of the St John's Wort into his preparations room behind the hawthorn screen and pummelled the seeds into powder which, when taken with a little broth and drunk, is an admirable cure for the choler, or, if mixed with butter and applied externally, makes an excellent ointment for blistered hands.

"And a more sensible and Christian use indeed than all yon magical nonsense," said Mungo.

# 13

## *Harvest*

And so the solstice passed, and slowly the days began to shorten. On the hill the bracken stood waist- and more than waist-high. Blue milkworts and white garlic flowers stirred the smell of the warm breeze. Yellow pimpernels, iris and tall foxgloves filled the shady recesses of the glen, and masses of golden honeysuckle spilled over the rocks to the burnside. From the loch in the lap of the distant purple mountain, the stony voice of the water echoed through the rustling corn.

Lammas passed uneventfully. The womenfolk kept their bairns closer to their skirts. Fearchar and Tomas and idiot Rob laboured long and hard on the stockade, erecting new staves and mending the old. Blind Manus piped over the working fields, or sat staring silently with his chin on his knuckles. Wat prowled the forest day and night with a boy by his side ready to run with warning. As yet, no enemy showed anywhere in the strath. Hazel nuts began to brown in their little frills. Marauding children sought the first blackberries, until called back by their mothers' anxious voices. No enemy appeared. But already the sun was spinning the earliest threads of autumn, and the time for harvest was near upon them.

Autumn: the first of the southering birds began to plough their furrows across the blue howe of the sky. The woodpigeon with the injured wing pecked the floor by Mairi's bed. "Where are you going, wee pow?" she asked. The bird stared upwards at the migrating flight and fluttered his one good wing.

Autumn: they sheared the sheep, the women again doing what was traditionally man's work. Big Malai sat on the beasts' rumps, while Sine held the forelegs, and Nessa snipped away delicately with the shears. They put fresh daub on the beehives and fastened them to the stockade as an extra line of defence.

Autumn: the nimblest women clambered up to repair the thatchwork roofs, and Mungo had more than one limb to strap in splints as an inexperienced thatcher crashed to the ground amidst cruel laughter. Beautiful Seonaid, the trooper's woman that was, more burned and bruised than ever in her life, was at last sent in from fieldwork and planked at the loom which at least she knew how to handle. There she sat happily pulling back the heddle bar that separates the vertical threads, and passing through the weft on the wooden shuttle known as the weaving sword. Slowly the cloth crept down the loom, and strong, warm and handsome it was from Seonaid's fine fingers.

Autumn: and Mairi clarted about in the dyeing vat. She used St John's bonny Wort for its soft ochre, and yew wood chips for the warm gold, and blackberry and elderberry, lichen and tree bark she used, until she was herself more colours than the rainbow, and the cloth from the loom was a brilliant pile of all the chequered tartan of Gaeldom, and Mungo had a splendid purple stole to wear for the altar bell that autumn.

The oak is in its lammas-shoots, the undergrowth crackles with the explosion of gorse and broom pods, the first stars of the constellation Pegasus—the winged horse—are burning on the eastern horizon.

And then it was autumn indeed, and the harvest time was on them.

Between Lammas and Michaelmas, the first day of August and the last week of September, the fields roared like bears, "Reap us, reap us, we are ready!" And the folk took up their scythes again, adjusted the blades for the corn, and trooped out to the Shirra's park beneath the tower where the barley awaited them.

Mairi sang,

> *My jockey is a bonny lad,*
> *A dainty lad, a merry lad,*
> *A neat, sweet, pretty lad,*
> *And just the lad for me.*

The words carried over the booming fields.

> *For when we over the meadows stray,*
> *He's aye so lively, aye so gay,*
> *And oft right canty does he say,*
> *There's none he loves like me.*

And the sky was all a glowing grandness. Only the oldest ones said they could mind such fine harvesting weather. It was so warm that many of the women hitched their skirts up to their thighs, let their blouses down over their waists, and worked in the long corn with their breasts wobbling. Mungo viewed them quite dispassionately. He had given up all that nonsense decades ago. But he noticed gentle Sorcha's bosom was all red bites, and that she fluttered to

Wat moth-like whenever the forest gave him up, and that the tough woodsman smiled at her, both proud and shy. Hm, thought Mungo.

Young Fearchar was excited as a new colt. He stripped himself to the loins and went at the scything with startling white teeth and flashing eyes. Hm, hm, thought Mungo. He noticed that the boy was always trying to find a place near Nessa in the scything line, and that some of the other women didn't like it.

> And he's aye hugging, aye petting,
> Aye cuddling, aye pressing,
> Aye squeezing, aye kissing,
> And winna let me be—

sang little Mairi, who had a flat chest and never a wisp of hair on her as yet, save what grew (abundantly) on her tangled stoury wee mop of a head.

Mungo the priest let them all see he was watching them. He stood up on the cart like Moses on Sinai, and put his fists on his hips, and glowered.

So the harvest went gladly and without a single drop of rain falling, and though their sense of foreboding had deepened now the coming of the riders was surely close, yet all things conspired to allay their alarm—the sun, the fields, the blue sky and the clouds that passed so gently across it were all such a peaceful picture; and soon these words were passing among the reapers:

"Maybe the riders winna come at all."

"It's forgotten us they have."

"God wouldna allow it."

"St John's magic is working for us."

And indeed all their troubles seemed to have run away from them.

The cream of it was that they were working the Shirra's well-tended field now for their own benefit. Not a single sheaf of the long-strawed and heavy crop would go into the tower to feed idle soldiers or their cuddies during long winter months when bairns had empty mouths. No, not one. A woman's voice was suddenly raised in a laugh. It was infectious. The laugh ran amuck. Everyone understood it; no one needed to explain anything. Soon the whole glen was laughing. Fieldmice scattered. Sparrows and finches took flight in a white cloud. *The field is ours!* cried the laugh. The folk swung their scythes happily, with increased vigour.

This time only twenty-four scythes were being used. Grand though the weather was, the village had known too many damaged harvests in the past to let new cut corn lie untended; for, profound as their belief in miracles and magic might be, the youngest wean tottering at the field-side knew the basic fact of peasant life: a ruined harvest means black starvation. And then no miracles would help. No miracles ever had. Hunger, they knew, was the one curse even God could not alleviate.

So as half the harvesters swung their scythes, the other half followed them in line across the first swathe of that great field, binding the sheaves. Fortunately, it being the tower's field and all, the stones that had blunted the scythes on the hayfield had been removed over long years and the whole well manured, but still there were thistles and nettles enough. No one liked the binder's job because of them. The women in the second line bent their backs to the corn and gathered it up with care. Some of the scythes had cut properly and left orderly swathes behind them, but others less used to it had laid the corn un-skilfully and the stalks were strewn in disorder. The binders cursed under the piping and the song of it. A badly constructed sheaf is a finger beckoning on famine. If too small, it will not stand; if uneven, the stooks which the sheaves shall make will lean crooked and may dampen at the base. The

straw band that ties it must be tight enough to hold the
sheaf when it starts to contract, but not so tight that it
prevents the drying. And all the while, as they worked the
sheaves, the women's red, chapped, gloveless hands were
closing in on hidden nettles and leaving iron-hard thistles
glinting bloody in the sun.

That first morning they cut the row twenty-four scythes
wide straight across the edge of the field, and then the
rows changed places. By noon, the women's fingers were
dry and harsh as old sticks. They ate, and most went to
the burn and soaked their near naked bodies, laughing as
they flung water at each other. Then they began again.

> *I met my lad the other day,*
> *Frisking through a field of hay,*
>
> > sang Mairi,
>
> *Says he, my hinny, will you stay,*
> *And crack a while with me.*

And back over the baking field the two lines trudged,
while beside them Mungo and Finella and half a dozen of
the least able women commenced the easier job of making
the stooks: setting the sheaves up in fours, leaning against
each other at the top, with their butts straddled well out
so the air could circulate freely. It took them a week, all
told, to scythe and bind and stook that barley field, the best
in all the strath it was, and not a day, and not an hour of a
day, was there in which the women did not say to themselves, "Ours it is! all ours!" Nor was there an evening
when, turning and looking at the stooks standing there
behind them in the moonlight, they did not feel a sudden
welling of strange, fine new pride in the knowledge that
it was their work and their creation, and, for the moment,
no one could dispute it with them by sword or by law.

For the moment.

Words whispering in the village. No, not words; not anymore. A word only. The word *Fight*.

"They wolfriding bastards will take the tower, so they will. We maun hack it down."

"Ach, they'd build another. We should take it oursels and fight from it."

"Pour boiling water on them from the ramparts..."

"The Father says it's no our place to fight."

"The Father says—!"

"The Father's a man. What does he ken?"

"Fighting's men's work, but."

"Ach..."

"It's no our place to starve either."

"Listen..."

Listen. Fight. Listen. Night. No one can listen in daylight: there is aye too much work to be done. But at night—at night the village, and the glen, and the whole strath itself surges with strange visions, apocalyptic dreams that clatter over the stony paths under the red harvest moon. Somewhere the riders are gathering; sometime they will come thundering out of the darkness on their fiery horses, the screaming angels of the night, the nightmares that loup down on us like wolves.

Fight. Listen. Fight. That is the food of our mouths we harvested today, says Finella, and I would leifer put a torch to each sheaf and let the red rooster crow from one end of the field to the other, than let they bloody murdering men take even one grain of what is rightfully ours, so I would. And Malai nods, and Seonaid, and Una, and Sine who says,

"When I saw that field the day, I kent then I was ready to fight for it."

Aye—fight. The final fury of the oppressed that slumbers long, a crude, elemental force, somewhere, and yet everywhere, in the forests, in the land, in the earth that gives its bread, and with the damp black soil clinging to the stalks and to the roots of the stalks, the hidden message: This land is ours! Who dares take it from us? And out of the forests and the land and the earth they had summoned that fury of theirs. We maun fight for what is ours, whispered Siubhan over her baby who gurgled. We maun fight for it! yelled Pedair and Ringean, the boys on the haycart. Fight, murmured Fearchar, kissing Nessa's throat. Fight, said the silence that came between Wat and his Sorcha after the gasping and the little cry was over, in the quiet darkness of the tower, a place of love now, and a habitation of owls.

Fight...

And Mairi peeped in at the giant Soldier where he sat motionless in the kirk. O Mairi, eyes so big, and yet pummelling her nose, sleepy she was from the field. And the huge fury sitting there, their Soldier, manlike and yet un-man, he was not man to any of them. And Mairi keeking at him, nosey wee girl, and then rushing to get out of sight as the Father's steps passed under the lintel and entered the gloaming kirk. And there she, jouked under the altar, heard his troubled thoughts.

"They want to fight," said her Mungo's voice, and it was dry as brown leaves. "There will be *killing*." The leaves fell in the misery of that word. "Listen," said the old man's voice, as he squatted stiffly, his joints creaking, beside his giant; "Listen. I want no killing, no butchering, no slaughtering—O none of it!—do you understand? Your great power is but to frighten and put aside they bad misguided men when they come; but I will no have them killed, no even the worst of them, black in hell's sin though he be. I winna have it! You understand me, Soldier? You understand?"

And in a voice that came from the cellars and that set Mairi shaking so that she was overturning the altar very nearly, the great Soldier answered, "Yes."

Mairi sneaked out the back door like a little mouse. The mild sky, the moonlit stooks...

Other night sounds. From the smithy, Una lambasting Sorcha, her daughter, and sore miscalling her for lying with a man unwed; and Sorcha's yelps, and Siubhan's patient remonstrances. And Mairi felt enough of a woman then to grin and nod knowingly all to herself.

Ah, harvest fields under the warm moon!

"Pretty weather"—that was the saying for it. It held all the time they worked the barley, and when they passed on to the rye and the oats, it held too, and then the reaping was over. From the shoulder of the learig, where a last and particularly fine acre of barley grew, Nessa cried out, "It's done!" and everyone cheered. Then Mungo closed his eyes and raised his arms above his head. The folk knelt, there on the land amidst the stubble. And Mungo said, the folk repeating his words,

> *Dhe beannaich fein mo bhuain,*
> God, bless this my reaping,
> *Gach imir, cluan, agus raon,*
> Each ridge, and plain, and field,
> *Gach corran cama, cuimir, cruaidh,*
> Each curved sickle, shapely, hard,
> *Gach dias is dual a theid 's an raoid.*
> Each ear and handful in the sheaf.
> *Air sgath Mhicheil mhil nam feachd,*
> For the sake of Michael, head of hosts,
> *Mhoire chneas-ghil leac nam buadh,*
> Of Mary, fair-skinned branch of grace,
> *Bhride mhin-ghil ciabh nan cleachd,*
> Of Bride, smooth-white of the ringleted locks,
> *Chaluim-Chille nam feart 's nan tuam.*
> Of Columba of the graves and tombs.

"*Chaluim-Chille nam feart 's nan tuam,*" muttered the

kneeling folk. Then they stood, and Fearchar held the head of the last armful of long corn to be cut, while Nessa, blushing, cut it with her sickle. The young peasant girl cut it demurely with all the grace of a queen. The folk cheered; they threw their sickles and binding hooks in the air, and cheered.

The last red evening of the reaping came down. The whole expanse of their glen was in stook, all the fields were tented with fourfold sheaves. They prepared the clyack sheaf, the last sheaf of the harvest, the one Nessa had cut. It was in the form of a woman. Her body consisted of stalks laid out in pattern some sixteen inches long. They gave her a dress of cloth and ribbon, and put a sprig of rowan on her to keep away witches. Then they sprinkled water over her and carried her down to the kirk where she was kept to be given to the ox that cut the first furrow of the ploughing.

The folk did no more work in the remaining hours of daylight. They were happy: they drank; they were drunk with the weeks of perfect weather, fair miraculous it was. They drank some more. And there was no a cateran in sight. Aye! They mixed the beer of their brewing with the whisky of their stilling, and their brains with both. Corn must stand in stook for up to ten days to mature before it is gathered in. They had gathered only a pickle of it so far, all intent they had been on reaping while the weather was kind. They would begin the gathering seriously, they said, tomorrow, and the next day (they said), and—yes—the day after that, but now they deserved their beds, they said, after such a grand reaping. So they went streaming back down to the village, and many staggered, and Finella nearly fell in the burn, and Rob the Gowk did fall in the burn, and Mungo waded through the deepest part of it with a red beaming face and his cassock hitched up. And at the door of his room, which he had difficulty with, Mairi stood sighing loudly with her freckled arms crossed and her wee face puckered into a very reproving frown. And as the shadows lengthened, different voices at different keys throughout the village could be heard singing,

> *And he's aye hugging, aye petting,*
> *Aye cuddling, aye pressing,*
> *Aye squeezing, aye kissing—*
> *Syne he fucked me...*

Then the voices trailed off in shrill laughter, and the shadows lengthened, and it was night, and when the first drop of rain fell, there was no one in the village awake to hear it.

# 14

## *The Storm, and What Came of It*

It was a measure of how preoccupied the folk were that
they had not seen the signs that were standing there, glaring
right at them. All that day there had been a strange commo-
tion in the animal world, as the beasts sensed something in
the air. That morning, when the first doors opened, two
rooks had been seen feeding on the village street—and that
was fey enough, for what could have driven *them* in from
the forest? Then the hens, shooed out, stayed huddled close
to their coups, while the kye in the neighbouring pasture
cropped morosely at the yellowing grass, syne shook their
heads suddenly and moved a few yards at a nervous trot,
then began to crop again. The air hung heavy and sullen
over the glen, pregnant with storm. A rare screech owl flew
from one side of it to the other, screaming horribly; but
the folk who raised their eyes to it were so saturated with
harvest they were deaf to its warnings. There was also

an unusually shrill tone to the blackbirds' and the woodpeckers' call that day, but Wat, prowling among the trees
as ever, eyes sharp for human foes, ears pricked for the
sound of hoofs galloping, failed to pay it the heed it
craved, and let it drown that evening in his hungry stomach
beneath a fall of whisky and beer. And though the spiders
who inhabited the stiff stalks of corn and the bracken of
the fields' verge were spinning their webs very short, or
breaking their webs, or not spinning at all, the folk were
blind to the creatures' distress and swung their blades
blithely, sang randily, and thought harvest, harvest, nothing but harvest, all the day long.

So night came and the village slept. Mairi and Mungo,
seventy years apart, sang the sleepers' duet, her tiny nostrils
snoring gently as a kitten's purr, his hairy caverns grunting
and snorting like a hog at a water hole. And Nessa slept,
and Fearchar, and Sorcha slept, and Wat, all too tired for
each other's arms. And all the women and the bairns slept,
and the two old men and the Gowk slept; and motherly
Siubhan slept, placid as milk, and Eoin, her wean, blew
nearly inaudible wee bubbles of sleep up to the ceiling of
the smithy. All lay at peace.

But around them there was unease in the forest. The red
September moon ever hangs low on the horizon, and that
night she was lying on the illuminated black treetops like
a martyr bleeding on a bed of nails. The fierce-faced otter
sniffed the air and dived to the depth of the swirling pool;
the darting squirrel sought the innermost recesses of the
oak; the night hunters crouched in den and sett and nest,
their prey bedded yet lower in their holes; the king stag
shook his antlers across the strath; and on the distant high
mountain the eagle barked into the splashes of rain that
were hitting the ledge and the sheer rocks of it—*krak!*
*krak!*—and the first low mutter of thunder answered his
call.

Beneath Mairi's cot, Faidh the foxcub jerked awake, his

ears up at the alert. The woodpigeon shifted unhappily on his perch. Then it came. The first wallop away off (it was on the mountain, and unknown to anyone it killed a wildcat and sent a scattering of stones plunging down a corrie); the second, a rumbling over the trees (it bent their tops, it shook a flutter of birds from them); and the third, the third was directly above the strath. It began somewhere in the west and rolled down the valley; it seemed to follow the course of it as though the strath were channelling its roar, river-like, as it rolled to the far-off sea; it crashed over the battlements of Thanehall, and the sentry on duty—who was a notorious sinner—flung himself down, weeping,

*O Lord, keep it from me!*

It shook the roofs of the next village some dozen miles off and sent every pot and pan that hung from the rafters trembling; it rolled up the glen (and in times past folk would have said that the wind giants were playing bowls in the lift, for indeed it sounded just like it, that rolling); it passed over their heads and crashed again a mile or so away. And the lightning hung in sheets somewhere behind the mountains, and the mountains were jagged graphs of rock leaping and jumping on the sudden silver page of it; and on the battlements of Thanehall it killed a man: not the sentry who was a sinner, but the sergeant who was devout, and who had come from the guardroom to see what was amiss—he never crossed himself again; and it kindled a roof in that next village which was a dozen miles away. And then the wind came and blew down the sheaves and the stooks everywhere; but not in their glen—no, for the forest walls were close and kept it out. In their glen the next thing that happened was the coming of the rain.

And that was the worst thing that could have happened. Corn standing in stook is horribly vulnerable to the weather. If it should be saturated and scattered in its maturing stage, then some may be redeemed by hasty and judicious labour, but most will be completely ruined and the staple food of the whole coming year will be gone at a stroke. And what then?

Over the village, and over the stook fields on which the folk had worked so unremittingly all that deceptive month, the heavens now opened and rain came pouring down in torrents.

Mairi woke. She opened her eyes wide, wondering what it was that had wakened her this time. She could smell Faidh close by in the darkness and ran her hand over his head. The fox was staring up at the roof with his ears cupped forward. Mairi listened. Suddenly the smell of wet soil was in her nose and she could hear the rain buzzing insistently on the thatch overhead. She leaped out of bed. Underneath the smokehole the hard earthen floor was an oozing puddle of mud and the water was pouring down as from a running pipe. She ran barefoot outside in her smock and the rain was lashing the ground. The moon was hidden. From the invisible fields, where these past weeks the dry breeze had whispered softly in the standing corn, came the sound of rain drumming the uncovered earth.

She ran to Mungo. Mungo was asleep, snoring, whisky on his breath. She held his nose, and shook the old man awake. "Father!"—her voice bright with urgency. Mungo's eyes opening, blinking. "Wha—who there?" She told him, in the darkness. Mungo, with a shrill girlish squeal, stumbled out into the storm. "O God—O Jesus—O Mary and Joseph—O!..." Mungo and Mairi both, running from door to door, kicking at the wood, shouting into the snoring mirk. Faidh barking and the village dogs barking. Mungo in the kirk, ringing the iron bell.

*Wake! Alarm! Wake!* shouted the bell.

And out came the folk into the downpour, naked and near naked and suddenly very sober, and they rushed into the fields, bare as they were, and clawed frantically at the stooks, pulling sheaves out of them, and dragging them down into the bothies, under cover. But no woman could handle more than a couple of sheaves at a time, and there were many acres of field, and many thousands of sheaves, and the rain fell from heaven and leaped up again from the earth and splattered their knees with mud.

The larger beasts, kye and oxen, pigs and sheep, all huddled together joylessly under their sheds. The goats and chickens crouched by the bothy walls. Brimming lochs formed in the potholes of the village street. The path to the learig ran like a burn, while the burn foamed over its banks and flooded the reed and rock and little flower land of its margin. The broad howes were slowly turning to a brown, soaking deluge, and still the white-footed rain came dancing demonically down the strath; and as women slid and fell to their knees tearing at the stooks, and the mud splashed at their thighs and stomachs, and the sheaves tore long scratches from their breasts and shoulders, the slender trees that were keeping the wind from them bent as bows against the lightning flash and shook their long hair and howled like banshees.

Sine put her mouth to Seonaid's ear and shouted, "We're losing it!"

It was a faint sound in all the roar.

Everyone was working—except blind Manus, who couldn't possibly do anything. Nevertheless, he felt he shouldn't be indoors while all this was going on, so he positioned himself in the middle of the village street like a totem with the rain steaming down his tan-coloured face. Fearchar, then Nessa, then the Gowk, all strove to harness up the cart, though there was no light but the occasional lightning flash to do it by. Eventually, they managed to drag the harness ox out of his byre and rope the miserable creature between the shafts; but as they were driving the cart out to the field the lightning racked through the bucketing rain right above their heads, and the poor ox, terrified into his first ever gallop, took off, snorting like one of the infernals, and up-ended them all over the stones at the edge of the field.

Out of the darkness came Finella and grasped Mungo by the shoulder. She shouted. Mungo was dazed by what was happening and couldn't understand her. Once, years past, he had looked into the loch and seen the face of a drowned woman looking up at him: she had been pregnant and had drowned herself for the sin of it, and she was floating there just below the surface of the water. "And that's just what she looked like," he thought, looking at Finella through the water. Finella spat rain out of her mouth and pointed to the kirk.

"*Uruisg!*" she shouted again in a moment's lull. "The Soldier! He has the strength of twenty! Call the Soldier, you gaping old gomeril!"

Mungo shook his head hopelessly. The rain redoubled. Finella shook him and pointed to the kirk, shouting wordlessly. The lightning went walloping over the whole glen and the old priest saw the women there for a second, motionless, bent like souls in torment as they hauled at the precious sheaves. The rain was whipping up a sort of fine white smoke all around them. Then the lightning was past, and again he could see nothing. He turned and stumbled towards the kirk.

The altar light was always burning. He leaned panting against the wall. "Soldier," he gasped.

The huge body stirred.

The next day the rooster's yard was an archipelago of islands in an ocean of mud. The proud bird crowed, dancing from one island to another, splashing his feathers in lochs, seas, lagoons. The sun rested his elbows on the golden gleaming sill of the mountain and looked down into the strath. The rainbow came and stood over the forest. The air was clean and rich with the scent of wet earth.

Every roof was dripping, every gutter was running, and now that the rain was over, the water could be heard falling among the trees, from thousands and from hundreds of thousands of branches, pattering like gnats' feet on the soft forest floor.

The folk were confident. They walked about with a business-like air, exchanging stories of the previous night, reminiscing about their hardships, and joking happily, catastrophe on catastrophe—ha, ha, ha. They were shiny-eyed with exhaustion, and the soaking had made their hair flat and dark, their cheeks bright and rosy. The harvest...was saved! They had sheaves everywhere. Their homes were full of sheaves, corn stored in every possible place: folded over the rafters like washing, sprouting out of pots and cauldrons, piled under their beds and on their beds, and even in their beds. They slept and dreamt on corn.

Yet how odd is the human race! Instead of giving thanks to the Lord for their salvation, the villagers went about with a weird guilty joy on their faces, as though they had just committed a wicked unnatural sin and got away with it.

News of their success spread. Ruined villages the length of the strath sent to them for help, and were turned away with nothing. A rider from Thanehall came and gaped at their miraculously dry, preserved harvest. The storm had wrought a desolation everywhere else. There was not a village in all the thanedom where the old and the young and the sick were not going to die of starvation that coming winter.

"A thousand sheaves," said the red fat-faced headman from the richest village in the strath where the defences were strong and the stockade could keep out everything except hunger and the tower was packed with soldiers. "A thousand sheaves and you can have what you want of us."

The women nudged each other and jeered.

"We asked you for help against the riders, and what was your answer?" said Malai.

"You can have every man, old and young, every mother's son of them. Seven hundred sheaves?" wheedled the headman, who had turned his dogs on Fearchar a month gone by when the boy came crying for help against the coming of the riders.

The women giggled.

"We asked you for help then, and what did you give us?" said Sine.

"Dogs!" said Nessa, and spat on the ground at the headman's feet.

"Five hundred sheaves?" sobbed the headman. Tears began streaking his red face, his whole fleshy body was quivering. "Four hundred? Even three—?"

The women laughed.


"But how was it possible?" said the rider from Thanehall, after they had proudly shown him their fine dry sheaves.

"Ah-ha," said the women, and winked at each other.

"And you, with hardly any men to help you," wondered the rider.

"Aye, us, with no men," said Finella. "And now we need none. The glen is ours."

The women shouted their approval.

"Ours! Ours!" they cried.

The rider sat back on his snorting horse.

"And what am I to tell the Thane?" he asked.

"You are to tell the Thane what the Thane told us," said Seonaid.

"Away and chase yoursels, for I canna be bothered listening," said Rob the Gowk happily.

"That is what you can tell the Thane," said Una. "Now go."

They were flinging clods at the horse's hoofs when the rider spurred off, his dignity plastered with farmyard clart.

Slowly the clear autumn sun dried the flooded land; the

rainpools returned to the sky, the upper skin of the earth turned once more light and dusty over the dark moist flesh of it, fieldmice ran again among the brittle stubble of the fields, and the woman who now sentried the nights in wakefulness had nothing to do but count the quiet passage of the stars.

When the sheaves were dry to touch, they stacked them and thatched them over with reeds. No more rain came. The autumn continued mild as the summer had been warm, and before the customary drying month was up, the stacks were ready to be taken indoors, where much of it fitted in the great barn, and the rest in the smaller barn, the hay having shrunk down in drying to leave plenty of space for it. They stored it in safety, for there were no rats in Scotland in those days, and brother mouse didn't steal enough grain to be worth the missing.

The Shirra had constructed a small water-wheel on the burnside below a drystone dam where these two years past the folk had had to pay for the privilege of milling their own grain. So in one wrathful day they wrecked the wheel and smashed the dam and dug out their old querns—the stone handmills—that the Shirra had ordered to be destroyed. Some of them had been destroyed, of course—the corbie soldiers had taken them out and smashed them on the ground—but these were inferior ones; the best mills had been carefully hidden in holes beneath the bothy floors. The Shirra was no fool; he knew fine what was going on, and his men rummaged for the hidden querns, prodding the earth with their spear shafts and using dogs to dig them out. Any householder found with such a quern was fined, or flogged, or had his wife given over briefly to the men in the guardroom for their enjoyment. Such a fate had befallen Una, Ealasaid, Eilidh, and one of Sine's bairns—wee Pol—was rumoured to be a tower child. It was all part of the price they had paid for their protection.

Now the querns were spinning again as the folk emptied

what grain was left in the storage jars and prepared the last bread of the old crop.

Una and Sorcha her daughter were milling. They were using Malai's quern: two stones, one on top of the other, the lower being fixed while the upper revolved round a wooden pin passed through a hole in the lower stone. Sorcha funnelled the grain in her hands and carefully let it trickle down through a hole in the upper stone until it rested on top of the one beneath. Mother and daughter then turned the upper stone together and the ground flour gradually sifted out between the stones onto a skin spread there for the purpose. They were careful not to lose a grain.

Sine and Siubhan were at the baking. The oven looked like a large clay hive. They lit a wood fire inside it, and after a bit, when it felt hot enough, Sine opened it and raked out the ashes leaving only the glowing embers within. Siubhan, meanwhile, was kneading the dough into loaf shapes. Wee Eoin lay beside her in his shawl. Siubhan worked in the heat with her arms bare and ruddy, and her face gleaming with beads of moisture. When the loaves were finished they let them stand awhile, shooing off the inevitable bevy of bairns who were there for a piece, and then they put them gingerly inside the oven on large flat stones. When they had done that, they blocked up the entrance with other stones, and covered it over with turfs to shut out all draught. And then they sat down beside it, and mopped their brows, and smelt the good bread that was making.

They began the threshing. It was a specially prepared floor by the great barn that they used, and it was paved over with wooden planks, every intervening crack being filled with pitch so that nothing would fall between them and get lost. There six of the biggest and strongest of the villagers paraded round and round in a sun-circle hitting the long corn with hardwood flails that had hand-staffs some five feet long to which three-foot beater rods were tied with leather thongs. Round and round they went like executioners, and the hand-staffs rose and fell, and the beater rods reared up and came crashing down on the bowed heads of the corn, on the whiskered barley, on the rye and on the oats of their precious saved harvest.

And as they worked, the folk gossiped the while. And this was all their claik:

"It's terrible, terrible, (says Una) that awful beast that we're using."

"Och, Ma! (says Sorcha) And him going and saving our harvest for us and all."

"Dinna cry me *him!* (Una again) Yon orra creature's an *it;* and *it's* no canny, the Father saying what he likes."

"Och, Ma..."

"For all that, though, (says Sine to Siubhan) we're all after coming out of the earth and going back to it soon enough too, and, say what you like, we're owing him the harvest."

"And do you think he's really a *man*, (says Siubhan, face all red over the warm oven) with all a man's parts and that?"

"Och, shame on you!" (Sine, giggling like a girl)

"No shame. (says Siubhan) Winter has gey cold nights, and we'll no be that tired in them either."

"Och, for shame..."

"We're lucky to have him. (says Fearchar at the threshing) Did yous lot see him out there? I never would have believed it! Fucking magic, so it was."

"Do you really think he can fuck?" (innocently says a big flaxen young woman, built like a cow)

*"Tha e 'na dhuine."* (He is a man)

"You women!" (Fearchar, horrified)

"Aye, well enough, but can we no have him out for the threshing? (says a third) My back's bloody killing me."

"Mine and all."

"He could swing three flails in each hand—bet he could."

177

"And one in his gob."

"And another up his bum."

"Shote! Here's the Father!"

"Hey, Father! Can we no have that mannie of your's for the threshing, eh?"

They called him *Math-ghamhainn*, which is to say "the Bear," for he resembled a great bear in many ways. He had come to them naked, though it scarcely mattered since bears and bulls and horses go naked anyway. But now, strange to say, Mungo told Seonaid that the Soldier needed clothes, and he gave her the creature's measurements. Seonaid scratched her head. Even though men went bare-legged and wore little more than a rectangular expanse of plaid which they wrapped about themselves as kilt and cloak combined, the Soldier would still need nearly four times the amount of cloth that an ordinary man required.

"Use these," said Mungo.

He gave her an armful of sarks which had belonged to dead troopers. Dead men's clothes! Seonaid shivered.

"Dinna fret," said Mungo, "for their souls are with the Good Lord and their spirits winna haunt you."

"Aye—if you say so, Father."

He gave her several plaids as well and asked her to fashion the clothes as quickly as possible. Seonaid nodded. She was so anxious to get rid of the unlucky things that she worked every minute of the daylight and on into the dark by light of the hearth flame, cutting and sewing together. By cockcrow she had completed a vast sark, and plaid enough to wrap a team of oxen in. Mungo thanked her, and took the stuff with him into the kirk. The other women came fluttering and asked Seonaid again and again to repeat the fearsome measurements to which she had worked—for they had seen the Soldier but twice, and once they had run away, and the other time was the night of the storm when everyone was seeing double. Some women, and all the men at one time or another, took to lingering around the kirk door in the hope of getting a keek at him, but Mungo wouldn't have it; and Mairi, who alone of them saw the Soldier every day, set her mouth firm—*I'm no telling*—and never a word would she say.

By her solitary hearth, Finella looked wise; and when they speired at her, she cackled toothlessly and nodded to the cat.

Mungo was troubled. He believed in the miracles with all his heart and soul. He made up his bit verses about the miracles of flowers and sunrise. But, verses aside, he had never thought to see a miracle occur in his own day, far less be party to it himself. And now that it had happened—slap! miracle, right on his doorstep—he was not exactly singing for joy. Quite the contrary: he was most grievously vexed. Miracles, he decided, were a sore dispensation, and his stooping old shoulders not broad enough to bear the weight of them.

This was what had happened.

That night of the storm...

Mungo standing there in the blast...

The rain lashing—the blow of the wind—the dangerous sky cracking from side to side...and the glimpses in the lightning stab of their golden life's blood, their harvest, washing away into the earth.

And old Finella's voice. Finella. The witch. She knew as well as he did that the Soldier was given to them for one purpose and for one purpose only—to defend their village against the coming of the riders—and that it is in the nature of magic that the slightest misuse must warp its power. Desperately, Mungo had hesitated there in the pissing rain; his feet had strained to run kirkwards, but he ordered them to be still, and they were still, and another stook capsized, soaking, ruined, and another winter's meal was lost forever.

"O God," Mungo had moaned then, and had looked for a miracle, but only Finella's ugly wrinkled face was to be seen, her finger stabbing at him. HUNGER. Suddenly Mungo had had a vivid picture—it was *the Sight*, no doubt about it—and his picture was of Mairi, starving, in rags through which her ribs showed, lying face downwards in the snow too weak to move; and the snow killing her.

"O God," he wept, "let it no be a sin."

And Mungo turned and stumbled towards the kirk.

The Soldier was lying there, covered in old plaids; his head was wrapped in a horse blanket, and, being a mindless creature of earth and wood, he wasn't breathing. The eternal altar light was burning, and for a minute (or perhaps it was five, for time as we measure it didn't exist in those days) Mungo leaned against the mottle wall with his breath hot-knifing him and the room spinning aromatically about like a censer. This night will be the death of me, he thought. "Soldier," he said softly. "*Saighdear*." Underneath the heaps of dirty cloth the huge figure trembled and turned, a sleeper prodded by dreams.

"Soldier."

Slowly, gently, with the kind motions the old man used when he bent over Mairi's cot, Mungo raised the tattered blanket and turned the plaids aside. He squatted there looking at the giant cold earth that was so mysteriously trembling. Then he put his hand into his cassock bosom and drew out the angel's little golden cross. "Soldier," he whispered, hanging the cross around the bull neck of him. (*Why am I talking like this to a lump of earth?*)

Immediately the Soldier's eyes opened. The irises were brown as his face, the pupils nearly black, the whites solidly white, like boiled eggs. He sat up and looked at Mungo.

Mungo's voice began to quiver. A trickle of rainwater ran into his eyes, and he wiped it out impatiently. (*He's looking at me.*)

"Soldier," said Mungo, "you were formed for a purpose

which was to protect this village from its enemies. Now we have an enemy called Hunger who is, God have mercy on us, even more fearful than the black bandits, and who at this moment is threatening us from the rain and lightning—and you see, Soldier, (*Why am I pleading with him?*) if the harvest's ruined, then no village, Soldier, nothing to protect any more, all a desert and a desolation. So, Soldier. You are part of the earth this harvest comes from, and we are part of this same harvest, of the barley and the rye and the oats, and without them we are dead. So this is what you are to do. You are to come with me now and together, God willing, we shall save this harvest."

Silence. The Soldier looked at him. The altar light flickered sickly over the great earthen face.

"You understand, Soldier?"

"Yes," said the Soldier after another pause.

"Then come."

Mungo stood up and the Soldier stood up beside him, bowing so his head did not smash into the rafters.

"Follow me now."

Mungo strode out into the rain, and he could feel as well as hear the ground vibrating as the Soldier came lumbering behind him.

*Why did he hesitate?* thought Mungo.

No—hold on. Dinna fash yoursel, man. If it were wrong, he wouldna be obeying me at all. No. That's all right then. Aye it is. No problems.

*Why did he hesitate though?*

Out they went into the crash bang wallop of the roaring sky. It looked for all the world as though there was a war in heaven, with armies of wee black devils chirling the gates and dinging at the walls of it, with the bright fire of burnings springing over the battlements, and all the crying of the wounded, and the shouting, and the flashing of fiery swords. The fields were now fit to wade through, and Mungo splashed and slithered in the muck, but the great

Soldier behind him strode onwards, covering six feet at a time quite easily with his great shanks, and at last Mungo called to him and clutched at his arm, and the Soldier lifted him off the ground and carried him against his chest as easily as a man might carry a chicken home from market. They came to the place where Fearchar and Nessa and Rob the Gowk had cowped the cart upside down in the ditch. It lay there still, with Fearchar and Nessa hugging each other bewildered, and the Gowk holding his sore head and moaning, and the ox God knows where, and the wheels turning and turning in the stottering rain.

*KEBRAAAK* went the lightning through the lift.

*WAAAAAAA* wailed the Gowk, and Fearchar groaned and Nessa snivelled beside him in chorus. Then in the white light she saw the Soldier with Mungo, wean-like little old man, in his arms, and she forgot this misery and instead her eyes grew huge and her mouth fell open and the rain ran into it as the tide runs into the red cave of a sandstone cliff.

Mungo pointed to the cart.

"Up with it!"

And the giant lifted it. He stood holding it upside down. Mungo clambered round onto his shoulders and sat collie-back with his skinny legs wrapped round the huge neck. To Mungo's command, the Soldier righted the cart and walked off with it like a wheelbarrow. When they came to a toppled stook, Mungo halted him, and the giant Soldier bent down, scooped up the fallen sheaves in one arm, and dropped them into the cart. The folk stood dazed in the rain, in the very pattering and pissing down of it, looking, when the light allowed them, at a sight none of them had thought to see this side of the Judgement Day: a great creature, so great the world had surely not its likeness on this shore of the dark sea, striding forth in power as a ravening and a roaring lion across the drowning fields, and Mungo, their old old priest, now a small wizened figure perched shoulder-high in sharp silhouette against the lightning shatter, conducting the whole hellish symphony of it all like a demented demon with his wispy beard jutting out and his hands waving. At last they realized he was shouting at them—and using words the bishop's latin secretary would never have dared scrieve on the vellum, for either the Romans had never had the unnatural vices and dubious parentage Mungo was now attributing to the folk, or else they had had the decency not to write of it if they had.

"Gerra fucking finger out, yous lot of whoreson gets!" the gentle priest of God was howling at his flock.

For a wee, the folk didn't hear or understand—the roaring of the sky and the splashing rain being above it all—but then they caught the sense of the words, or the gestures, or saw what the old priest and that huge lumbering creature were doing, and they came louping over, not minding the slithering dirt now, and soaked beyond caring anyway—they couldn't get any wetter if they went and stood up to their necks in the loch—they began tearing at the stooks and flinging them into the ox cart that the Soldier was pushing that night of the storm.

And so it was that the Soldier, who was created a mindless thing of earth and wood, came to win the praises of the people of the glen, and the village that was in the lie of it, between the folds of that far away stretching forest under the northern sun.

And the women were happy. Perhaps, went their shameful talk, they could mate with him and mother a clan of tall young giants who would rule the whole strath, perhaps the whole of Scotland, and to bugger and arselins with every fleabitten bandit and trooper then, every thane and squabbling chieftain, even with the fabled King himself far off in Dunedin and all the bishops of the Roman Pope, for with such a power as this, they thought, some of the bolder of them, they need bow the head and scrape out the pocket and the harvest barn to no one; if only their children had the power of the Soldier.

And why no?

After all, there were old tales told in plenty of the secret land of green good nights, before the yellow bird of dawning first flew over it from sea to sea and named it Scotland: there, when the first daughters of the folk lay with tree—gods, and wizards made themselves wives out of the flowers; there in that land all things were possible.

And so all were happy. All save the priest. Mungo alone was sad.

# 15

## The Soldier

"God be praised, it's saved, it's saved!" cried Mungo.

(*That night of the storm...*)

Wee Mairi stood bewildered. The water was streaming from her. She took Mungo's plaid.

"Saved, God be praised!" cried Mungo. He knelt at the altar crossing himself and muttering his thanks to heaven. Mairi began wringing the water out of a plaid twice its normal weight with it. The Soldier stood behind her. Strange—he was so big she had no fear of him, and so naked she had no shame in his nakedness, for he was naked as the animals are. He wore the green odour of the forest about him like a cloak.

He was standing there behind her, a huge statue (herself hardly above his knees), and his head and shoulders were lost way way up in the roof. Only his eyes shone down, two pale stars in the darkness.

Mairi tutted. If she and the Father had shed puddles of rainwater on the kirk floor, a whole loch was forming round the Soldier's boat-like feet, and she would have to mop it out in the morning. Indeed, miracles are unco things if they do but increase the housework! She put her fists on her hips and shook her head at the Soldier. An expression came into the pale lights looming over her, but she could not tell what it was, nor was she much interested just then, seeing the work she would have to do.

Mungo finished his crossings and his prayings. He stood up with his joints cracking and turned to the Soldier. Whiles he looked at the floor, whiles at the walls, then gave a furtive glance up at the giant's face. He was disconcerted to find the pale eyes looking straight down at him. It was the first time he had felt such an embarrassment in the presence of his own creation.

"You did a grand job of it, Soldier," he said, and smiled. He was a sincere man, and the insincerity of his smile pained him. Mairi turned and looked at him in astonishment.

"A grand job," said Mungo, and took a couple of steps forward, rubbing his hands. "Kneel down now," he said, "and I'll take the cross from you."

The Soldier said nothing. The water was still dripping off him—drip, drip, drip—so much of it the earthen floor couldn't absorb it all, and pools formed, and little creeks, on the hard much–trodden surface. Mairi took a mop to it.

"Soldier, do you no hear me?" said Mungo. "You have done the job of the night. The time has come for you to rest until you are needed once more."

The Soldier looked straight at Mungo there below him. There was a weird gleam, something almost like defiance, in his unthinking white eyes.

"Soldier, I order you, kneel down!"

"No!"

Involuntarily, Mungo took a step backwards. He was shocked. What was happening?

Without being commanded to do so, the Soldier moved slightly on his massive feet. He shivered like a dog. Water sprayed from him in huge drops.

"*Saighdear fliuch,*" (Soldier wet) he said quietly, pronouncing the Gaelic words with difficulty.

Mairi, whom the spray had hit, laughed at the daftness of it, but Mungo was horrified. It was the first time the Soldier had spoken without being spoken to. Besides, where had this mindless creature learned the words?

The Soldier didn't seem to know either. He stumbled like a bairn at the learning. After a while he said,

"*Saighdear fuar.*" (Soldier cold)

Then, after a while longer, and with a great effort, he said,

"*Saighdear fliuch agus fuar.*" (Soldier wet and cold)

Mairi laughed and clapped her hands. Mungo heard other laughter. The shrill cackle of the witch–woman, Finella.

(...*and the rain's lashing.*)

And as the days passed, the Soldier became more and more human. Mungo viewed the beginning of the process with trepidation, knowing (and he alone of them all had the foresight to know it, and to admit his knowledge) what the end must inevitably be: that the Soldier would become a fully-fledged human man, with all the virtues and all the vices—for how could he not have all the vices?—yet with a strength that was abnormal, and a mind too, and a destructive power that could not be contained by any secular authority whatsoever, against which there was neither remede nor defence. Mungo was the possessor of a weapon too terrible to be used, and one which had already grown out of his control.

Hair began to grow around the Soldier's sexual parts—mind, he had been made man-like in all appearances. Mungo ordered him clothed; told the Soldier to remain indoors until his apparel was ready; and indeed the Soldier stayed in the kirk while Seonaid worked at the giant clothes for him, sitting patiently by the altar with his hands on his knees. Mungo and Mairi dressed him as though he were a helpless invalid, and he raised his arms and his legs and turned first this way then that as they commanded. Then he stood up incautiously, and smashed a hole through the roof with his head. Mungo had him housed in the barn, moving part of the crop into the kirk to make way for him. The worship bell rang amidst piles of golden sheaves.

About the village the Soldier took to wandering like a big bairn. Folk lost their fear of him and laughed instead. When he saw them, the Soldier laughed too, his voice booming like a great drum. He picked folk up and ran off with them; he put children on his shoulders and leaped over the stockade; silently, he picked up blind Manus while Nessa sang in gibberish Latin and Fearchar tickled his feet with goose feathers, and the old one thought he had died and was being carried to Heaven by a winged angel. People gave him chores to do. They said, "Soldier, do this," or, "Soldier, do that," and the Soldier did whatever was asked of him. One day he went into the forest with Wat, and came back with the trunk of a pine tree over his shoulder. Then they asked him to move some large sunken rocks that strewed a piece of open land at the foot of the glen and made it impossible to plough. The Soldier moved them, using the tree trunk as a great lever; then he rolled the rocks away and kicked them into the loch like chuckie stones, doing in one afternoon what generations of folk had failed to do with ropes and teams of harnessed oxen. He found a cow that had strayed and brought the beast home, tucked under his arm.

The Soldier began to eat. Fortunately, he showed no interest in red meat, but he ate whole loaves at a gulp. Soon Sine and Siubhan were baking extra loaves for their *uruisg*, and the great creature stood waiting by the oven with all the village bairns around his feet. One day, however, when the two women had gone for fresh flour, the Soldier shoved his hand into the oven. The roar he let out shook birds from the trees half a mile away. He beat at himself to extinguish the flames, and then sat growling with his hand in his mouth. Everyone hid. Mairi came and stood on the Soldier's knees and took the huge hand in both her little ones. She bathed the place with St John's Oil from Mungo's preparations room, a mixture made of the flower and leaf of St John's Wort chopped small. Mungo stood at a distance looking at her. That a tree should cry with pain when possessed of a human voice, confirmed what he had always believed, that all created things have sensibilities even if we are deaf to them. He also saw that from where she was Mairi could pluck away the cross that was around the Soldier's neck.

Mungo was about to walk up to her and whisper, "Mairi, pluck away yon cross," but instead he found himself smiling at the oddly matched couple—wee Mairi whom he loved more than he had ever loved any other living creature, and the huge innocent giant who could crush her between his fingers, and who was letting her do whatever she wanted with him. And Mungo walked closer, and he saw the Soldier's eyes, and the uncomprehending but gentle look that was in them; and the old priest stopped again, and when Mairi came to him, Mungo said nothing about it.

One day Mairi came up to the Soldier holding her woodpigeon in her hands. "Look," she said, "he's ready. His wing's healed up right fine. I'm going to let him go." She walked out of the village. The Soldier lumbered behind her. "I wanted to keep him," said Mairi, "but he belongs in the wood, the Father says, and it's no right to keep him here. Maybe he'll come and see me sometimes, but. What do you think?" she said to the Soldier. "Anyway, he might," she said, without waiting for an answer. "I'm going to pray so no hawks harm him. Hold him careful now," she said, putting the little bird into the Soldier's enormous paws. She knelt on top of the learig and put her hands together with her fingertips touching and her chin resting on her thumbs, and said things into her fingers that the Soldier didn't understand, but he stood beside her and waited for her to finish. She stood up and turned to him. The Soldier didn't know what she was going to do, but it had something to do with his hands and the funny fluttering thing that was in them, so he lowered them to her. Mairi stroked the hard little poll. "Aye then, wee yin," she said, "the blessings and the peace be upon you, and mind they bloody hawks. Hawks," she said to the Soldier, "and him all alone too, poor thing." She opened the Soldier's fingers and the bird flew out. He swooped several times around them before flying off across the burn into the noisy forest. Mairi wiped her eyes and turned to go. The Soldier stopped her. He put his great slab of a hand on her tousled head.

"*Mairi math*," (Mary good) he said. He picked her up. Mairi held on and kissed his rough scratchy cheek.

"Soldier good too," she said.

But with the Soldier's humanity, so too grew the people's greed. Mungo heard them, the whispered·talk that ended hastily when he approached, the bold eyes that sometimes caught his glance. Finella said to him, "Do you blame them? Why should they need your precious Jesus indeed when they have a saviour of their own?"

"God forgive your blasphemy, woman! He is the instrument of God. We are all the instruments of God. Yes, the very wolfriders are instruments of God!"

(*O Assyrian, rod of mine anger...*)

"What kind of loving God is it then that needs

criminals and murderers to reveal his nature?" So spoke Finella contemptuously, and spat on the ground.

The worst of it was that, even if the old witch was beyond redemption, the young folk were now beginning to look to her for guidance and neglect Mungo and his kirk. Her pagan creed—what was it in the end but one of simple survival? Sacrifice such as Christ's was alien to it. So now, look, when other villages sent to them for help, what did they do but laugh? Mungo pleaded otherwise, and indeed they didn't laugh at him: no, they listened, they looked attentive, they said nothing. They did nothing. And what could he threaten them with? Divine wrath? But God had never answered their prayers. Those who prayed and those who did not all died just the same, and it was all one. And could God keep the riders from them? Had God troubled to stay the riders' hands that day of the butchery when their men had died? They had the Soldier, a solid body, and he would defend them, they said. "Yet he will no kill!" said Mungo. They laughed heartily at that. Soldiers are for killing.

Mungo told his troubles to the altar. He could read and write only a little (no one in the glen could do either), but he had learned whole chunks of scripture off by heart, hearing it recited by monks in his youth.

*Woe to them that go down to Egypt for help; and stay on horses, and trust in chariots, because they are many; and in horsemen, because they are very strong; but they look not unto the Holy One of Israel, neither seek the Lord!*

And are we now to go down and live in Egypt, and the people who have been slaves to become slave owners? he said to himself. Better to live in a land of thorns and briers.

Better to live.

And on one side of the altar was Mairi, and on the other was the Soldier, and in that gloaming room both were looking at him curiously.

One evening shortly thereafter the Soldier came to Mungo and sat at his feet, just as Mairi was wont to do. He simply sat there without sound or movement. Mungo continued his work. He was making a mix to cure the inevitable kidney pains winter would bring on by powdering the rootstock of wood avens in his mortar. Folk attached so much importance to the little yellow plant, that doctors were taking to calling it *herba benedicta*, blessed herb. Sufferers would take the powder mixed in ale or whisky, or boil the roots in water and drink off the strained result. Vainer women even made an ointment of it to remove blemishes from their skin, as Seonaid did. And because whooping cough also seemed to afflict bairns most in the months of the year's turning, Mungo was simultaneously preparing for a village of hoasters. A string of red bearberry leaves was drying over a peat, and he would powder them when they were ready, and administer them on a wooden spoon to weans wrapped up in red cloth.

The great Soldier and the tiny flowers with their creeping rootstocks and radical leaves all smelt of the green place.

"There's a plant in the south folk cry wolf's-bane," said Mungo, working his pestle. "What it is I dinna rightly ken; but if there were a plant called folk's-bane or bandit-bane or war-bane, yon would be a mighty precious thing indeed."

(You are our war-bane, he thought, but held his wheesht.)

He worked in silence, save for the scraping of mortar and pestle. "Is it something you want to ask, *Saighdear?*" he said.

The Soldier coughed and swallowed just as a man would do. Then he raised his huge hands and pressed them to his head.

"*De tha so?*" (What is this?) he asked.

Mungo didn't understand.

"*Saighdear. Duine?*" (Soldier. A man?)

"No, you're no a man," said Mungo.

The Soldier thought for a bit.

"*Saighdear. Duine mor,*" (Soldier. A big man) he said emphatically.

Mungo bit his lip.

"You are no a man—no as other men are," he said gently. "You were made out of the trees and earth, Soldier. By the powers of God you were made to fight for us and defend us. Manlike you are, but no, yet no a man."

The Soldier suddenly gave a great sob.

"*Tha mi bronach! Tha mi leam fhein!*" (I am sad! I am alone!) he cried.

The very walls shook. A great feeling of pity and sorrow came over the old priest as he looked at this great, powerful, lonely creature he had made. The Soldier was still sitting, now holding his ankles in his hands, but even bent double his chin was above Mungo's head. If Mungo had moved fast enough, maybe he could have snatched the cross away at that moment.

But Mungo wasn't thinking about that at all.

"Everyone loves you. You have helped us. Don't be sad."

The Soldier shook his head.

The Soldier went to Finella. He sensed that she didn't like to see him looking weak or foolish. So he stood upright. (He had to stand outside her door or his head would have broken the roof.) He clenched his jaws and put his fists on his hips. People were most impressed when he acted like that.

"*De tha so?*" he asked of her.

Ah, my heart! The most powerful Soldier in all Scotland, you are. Our right arm in the days of struggle. Our axe against the roots of rottenness. Our revenge on the whole race of murderers—pride of my soul, light of my eyes!

"*Tha mi leam fhein,*" muttered the Soldier, turning away.

Aye, great one! Alone as the heroes are always alone.


The Soldier met wee Mairi.

"*De tha so, a Mhairi?*" (What is this, Mary?)

Mairi reached out and touched him.

"*Na biodh eagal ort,*" (Don't be afraid) she said.

"*Is caomh leam Mairi,*" (I love Mary) he said, picking the wee lassie up in the crook of his muckle great arm.

Yap! yap! from underneath them.

"*Is caomh leam Faidh,*" said the Soldier.

# 16

## *And the Red Rooster Crowed*

The rains came again, light drizzles over the cut fields, mists that smoked out of the sunrise, showers that ran down the clouds and jumped onto the treetops with hissing grey breath. Sometimes it was difficult to tell whether it was dew or rainwater that glistened so on the innumerable webs the spiders had hung everywhere, as every autumn, stitching together shoots of long grass and turning bracken clumps into shimmering cities of silk. In the morning, those nights when he had slept out under the boughs, Wat, stretching, had seen himself surrounded by whole rainbows of moisture sparkling on thousands of gossamer strands, and he had paused in lighting his breakfast fire to watch a spider run down the middle of her web and shake it till it was dry and near invisible again. For now autumn was old and crouched on the slopes of the misty mountain and capped the alders of the strath with its dull golden glow, as Wat the woodcutter walked through the browning forest with his axe on his shoulder and a laddie, Ruadh, trotting submissively by his heels.

Wat walked happily. There was a loving ache in his groin such as he had not had for years—he wrinkled his hardnut brow—aye, for more years than was good for a body, spending all its time in the woodlands where even the deer grew lonely. Happily he walked through the falling of yellowed birch leaves, and he thought of Sorcha's milk-white body, and her limbs flailing in the dusk of the deserted tower where the old Shirra had once tortured men. And O! but this was a sweet torture, her gentle eyes cried him as she trembled and gasped and gave that one last jerk and lay still under his thrusting; and when he sighed long and contentedly, her fingers would cease scratching and lie quiet, then stroke that place between his shoulder blades he could never reach, and she would murmur petting cradle words into his torn ear. He loved how she did that.

Wat walked warily, all alert, sniffing the air like a wise beast. The first winter chill was on the wind blowing in from northern icywaves; the sun was shining as through a coating of thin blue ice. Warily he walked though his feet were mere whisperings on the soft floor of leaves. The capercaillie was beginning to forage among bracken and pine needles for winter feed; groups of adders were slithering to hibernation under tree roots and in brushwood dens; in the distance the brown woodcutter heard the high yap of a mating fox.

Wat wasn't looking for wood. He was looking for men. It was no killer boar he sought today with his axe, but the worst killer of all. Once, twice now, he thought he had seen white on the mountain top. One night he had heard the voice of an elk. If they bastards are coming, they'll be on us afore the antlered folk seek the low ground! His fingers tightened on the handle of his axe. Aye, but it's lovely breasts my Sorcha has!

It only takes a moment to die; and with too much of his attention lying back in the womb of that previous warm night, in the tower, in young Sorcha's loving arms, Wat missed the moment that might have saved his life.

The beast came hurrying down the path right towards him, as though the man wasn't there, leaping from mossy stump to black boulder, through the green chequered sunlight, pattering over the grid of fallen branches and decaying leaves. Wat was staring straight at the yellow cheeks of the polecat before the creature seemed to see him and darted off to one side with a flash of its bottlebrush tail. What the—? Suddenly Wat's whole body jerked. He stood quivering like a dog. In front of them the trees were beginning to thin out and plunge down into a small glen where there was a croft standing solitary, a single family's abode. The hair began to prickle on Wat's neck. He crept forward into the open. Then he heard it.

*FAOL!*—WOLF!

Motioning the boy Ruadh to do the same, Wat dropped into cover. The first thin thread of smoke began to curl over the trees. Wat edged forward a little further. He heard a horse's neigh—then another and another. Forward a bit more... Very, very faintly, he heard a woman scream. Wat had heard enough. He turned to Ruadh. O my God, the boy was standing right out in the open with a panic–striken look on his face. Over the rise out of the glen came a rider. He saw Ruadh too, and with a whoop of terrible joy he spurred towards him. "Run, laddie!" Wat shouted. The boy turned and stumbled back towards the forest. "Run!" The rider was between Wat and the boy and coming quickly, his long spear lowered, aiming straight at Ruadh's back. Wat judged the distance, raised his axe, and flung it with all his strength at the horseman. The blade missed, but the handle hit the horse's neck. The startled beast reared up, an overhanging branch struck the rider on the head, and he dropped unconscious from the saddle. Ruadh reached the forest in safety. Only then did Wat turn to face the hoofs that were thundering up behind him. His hands were empty and he had nowhere to run to. *Please God!* God wasn't listening. A blade flashed in the sunlight: Wat's body fell to one side of the path, and his wizened brown head, which Sorcha had cradled to her bosom, rolled off on the other. His legs kicked once, and he was still.

"Father! Father!"

Ruadh arrived at the stockade, tearful, screaming, his words a whummling spray of fear. The kirk bell rang urgently. From wherever they were the folk came running, down from the rigs, up from the burnside, across the fields they came driving the kye, every last goat and sheep and pig, every cow and ox, the very chickens scattering in among the tangle of hurrying hoofs and legs; and the women raced for their bothies and disappeared indoors for a moment, then emerged again with scythes and sickles and long forks in their hands, and they congregated within the stockade, the gate pulled shut, Fearchar there with his bow and quiverful of arrows looking bold and feeling sore afraid underneath, and out of the kirk came Mungo, and the huge Soldier came behind him, his sun-tossed shadow vast as the very tower from whose roof the woman sentry shouted: "Smoke! I can see their burnings! *They're coming!*"

Down the strath came the wolfriders, a hundred strong, and the ruins of isolated crofts and solitary clachans wept red flames behind them, and the smoke called down the whistling wind that heralded their advance. They were terrible and cruel-looking men. Some wore long hauberks of chain mail painted black and criss-crossed with leather thongs; others wore short sarks of the metal stuff, blood-rusted, and covered with thick jackets of shaggy animal hide; some wore iron helmets, Scottish and Scandinavian, some with flat nose-pieces, some conical, some round as pots; others wore no helm but only their own masses of greasy hair. Some were drunk, swaying in their saddles and shouting obscenities over the waiting fields. Tied to many a saddle girth were the heads of those they had already slain in the strath, and Wat's was there too; white-eyed they were, with open mouths and long slivers of red raw flesh that dangled from the torn throats of them.

And in front of them all, before his own fearful wolf's-head totem bobbing on its tall pole, *he* rode, the leader. O bonny and cruel he looked, there on his proud black horse, his legs out-thrust in the long stirrups, the plaid lying over his saddle, and the war cloak of wolfskins on his back clasped to either shoulder by a golden brooch, while around his stallion's hoofs billowed the smoke of the tortured valley.

It was about noon when they crested the learig and came within sight of the village. At once outriders galloped off left and right, riding in the shade of the trees, passing the stockade a long arrowshot away on either side, and meeting each other again behind the village in the lee of corbie tower. Then they returned as they had come and reported to the leader that no troopers' spears showed over the battle-ments of the tower, and there were no tracks of warhorses to be found anywhere among the cattle hooves that had stamped the glen. The leader nodded grimly. He raised his right arm, and the column of horsemen halted. He made a sweeping motion with it, and the riders fanned out until their line stretched across the entire width of the valley from forest to forest, from stately pine to gentle alder. They splashed across the burn and rode down over the fields where the harvesters had worked.

In front of them was the stockade. They saw the glint of steel beyond it, as scythes and sickles were raised. They saw the long skirts of the women and grinned. They weren't afraid of women with knives. They heard the lowing of the beasts. The stockade gate suddenly opened and a small robed old man came out. The riders guffawed. They had seen it all before, but it never ceased to amuse them the way these old priests would come flapping out with their mouths full of pious blethers. Sometimes they let them haver on a bit. It didn't matter, no really. They killed them all in the end—crucified, some of them, some strung up by their genitals, others dancing with their feet in a fire. Beside his leader, the standard-bearer was laughing so hard he was swaying in his saddle. He was thinking about what he was going to do to Mungo. Laughing, he leaned back and closed his eyes, the better to enjoy the picture; still laughing, he leaned forward over the pommel, opened his eyes, blinked away the tears that were masking them, and—froze with his mouth wide open.

Behind Mungo in the stockade gate stood the Soldier.

The entire line of riders came to an abrupt halt.

Tall in his saddle, the bandit leader swallowed his breath in a long sigh and blew loudly down his nose. "O shit," he said. He drew his heavy claymore. A moment passed and the line of spears came down behind him.

*Shit, shit, shit! I shouldha kent!*

He smiled sourly.

*Aweel jockey, but you ken now.*

Now the leader of the wolf-men was no jessie, no him. He had encountered folk of the were-world before this. The very sword he had in his hand (a hefty great claymore it was), why he had won it as a laddie digging his way into the death-howe of an old chieftain up in Sutherland, and the chieftain's ghost had up and fought him for it—aye. A hell of a fight that had been, down there among the rings and brooches and horse bones, for ghosts in those days were no whoowhoo spirits of white mist, but the very walking corpses of the dead, evil as in life, forbye twice as strong; so a long afternoon had passed there, battering in the mirk, before the leader staggered out into the sunlit world again, bleeding like a sheep, but with the red sword triumphant in his hand.

Nor were the riders at his back exactly a lot of cock virgins either. You couldn't live the life they led among the forests and in the lonely places without encountering bogles in some form or other. Fintan—him with the red face and beery belly—had once fought an *uruisg* half way up Strathnaver and had only pacified it in the end by chopping the creature's head off and laying it below its left thigh; then damn me if the thing didn't come to life again just as Fintan was taking a breather and chase him back down the strath swinging an oak club in one hand and holding its severed head bellowing away in the other. Feuch! Why the Lord had created such a tribe of boking creatures in the first place took some understanding. Harald, who was a Lochlannach and a pagan, said they were the spawn of Loki the devil-god, him that killed young Baldur. Others, more Christian-like, cried them the children of Cain—and you'll all ken who yon bugger was. The only sure way to kill the undead, said Harald, was to cut off the head, put it below the left thigh, and then burn the whole bloody body to ashes and scatter them on water making the sign of Thor's hammer, so the beast couldn't come alive any more.

Well, here it was then, an *uruisg;* and Jesu's nails and Thor's hammer indeed, but it was big! The one and only comfort the leader found was that the creature didn't seem to be armed; but even so, there was the strength of twenty, thirty men in those limbs. Aye, right then! He turned in his saddle. Yous for it? Good—all the lads in line there with their spears down, and nobody wavering, even if there were a few gey whey-looking faces. He stood up in his stirrups and waved his claymore high above his head.

"*Faol!*" he shouted. "Wolf!"

And his men shouted and shook their spears. "*Faol!*" The wolf's-head danced.

"*Faol!*" shouted the leader again, even louder; and his men repeated it. He shouted it a third time, and their roar rang in the trees like bells. Then he urged his black stallion forward at a walk. The line of a hundred horses came down behind him.

Mungo cassock-priest stood waiting for them, a few paces before the open gate. The Soldier stood behind him, muckle fists on muckle hips. Both were unarmed. Most of the women stood in a tight schiltron within the gate, armed to the teeth. In addition to their harvesting tools, a good many carried regular spears and swords, looted over the years and stashed in the thatch against such a day as this. Old Finella had a long spear in both her hands and a cooking pot reversed helmet-like on her head. Daft she would have looked at any other time. Blind Manus was there too with the smith's hammer, and Tomas stood by his side with a mattock and a wooden chair. Fearchar straddled the stockade, bow at the ready. Bairns old enough to be of use sat on the nearest roofs with slings and handfuls of pebbles.

A horse whinnied in the forest. A sudden glint of white in the branches...

The horses of the riders snorted nervously and the men began glancing toward the trees, as though wishing to run in there, and at the same time fearful of what they might find if they did. To hide their unease they laughed and shouted loudly, giving the wolf-cry of the band again, and again, and again.

The women answered them. "Swine! Bastards! Vermin!" they screamed, clashing their weapons.

Mungo walked forward towards the riders with his

hands outstretched and his mouth full of words. Seeing him, one of the riders called Niall Crooked-mouth put spurs to his horse's flanks and came forward at the charge, leaning over the tossing mane with his long spear tucked under his arm.

*"Buaidh no bas!"* shouted Niall, which is to say, Victory or death, for he was a brave man for all that he was a robber and murderer. The shiny leaf blade was pointed at Mungo, who stood to receive it unmoving, with his eyes very wide and a shake in his voice.

Like a thunderbolt came Niall, and clods of earth shot from his mare's stamping hoofs. Then from atop the gable-end of the nearest house wee Mairi's voice came trebling—

"Soldier, Soldier, save him, *Saighdear!"*

—and instantly the Soldier was by Mungo's side, had pushed Mungo behind him, and Niall, unable now to stop his mare, cursed viciously and thrust his spearpoint straight at the Soldier's face. A blow took his horse full on the nose, the startled beast sat back on her haunches, Niall was torn from the saddle by the very spearshaft he clutched, and his mouth, still cursing, smashed into the ground at Mungo's feet.

A roar from the women and a clashing of iron.

There were other men there as brave as Niall. Two of them spurred towards the Soldier, and mindful of Harald's advice they had discarded their spears and were swinging axes. The pole of Niall's spear clubbed them both, splintering as it did so, and they fell senseless by his side.

The line of riders stopped and several arrows were discharged. To no avail: they stuck in the Soldier's unfeeling body with wooden thuds, and he brushed them away.

The Soldier laughed like a boy being tickled.

More arrows came. The Soldier laughed louder, so startling some horses with his bellowing that they turned and galloped off, dragging their riders with them. An arrow transfixed Mungo's shoulder, tearing the rough dark cloth and the scruffy white body within, and ripped out through the cloth again, a good six inches of it, red dripping elm wood topped by a glinting triangle of blood.

The women howled and screeched. Finella gripped the stockade and spat a stream of venomous curses. An arrow thumped into the log by her face. Another arrow hit big Malai on the leg, and Malai skirroched and sat down heavily in the gateway. An arrow arched towards the gable and combed a scarlet scratch through Mairi's hair.

A strange fury took Mungo then. He shouted something, pointing straight at the leader and his wolf's-head totem with one trembling arm. No human being heard him that lived. Niall, groaning on the ground with his jaws shattered, found himself being lurched upside down into the air. The Soldier was holding both his ankles crushed together in one massive hand. Niall screamed in agony as he swung helplessly high, high into the air; and then perhaps he lost consciousness altogether the moment both his ankles snapped—*crack! crack!*—so that he felt nothing at all when, from twenty feet, his body was brought whirling down onto the head of the standard-bearer who had laughed so, and the man's iron helmet met Niall's chest and shattered it, and Niall's weight drove the helmet down into the skull and split it in pieces, and drove the broken skull down into the brainpan, and the brains spurted out the man's mouth as he fell, and the hellish wolf's-head fell with him on its long pole and lay a useless thing on the earth.

Then the Soldier swung Niall's dead body once more, a second rider lay in the blood, and he never moved again.

Out of the gate the women now came pouring, old Finella and beautiful Seonaid, each with a spear; plain Sine and gossiping Una with scythes; Una's daughters, Sorcha and Siubhan, waving sickles: gentle Sorcha who had seen her lover's head dangling from a saddle and was weeping for vengeance; mild Siubhan whose white breasts Mungo had seen and loved at the haymaking. And Nessa came with a harvest hook and a long knife, and all the others, dead now to everything, even to hate, moved only by a desire to destroy these raging mad dogs that had killed so pointlessly and plundered so rapaciously for so long. And the men too—Tomas and blind Manus together, no hesitation now about fighting, either of them. And on top of the stockade logs young Fearchar fired arrow after arrow after the fleeing riders, while from the roofs, Pedair and Ringean and all the bairns who had muscle sent their slingshots spinning and dinging down on the helms of those who came within their reach.

Rider after rider fell to the earth. One or two regained their saddles, but the smell of the Soldier, and the strange forest sound, had the horses in a panic and it was difficult to remount. On foot the heavily armoured riders were at a disadvantage and a couple of dazed men were killed before they could even draw sword to defend themselves.

Alone in all that rout the leader held his ground. He spurred his great black stallion back and forth in front of the women swinging his claymore in both hands. He cut the heads off scythes and spears, ignoring the arrows and stones that came flying at him. "Cowards! Yellow-bellied bastards!" he roared at his men. "Stand and fight!" Some of the band tried to turn their horses back into the fray, but none of the beasts would face the Soldier, and they shied off, kicking their legs. One man, a young Hebridean named Raonull, came running back on foot with raised sword and shield, and at first the women gave way; but a scythe cut his legs out from under him, and he fell, and a sickle ended his life. Soon, as the others a field away tried vainly to control their snorting, rearing horses, the leader was left alone.

Mounted though he was, he made no effort to escape. He realized that his authority depended on not losing face, and to be beaten by a pack of women—even if they had that damned walking tree behind them—would end his rule for good. With nothing to lose, he smashed the head of a tall woman called Marsali, and laughed. He shouted at them, shaking the blade: "Come on, you bitches! Come on, you dirty whores!" He slashed a raised axe out of a woman's hands, and the blade spun away in an arc and clattered against the stockade. Controlling his mount with his legs only, he hauled the beast round and spurred back again, swinging his heavy sword. The women cowered from him. He laughed: there was blood on his blade, he had put it there, and he shrieked with pleasure at the sight of it. There was the women's cold hating hiss, and the whinnying of the terrified horses—and he laughed even louder. Then *It* came, and it occurred to the leader that this demon was the thing that had eluded him for so long, Death itself stalking out of the ground to get him. The leader swore savagely and slashed out, but the blade rang and fell from his shaking hand. Then the Soldier picked up the black horse and flung it aside. The saddle girths broke and the leader of the wolfriders rolled on the ground. Stunned, helmetless, he managed to pull himself onto his haunches. He groped for his sword, but it was out of reach. *Faol!* he cried, as the scythes and sickles came and waved over him. *Faol!* he cried, as they tore at him, rending his wolfskin cloak and slitting the straps of his mail hauberk, opening him like a lobster. And at the very end the leader found his dirk and stabbed one of his killers in the thigh. She screamed and fell. He laughed, and the blood welling out of his mouth broadened the lips of him like a demented grin. *Faol!* he gurgled into the falling blades. And then the red sun that the wolf had chased for so long finally rose up and exploded behind his eyes.

The black stallion scrambled to his feet. Strange to tell, none of his legs had been broken. He shook himself. He was saddleless: the girths were broken; the bit also had been torn from his mouth. The warhorse stood blinking, trying to realize what had happened to him. For the first time since he had been taken from the herd he was tied by nothing, neither by rope nor by leather nor by fence. He glared red-eyed at the carnage, then turned and galloped away. His hoofs beat over the fields, and the surviving riders shouted and tried to catch him. His hoofs beat over the rigs, and the watchful birds of the lower branches rose into the air. His hoofs plunged into the green shade, and the soft floor of the autumn forest muffled their thunderous passage.

I'm free! thought the black stallion, though he was badly shaken, and his mouth was sore from the bit, and his back sore from the saddle. Free! They *duine* bastards! Who would have thought they had it in them? The stallion laughed and shook his head, there, below the trees. His laugh, equine as it was, was not the vindictive violent laughter of the leader seeing his death. It was a laugh of pure contentment, a sigh of great release. Once, his herd had fought like the *duine*-folk back there, for the wise king-horse had known the virtue of collective defence. When the wolves came down on them, they had formed a tight ring and kicked out with their back hoofs. His own father had brought a wolf down with his teeth, and leapt forward and stamped the grey dog to death. Then the wise king-horse had died, and other wolves had come, and the herd galloped in flight, the stallions on the outside and the mares, the foals and ponies within. He was young and weak and had fallen behind. His mother had stayed with him, and she had fallen with a wolf's teeth in her throat. Then a hunter had killed the wolf and skinned it, and taken the foal with a rope around his neck, and trained him to be *duine*-servant in war; and terrible he had been too, with the wolf totem behind him and the wolfskin leader on his back, pawing the ground and breathing black fire in the snort of his nostrils. But always that rope had been on his neck.

He had loyally risked wounds and death for the leader, yet now the leader's fall was a release and a great joy to him. The horseman's word was broken.

Hoofs in the forest. Even before he heard them, the black stallion knew they were there. Then he heard the whinny which every horse in the days of the forest's greatness knew from the sunrise to the sunset shore: and the white flank shone amongst the dark pillars of birch and pine, gleamed and glittered there amongst the bracken and the alder's spray, as though the Moon herself were come to earth and were walking free in the morning, in the living turning greenness of the world that was before men and the clamour of them. And when he came to the place, to the naked hollow surrounded by the black walls of rock, topped by the waiting masses of the forest, not a killer's eye shone anywhere on Wolves' Crag as the black stallion stopped, and stretched his forelegs, and bowed his head.

"Lord Goban," he said.

## 17

## How They Made the Michaelmas Struan

*Ah, Soldier*
*Soldier, what are you?*
*Soldier.*

It was a late Michaelmas and there was dancing in the village. The folk were celebrating *Micheal nam Buadh,* Michael the Victorious, saint of the sea and horses, conqueror of the powers of darkness. They had cleaned the blood off their red weapons, and returned scythes and sickles, hooks and mattocks, to their nails on the wall to await the springtime field. The spears and swords, and those they had taken, went back into the thatch.

Two of the women were dead. They were gentle mounds of new earth within the kirkyard. Seven of the bandits and two of their horses were dead also. They didn't want to bury them anywhere in their glen, though they were afraid to leave them to the birds in case their ghosts should come walking; but Mungo said their souls were bound for the other place, and Finella having a memory of the Norsefolk and of dead vikings being pushed northwards in burning longships, they made a pyre in the field behind the tower and burned the seven men there, and the horses with them. The women had taken the wolf's-head totem and set it high on the tower, but Mungo clambered up and cast it over the battlements. It turned several times in the air, and fell into the flames. The red rooster crowed.

There were four prisoners, including fat Fintan. The rest had scattered. They also had six captive horses. At first they had intended killing the prisoners, but tempers soon cooled, and instead they were brought before Mungo and Finella for their judgement. Mungo preached damnation at them, told them about their wickedness, asked if they repented (they did), asked what work they could do for the village in contrition (they shuffled their feet, glanced about uneasily). Finella filtered some grain through her fingers, said it was a pity for seed to be wasted, and with winter coming on too (men are men in the end, no matter what else they are). The women sniggered lewdly. The men were led away and imprisoned in one of the bothies. The horses were kept for use in the spring ploughing.

The Soldier they didn't know *what* to do with. No. He had stood and watched the burning with folded arms. No. He had killed two men and his eyes were gleaming. Mungo was afraid that—not having an immortal soul and hence no conscience—he would become crazed with killing and want to kill again. And again. Mungo told him to kneel down so he could remove the cross, and the Soldier refused. When Mungo sighed and said that at least he could take the arrowheads out of the Soldier's body, the Soldier pushed him away brusquely.

The Soldier walked through the forest slapping his arms. He broke down a young tree with a blow from his fist. He began to eat meat. He waded into the loch in pursuit of trout and swallowed them whole.

And the women? Well, they no longer talked, daft-like, about their Soldier becoming thane, or king, or fathering a race of heroes, or any such blethers. They were simply looking forward to the ploughing and the next sowing, being, in the end, peasants like their parents and their parents' parents before them, here in this same strath in the forest's shadow. The Soldier, what was he to them? He had come. He had averted the twin afflictions of hunger and pillage that had threatened them this season past, and not being accustomed to looking for danger out of the season in which it threatened, they were happy, and talked about a winter with full granaries and no hardship, and how fine the horses would be at the ploughing. He had come, aye. Now, secretly, they just wished that the Soldier would go away.

It was a late Michaelmas, what with one thing and another, battles and the like, but Michaelmas is one of the high points of the year, and they were not for missing it. True, there were no carrots in Scotland—indeed there were none anywhere in Britain—in those days for folk to pleiter with, making a *Domhnach Curran*, Carrot Sunday, as they would do of a Michaelmas in centuries to come, the women inspecting the phallic vegetables to discover their future lover-luck; but the bairns made themselves crowns of reeds and decked them over with heather, and went searching for pine cones on the forest paths, and said words about those of appropriate size and shape which made the lads redden up and blush, and all the lassies giggle. And that did well enough.

Then there were the races. It was pleasing to the saint, him being mysteriously a horseman as well as a boatman, to gallop cuddies on his name day. Well, there had been more than enough galloping of cuddies in the glen that season, you would have thought; but no, they must race the six captive beasts around the stockade from gate to gate, and Fearchar and Nessa (both of them with deaths to their credit), and Malai, who would limp the rest of her life, and Ealasaid, and a wheen of other women, two to a cuddie, with bairns running beside them and clinging on to the horses' rumps, all went thumping and splashing round the village and over the burn, kicking up a fine stour, and everyone stood and clapped and shouted them on. Rob the Gowk (who had been asleep under the haycart all through the battle, which says a lot for him when you think about it), well he did his level best to get seated on a great trumpeting chestnut brute; and he jumped over it, and he fell under it, and Pedair and Ringean, who were holding the beast, were splitting their sides very nearly; then at last the cuddie lost patience with Rob altogether and kicked him, wham! right in the balls, and Rob squealed worse than a stuck pig; and the bairns just about died laughing at him, sitting there with his bum in the burn, rubbing the tender place, and greeting his eyes out, before their mother called them in and cuffed them for all they were worth.

Sine and Siubhan, the most accomplished bakers in the village, were making the cake called *Struan Micheil*. It was a gathering of all the fruits of the harvest, of the oats, the barley, and the rye, which were taken and milled in equal parts, then mixed with a peck of meal moistened in sheep's milk, and the whole baked on a lambskin. As the struan began to harden in the heat, a thick dressing of cream, eggs and butter, whipped, was spread over it with a brush of cockerel feathers. Finally it was given a careful covering of cranberries, bilberries, brambleberries, and caraway seeds. Sine and Siubhan stood back to admire their work. Every bothy was making one, but theirs was ever the best, and so they had been asked to make the *Struan Comachaidh*—the great communal struan for the village. Wee Mairi's tousled head popped up between them, and she stared at the cake with big eyes and a dripping mouth.

"And here's the bit for yoursel, Mairi."—Siubhan, breaking a piece.

"And for my Soldier?" said Mairi with her mouth full.

The women looked at each other.

"We have one here for yoursel and the Father and—and other kirk folk," said Siubhan, and put a *Struan Treo*, a family struan, into Mairi's hands. The wee girl ran with it to find her Soldier.

> *O Jellon Grame sat in Silverwood,*
> *He sharpened his broadsword lang;*
> *And he has called his little foot-page*
> *An errand for to gang.*
>
> *'Win up, my bonny boy,' he says,*
> *'As quickly as you may;*
> *For you maun gang for Lilly Flower*
> *Before the break of day.'*

There was a dance that evening outside the kirk, and blind Manus (who had wetted his hammer's head in blood, syne put the thing away swearing never to use it for any purpose again) took up his pipe and put it to his lips, and joyful windmusic rose over the quiet glen that had heard the screaming of horses and the shouting, and the women danced.

The Soldier sat alone in the shadow of the barn and looked at them.

The women danced, though it was a sad thing to have a dance without men, for young Fearchar danced with Nessa only, and Manus was blind, and Tomas was old, and Rob was a Gowk, and Mungo a Priest; but then they minded on the four prisoners who were in an empty bothy all barred up with wooden staves, so they let them out after telling them that the giant Soldier would come and eat them alive if they even once tried to escape; and the four bandits joined in willingly enough, being pulled from one hot partner to another until they fairly were exhausted.

And the Soldier sat alone in the shadow of the barn...

Mairi danced "The Carlin Of The Mill-dust" with Pedair. They numbered perhaps twenty years between them. Pedair carried a long reed in his right hand, symbolizing the magic staff of St Columba or the druids—opinions differed. He and Mairi danced round and round each other, gesticulating with their arms raised, crossing and recrossing, changing and exchanging places. Pedair waved the reed over his head, then over Mairi's, touching her with it on the hair, and Mairi fell down as though dead at his feet. Pedair then began to keen for her death, spinning round and round with his head in his hands, then clasping his hands to his heart, making a grand show of misery. Then he knelt down by Mairi's left hand, lifted it, breathed on the palm, and touched it with his reed. Immediately, Mairi raised her arm and began waving it above her face, while Pedair danced, rejoicing. He then touched her right hand in the same way, then the left foot and right foot; and all Mairi's limbs were waving. Finally, he bent over her and breathed into her mouth; and touched her heart with the reed. As soon as he did that, Mairi came to life. She jumped up, laughing, and the two began dancing together again, whirling round and round as fast as they could go.

It was the resurrection, the bringing of life out of the earth.

The Soldier understood dimly that Mairi was only playing with the *duine* boy, that she wasn't really dead when she fell down; but still, no one knew whether or not his eyes were full of pain at that moment, because no one was looking. The next time someone did look, he was just sitting there, the great lump, gazing at them, and his eyes were as expressionless as two knots in a tree.

Dance! They had other dances too. There was "The Combat Of The Cocks," "The Waddling Of The Ducks," "The Reel Of The Black Hens," "The Battle Of The Warriors"... Siubhan stood over a scythe and a sickle and a scattering of grain holding her Eoin, who was the youngest one, and Mungo and Finella, the oldest ones, danced round them, hooching, with their arms high. Fat Fintan, the prisoner, and old Tomas, who had damn nearly killed him with his mattock, performed a passable sword-dance over a couple of rusty blades.

They were in the very midst of all the piping and the kicking, the jumping and the laughing, when the woman sentry who stood now, a permanent fixture, high on the tower, hit the metal bar that hung there with a hammer and cried down, "Riders! Riders in the glen!"—and in an instant all was quiet.

There were three riders.

And who were they?

One was a tall gallowglass; he held the banner of the Thane, a rampant cat with flared claws. One was a page boy, lithe and freckled on a prancing pony. Before them rode the Thane's herald—not the common messenger who had been here before, but a grand duinewassal, richly clad and full of fine persuasions. He dismounted before the gate and begged entry, all politeness. The gate was opened to him amidst a great barking of dogs. His two companions remained outside. The folk turned their backs on them and resumed their dancing.

The herald greeted Mungo, rubbed his hands, and said it was grand to see the "simple folk" enjoying themselves, so it was; and then he chuckled at nothing in particular, and drew Mungo aside with his hand on the old man's elbow and a rosy smile on his face.

Manus's pipemusic spun threads between the lengthening shadows on the village street.

"Is he here?" whispered the herald urgently.

By the corner of the barn a gigantic shadow moved. Inadvertently, Mungo's eyes flickered towards it, and the herald followed their direction.

"Ah—!"

The herald jumped back a full yard and collided with a bothy wall. He remained leaning against it, his hand on his sword hilt and his lips sputtering frenzied prayers.

Evening, and the night was coming quickly. The east was all a darkness, and the first stars shone there.

"I am sent from the Thane," said the herald, "with these two demands. The first," he said, "is that the prisoners' heads and the weaponry and the horses you have taken shall be collected together, and shall be sent to Thanehall under guard, to await the Thane and his pleasure." But even as he spoke, his eyes were on that shadow there, beyond the leaping dancers.

Folk kindled a fire of leaves. Tiny yellow flames joined the reel. Immense shadows gesticulated on the dark walls. One still, silent shadow stretched out into the night.

"I regret the Thane can have neither the prisoners' heads, nor the weaponry, nor the horses that were taken," said Mungo.

The herald's invincible smile narrowed to a dangerous tight slit over his teeth.

"For those who took these things from our attackers have already decided on their fate," said Mungo.

The herald sneered. What village is it where the folk determine what will be, and no their rightful masters? Forbye folk who are in great part *wimmin?*

"This village—under God," said Mungo quietly.

"You could hang for saying that, priest."

"Aye," Mungo sighed.

"There is a second point on which your neck—may I

216

say your very soul?—is in jeopardy," said the herald, and once more he was wearing his smile. "You have by report (and I can see the report is true) acquired the services of an—how can I put it?—an *uruisg*, a hobgoblin, a brownie, a familiar spirit. No, my friend," he continued, raising a palm to squash Mungo's objection, "these are no my words—O no mine, for I have no knowledge of such wanchancy matters—they are the Bishop's words. Aye. For hearing of the existence of this, this *thing* of yours, what did our noble Thane do, but (concerned for your poor soul as he is, bless the man) send to the Bishop's palace at Inverness asking if you had, perchance, strayed from the straight and narrow path Mother Kirk has laid down for all her mortal children, into the dark and mirky realm of necromancy and the sly fiend. My lord the Bishop was sorely fashed (he is, besides, our Thane's cousin and frequent hunting guest, as has perhaps slipped your mind). So fashed was he over the state of your soul that he just sat down and howled and wept, seeing (as he put it) the flames leaping about you, and the wee demons with their hooks embedded in your flesh ready to drag you down into the waiting pit. For what is this (says our lord Bishop) but the work of a warlock, this raising of an imp of Satan out of the pagan places—and by one whose unco ploys in the past have caused us such sore unease. O erring son of the kirk! (says the Bishop) will you no come back? I will pray for your soul, lest the heresy and the abominations of devil-worship you have committed become so deep-rooted that they maun be burned out of you with the red flames and with the yellow! For is it no written 'You shall not suffer a witch to live'? And down on his hunkers the Bishop goes and prays away, and all his palace-load of priests with him, *O erring son of the kirk, will you no come back?* And in case you dinna hear or heed his loving words, a stake has even now been built before the palace gates, and a man with a black hood stands there to help you part company with your sinful flesh. Now is it no fine to have so many famous folk pishing themselves with concern for the state of your own good soul?"

Manus's pipe arced like a rainbow over the laughing shadows. Folk were giving each other small struans, known variously as *Struan Beag* and *Struan Cloinne*.

"We have, of course, a *Struan Mor* for the Thane which you will take with you when you leave," said Mungo.

"Of course," said the herald, "there is another way of looking at the whole issue entirely."

*Then went the Pharisees and took counsel how they might entangle him in his talk. And they sent out unto him their disciples with the Herodians, saying, Master, we know that thou art true, and teachest the way of God in truth, neither carest thou for any man; for thou regardest not the person of men. Tell us therefore, What thinkest thou? Is it lawful to give tribute unto Caesar, or not?*

"The Thane is greatly impressed," said the herald, "with the power this monster of yours possesses. Just think, priest (and mind, these are the thoughts of your Bishop too), what a Soldier it would make!—what a Soldier it has made! But why stop at wiping out some bandit rabble? Think what it could do if it were properly instructed in the art of war, and proper weapons were made for it! Our Thane, who is in all things a wise and benevolent ruler, and his cousin the Bishop (God bless and preserve them both!) would have a power at their backs that no one could ever challenge. Whenever a strath was threatened, then our Thane could send his power and the threat would vanish as though it had never been. Whenever a kirk was defiled or a holy sister violated, then our Bishop would have that power to chastise the wrongdoer. Imagine that, priest! Protected by your Soldier, we could have a peaceable united God-fearing land at last! A Scottish angel with a fiery Scottish sword that would guard our Scotland for ever! And, as the Bishop says, *God wills it!* That is, in short, our Thane's second demand."

*But Jesus perceived their wickedness, and said, Why tempt ye me, ye hypocrites? Shew me the tribute money. And they brought him a penny. And he saith unto them, Whose is this image and superscription?*

"It is finely baked, the big struan we have for you," said Mungo. "Two of the womenfolk are very fine at the baking. When they work on the eggs and the butter, the rye and the oats, the cranberries and the brambleberries, they bake a song, so they do, a thing of most surpassing excellence, which I believe the Thane has sampled every year from us now without complaining."

*And they say unto him, Caesar's.*

"I dinna doubt," said the herald, "that some satisfactory arrangement could be entered into regarding the prisoners and the weapons and the cuddies; regarding the taxes you pay, perhaps, the garrisoning of the tower, your own comforts, even. I ken well," the herald tapped his nose, "that my lord the Bishop has one or two rather more lucrative wee posts at his disposal than this. And as for yon stake—och! think no more of it. Mistakes often happen, slanderous tongues often wag, but no clever man went to the stake yet. You catch my meaning?" And he grinned a long sleazy grin.

*Then saith he unto them, Render therefore unto Caesar the things which are Caesar's; and unto God the things that are God's.*

"I mean, priest, you have the drift of my words?"

But the things which are Caesar's are not necessarily all those things which Caesar wants.

"And you will find a jar of whisky waiting for you too," said Mungo, "for it's a long ride you will have back to Thanehall, and the nights are drawing in, and gey cold they are too, this time of year."

"Perhaps I havena made mysel clear," the herald hissed,

and an inch or two of his sword blade gleamed sudden in the firelight.

"O you have, dinna bother," said Mungo. "*Saighdear*," he called out. "The gentleman is leaving. You will help the gentleman to his horse."

With a speed that was amazing, considering the size of him, the Soldier's soaring shadow detached itself from the barn. He strode over the fire, and the flames went berserk in the wind of his stride, the dance fell apart, the pipe stilled. The herald stopped long enough to get one eyeful of the colossus that was bearing down on him, then gave a bit yelp and took to his heels. His dropped sword rang hollow on a stone. He and his goggle—eyed escort were a muttering of hoofs fading down the darkness of the glen.

All the stars were out by now.

Autumn night...

The tang of winter in the air.

"He hasna taken his struan," said Mungo. "Such a pity, for I had it here to give to him."

Manus put away his pipe. The folk finished their dancing and went home. Brief lights came on in the bothies. The fire before the kirk died down.

The Soldier wandered disconsolately round the stockade, snuffling and moaning to himself. Mairi ran to him. The Soldier took her up on his shoulders, broad as an oak beam they were. Ten feet up in the air, Mairi's chubby legs kicked and flailed. She held on to the Soldier's ears. Mungo watched them disappear out of sight. He stood alone by the wall of his kirk. After a time he found old Finella standing near his side.

"This is surely the closest you've ever been to Grace," said the priest, jokingly.

The old woman made a grunting noise in her throat.

"The sky folk have lit candles for us," said Mungo, nodding to the white lights.

"Aye. Bonny," said Finella.

The old couple stood for a while looking at the stars.

"We have to make an end of him," said Mungo.

Finella said nothing.

"Our Soldier wasna created to wage war for the glory of thanes and bishops, only to defend a village. If they take him for their army, and put a mail shirt on him, and give him a muckle claymore, then who kens what will happen? No me. I dinna even ken what moves him. He has no soul, yet some kind of spirit is within him, for all that he is earth and wood, and I have no understanding of that spirit or of what it may direct him to do."

"No more have I," said Finella the witch.

"If he disobeys their orders," the old man continued, "they will punish the folk; maybe even burn the village after all. How could we stop them? If he obeys their orders, then—dear God have mercy!—we will have created a weapon that no one can control, no even the blind men that wield it. How should I explain mysel on Judgement Day when all they lopped hands and broken heads come together again and point at me, saying, 'Him! It was yon old hypocrite that set this fury on us! Yon blasphemer who betrayed his Lord of Love! Away with him! Throw him to the hounds of damnation! Let hellfire blast his filthy soul!' O the thought of that!" said Mungo.

After a tactful pause, Finella said,

"It is fortunate I am no a Christian to face such fears. I had natural wrongs to avenge, and outside yon gate I did it."

"Indeed, I saw you."

"Aye. He's torched his last bothy, yon man I finished with," said the fierce old woman. "A spear in the thrapple is a cure for many ills."

"Your medicine was most effective," said Mungo.

"Yet harvest is a thing to be celebrated. Killing isna."

"Aye. Indeed."

Silence. Then Finella sighed.

"He was beautiful, our Soldier," she said.

"He was very beautiful," said Mungo.


Finella went.

Mairi came.

"Father," she said. "It's awfy late, Father."

Mungo turned his sad eyes on her. He put his hand in her hair. The long arrow cut had grown a hard dry scab.

"Wee yin," he said. His voice was a gentle cry, a curlew in autumn. "*Cha chaomh leam neach ach thusa,*" which means, "I love no one but you."

Mairi nuzzled up against him.

"I ken that, Father."

They broke a struan between them. Each bit a piece and put it in the other's mouth, the old man of eighty odds, the wee girl of ten.

"What ails you, Father?"

"Mairi my lamb," said Mungo, "you maun take the cross from our Soldier..."

"Mairi my hinny," he said, "the cross is a burden too heavy for some folk to bear..."

"Mairi my heart," he said, "even Lord Jesus died of it."

Mairi wept.

"Why, Father?"

"He is earth and wood and of the forest, and the forest is wanting him back, Mairi."

An owl flew wailing overhead.

"You hear?" said Mungo. "They are asking for him. They are saying, 'Where is our Soldier? Why is he no coming back to us?'"

"Father, I canna."

"Lassie, lassie, I will take the cross from him mysel, only you maun get him, somehow, to bow his head down to me so I can reach it. I've had two chances already, and let them both go by. If I fail again, Mairi, they're going to take him for the Thane's army and make a butcher out of him. Mairi, he has to go back to the forest. He isna a man, and nature's other creatures are all innocent of the sin of Cain. It would be a weight that would destroy him."

There was a long silence between them then, and they heard only the forest sounds. And indeed it seemed to Mungo that there were voices there that cried out, *"Saighdear, Saighdear, come back to us, Saighdear."*

"I will for you, Father, and God forgive me," said Mairi.

She turned and ran off into the night.

Mungo picked up the bit of struan she had dropped, and turned it over and over in his hand. Never had the old man felt more wretched, never more unworthy of the cloth he wore. His heart was a hard cold clenching fist. The fact that he had just sentenced himself to death by burning troubled him not at all.

He walked for a while, wearily, through the village. Hearing sounds from the smithy he went and stood ·in the door. Una and Siubhan and Sorcha, her daughters, were exchanging some story. They were laughing. They didn't see him. All was as it should be. The fire cast a glow on Sorcha's full warm face. The old man could tell that she was pregnant, and wondered if she knew it yet. Perhaps, after they have killed me, the priest who comes next will christen the wean. I will leave word for him to do so. Some young priests these days make difficulties over illegitimate births.

Una made ready for her sleep. Siubhan looked at her Eoin's wee sleeping face. Gently she sang,

> *Lally, lally, sleep my baby,*
> *lally, lally, sleep my dear.*
> *Your coat is of many colours,*
> *lally, lally, sleep my dear.*
> *I made it of the skins of martens,*

*lally, lally, sleep my love.*
*Your father is a mighty warrior,*
*a hunter with a spear and club.*
*There is no man who is bolder,*
*lally, lally, sleep my dove.*

And pregnant Sorcha sang,

*In the mountains he hunts the wild boar,*
*in the hills the stag and the grouse.*
*He takes the fish from the falls of the Inver,*
*lally, lally, sleep little mouse.*

And Una sang,

*No man is braver, no man is bolder,*
*no man is stronger with sword and with spear.*
*When you are a man you will be a great hunter,*

*lally, lally, (sang Siubhan) sleep my dear.*

# 18

## *How the Soldier
Came to the Forest Again*

Mairi ran through the night.

Hers was a lonely soul. Being both orphan and house-keeper to the kirk, she was old beyond the bairn years, yet younger than the widowed women and loveless maidens with whom she was surrounded. And so, in a strange, yet real, way, she had come to love the lonely lumbering giant from the forest, much as in another age or in another country, a ten year old girl with freckles and a tousy wee head might give her love to a pony, a cat, or an eleph-ant, and think all the world was in the loving of it.

So Mairi thought of her *Saighdear*. So she loved him.

She came on him standing by the stockade. He had just broken down a part of it.

"Soldier hate everybody," he said. "Soldier not wanted any more."

"I want you," said Mairi.

"Soldier break everything! Kill everyone!" the Soldier shouted.

"I want you," said Mairi in a choking voice, and pressed her face into his leg.

The next day and the next, Mairi walked with the Soldier, and could not bring herself to take the cross from him, though he carried her about his neck. On the third day they went to the lochside. The Soldier waded out to catch trout. He guddled for them, letting them swim over the cradle of his hands, but was too bad-tempered to catch many. Whenever one escaped, his temper got worse. He smacked the surface of the water with his fist making strange throaty noises that Mairi listened to carefully, but it was not human talk. His eyes were like fire, red and bright and dangerous. The little cross glinted snell in the sunlight.

*He isna a man. The Father says so.*

Mairi sat watching him from the shore. She was cold and hugged her bright plaid around her. The Soldier seemed to feel nothing. He walked through the bitter freezing water, and it didn't reach him.

*He isna a man.*

Mairi huddled herself up on the grassy bank. The loch was just about full. In some places the hillside had fallen into it: she saw a raw red streak of earth, and one tree overhanging, half its roots spilling out. Elsewhere the slope was gradual, the heather stretching down towards the water and stopping just short, with a narrow frill of grass ending in broken earth and little stones. Here and there were large rocks, one a big bare boulder, pitted with the mysterious scars and holes the ice giants had chiselled in it long ages ago, now a place of gulls, white with their droppings. Beside Mairi, the head and shoulders of a rock jutted out of the hillside. The surface of the loch was a foot or two under its chin, and the stone was green with looking at it. On the back of its neck was a cup of ivy, darker than the stone, and dotted with pale flowers. It was the last flower of the year. A swarm of insects was feeding on it. For them it was the last flower of their lives. Mairi rolled over and took some of the flowers in between her fingers.

The Soldier returned to the bank with a couple of fish in his fist. He bit one in two, and spat half of it back into the water. He tossed the other one onto the bank. The fish was not just dead, but ground to an unrecognizable pulp. Mairi said something that was meant to be funny. The Soldier grunted and lay down beside her. As far as the knees, his legs were still in the water. Mairi saw the swirl his feet made on the bottom of the loch where the cold sunlight shone on the pebbles. A little fish darted among some near-black fronds of weed. A small white stone shone.

*The Father says so.*

*He isna a man.*

*The Father says so.*

And Mairi stared at the white pebble, fascinated by it. "Mairi want?" said the Soldier suddenly. His voice went booming over the water.

*He isna a man.*

He bent over and scooped the pebble up. He handed it to Mairi. Reluctantly, she took it from his hand, his huge clumsy hand. It shone wet and sparkling in her tiny palms. The Soldier smiled. He lay back again on the slope, his head in the heather. All the fire and anger went out of his eyes. He looked up at the clouds, then closed his lids. The golden cross glittered about his neck.

*The Father says so.*

*The Father says so.*

Mairi plucked some of the ivy flowers and put them in the Soldier's hair. She sat silently by him, choking on her tears. Then she looked a long time into his face. It was without human expression. He was breathing slowly and

227

deeply, as a cornfield breathes when the wind runs through it. Mairi touched her fingers to the chain holding the angel's cross.

"Mairi beautiful," said the Soldier's voice.

Mairi closed her eyes. Where her fingers pinched it, the chain burned and broke. The Soldier sighed as though his heart were breaking. Mairi lifted the cross from him. He sighed again and became lifeless. Mairi lay sobbing across the Soldier's body. When they finally found her, she was lying in a dwam, all glaikit, with no tears left to come. They didn't know what the little stone was. Someone's foot skiffed it, and it fell back into the loch.

Mungo carried her home and laid her in her cot.

He came back for the Soldier with Fearchar, and Rob driving the cart. Mungo stood over the huge figure and prayed a while for him, just as if he had been truly human after all. There was winter in the wind that lashed the old man's hair. Then they carried the body away.

Mungo said the Office of the Dead for the Soldier that night in the kirk. Mairi sat with huge staring eyes and said nothing. Mungo talked to her. She didn't answer. He kissed her brow. She didn't move.

He took the cross and laid it in a secret place behind the altar. The next day it had disappeared. Maybe the angel came for it.

They filled several large storage jars with grain and sent them down the strath, and with them Mungo sent word to Thanehall that the Soldier was no more.

Then he waited for the fire.

Strangely enough, nothing happened to him. Perhaps the Thane was secretly glad this terrible new weapon was not to be thrust into his hands after all; perhaps his captains doubted their ability to control it; perhaps the Bishop, for all his bluster, didn't want the long and embarrassing questions which a heresy trial inevitably involved. At all events no one came to arrest or to kill the old priest; and the womenfolk, who had been ready to defend him, nodded to each other and said, aye, it was all right, everything was going to be fine; winter with all its hardships was coming to close the doors of their world, and in the short days neither soldiers nor bandits sought a battle.

One last uncanny thing happened before the winter. Mairi disappeared. So did her wee fox, Faidh. One morning she simply was not there, and Mungo found her cot empty, just as she had found his that day of the haymaking.

As the days shortened and shortened, Mungo waited for her to come back. He ordered the folk out to search in the cold forest. He went himself, slowly, feeling all his age and infirmity on him now, covering the miles under the evergreen branches to the lochside, to the flat rock where he had sat watching the moonglade and hearing the heron's cry, to the mysterious Crag, to the foot of the mountains... He returned old and done. Thereafter he walked with the aid of a stick. Finella shook her head and spoke wise words to her black cat.

Mungo stood on top of the tower as the days shortened still and shortened. He strained his feeble eyes scanning the face of the forest, though no one knew what he could possibly hope to see; and at last Siubhan and Sorcha came and kindly helped the old man down the difficult winding stair and past the hall where Luath, the Shirra's old dog, still waited. And Finella shook her head and spoke wise words to the cat.

Mungo sat alone in the empty kirk at night. Fearchar cut the wood for him, Nessa carved his bread. But at night there was no gentle breathing from the wee girl's room, and in the morning he tried to imagine the sound of her voice, but there was nothing there. He talked to her hedgehog, and gave the creature milk in a wooden bowl. The hedgehog put his paws on the lip of it and drank noisily while Mungo told him about Mairi, and his fears, and how much he had loved her. And Finella shook her head and spoke wise words to her cat.

Mungo stood on the learig near where the fires were kindled, and Finella stood by him, and they found words.

"Is this your witchery?" said Mungo.

And old Finella told him what was being said among the folk: that Mairi had been seen walking into the forest at night under a full moon, with the little dog fox trotting beside her and around her and before her, sniffing out a path, and how Mairi followed him. The Soldier was waiting for her on a great white horse, so the folk said, at the end of that path through the forest. For they belonged there, both the Soldier and the girl, as the trees and the birds belonged, as the owls and the wolves.

"On a great white horse?"

Mungo looked at her with glimmering understanding, but without any words to put to it.

"Listen!" said Black Finella suddenly.

The two old folk cocked their heads. It was the month of the red roaring. They heard the stag on the hill. They heard the green door open to the place of beginnings.

"The Song of the Forest," said Mungo.

"Goban," said the ancient woman. "He's taken them back."

"He's taken them back."

In the land of Holy And Wholly My Own, at one with the reeds and the foxglove, at one with the hawthorn and the wild broom, where there are neither laws nor chains nor crosses, and the heather does not yet know the foot of man—there Mairi rides for ever with her Soldier through the forest on the back of that swanwhite stallion, and the green wind blows bonny through hair and mane.

## 19

## *The Green Door*

Then the month of the roaring was passed, and the drift of deer down to the lower hills and corries, and the heather redolent with the scent of rutting stags; passed were the violent antlers slashing at low branches, and the great beasts that roar at sunset, black against the red evening sky. The oak and the rowan, the aspen and elm, all wore the foliage of late autumn. Solitary amid dark firs, a golden birch burned like a flame. The aspen leaves stopped trembling and they fell.

Now comes the cold. Slowly the white walls of winter close on the strath, and on the glen and the village that is in it. Over the forest in those days of boar and elk and beaver, the November rains grow chill and snell, syne the air tingles with the sharpness of the ice, and the first black fingers of it close on the rocks by the lochside.

Mist pours over the corrie crags in grey falls; mist hangs over the forest in grey auras, and crossbills comb its tumbling grey masses as they feed in flocks on the crowns of the pine. And on the highest peaks, distant Ben Nevis, Ben Macdhui and Braeriach, the first new snow falls on sheltered icebeds that never thaw.

And the cold comes, it comes, and the wet mist, and the warning echoes over the land. The last summer migrants take to flight, the swift and the swallow: *weet-a-weet* cries the swallow, turning southwards. Those who can escape, do; those who cannot, burrow into oblivion. Wood mice search for acorns and beech mast to see out the coming hardships. Hibernating bats look for damp places, caves and empty water-near trees; frogs thrust into the still soft mud of the burn walls; bears curl for sleep in the forest and will not waken till the spring. Then the salmon come, heavy with spawn, fresh-run from the green deep sea. And others: birds of the Arctic; the brambling from the birch woods of Tromso, and the chaffinch; the whooper swan—*whoop, whoop*—from Iceland sagaland above the salt furrows of the longships, bird of Egil and Gunnar; and the little snow bunting from the place where words freeze on the air. And swanwhite, feather-white, light and deadly is the first snow that falls on Ben More, Ben Klibreck and Morven. And the mist of the curling valleys is rose-coloured in the winter sun, and the last stag calls there.

Cold. Cold. The first corries receive it now, the falling whiteness. The floors of the higher glens are white and featureless. The hills are patched with snowdrifts. Soft the light is. Even at noon the sun fails to climb much above the frozen mountains. The heather is withered, grass brown and harsh. Wild roses and moss campion grow in the glare of the snowfield. Down it comes, and the forest hides its colours, its yellow and green colours, its red and brown colours. The flowers of the rainbow kneel and bow their heads to the earth, the bracken bends, the burn drips over ice, the humming of its waters is a tinkling among icicles. In the bitter air, the frozen moisture of the mist falls as the thinnest rain of crystal; in the bitter air, fern patterns of fog-ice grow on rock and trunk; in the bitter air, black trees go walking in blue-tinted cloaks of mist.

Winter is a time of calms and storms, and this year it blows hard and heavy on the glen where the village is. Over the grey coast the wind comes howling, and where the forest does not prevent it, it torments the shuddering earth with lashes of hail. In the hidden places heartbeats slow to one tenth of their normal pace. Aye, the very folk hibernate, and the weakest die, man and toad alike, woman and crow, for the food floor is hard and covered, and the blood turns slow and chill. In the village, they herd the kye into the tower after boarding up all the arrow-slits and warming the damp stones with fire—to the joy of bat and owl who live there now. The beasts press together lowing in the yard, and Luath stands at the top of the stairs and barks. In winter.

Still the snow falls, for it is colder then in those days of boar and elk than now, and winter is the time of great snow, and a black running of clouds. Folk count the dawns of the season. The loch freezes out from its banks, and fishers from the hungry villages go there in hope of finding the dark shapes of salmon in the grey-tinted middle pool where the water still flows. But in the happy village under the tower, querns hum by day, the oven glows red, and round it the earth is soft with the warmth, and the frost runs from it, and the snow. By nights full of stars and howling wind, bairns who lie awake hear the tales their elders tell then of creators and heroes and the wood of tender leaves where time was once a child, and the youngest, whose memories have just been born, ask, Will it ever come? that wonderful Spring they do not know. And in the tower they fork long yellow-stalked hay to the kye, and it is a warm place of dung and thick steaming breath. In winter.

December is a milder month by and large than those bitter twins which bracket it. It is a time when snow gives way to rain, dreich, miserable rain indeed, yet here and there it opens the door of the snow and underneath the grass is found green and growing, a vision of future well-being for those who can survive long enough. It is a time when the storms and howling turn into peaceable days, and the world seems still and calm. Then the evergreens wear shimmering dresses, boulders are white castles, and a thin crust of frost tops the undisturbed snow. Footprints harden along the village paths. In the forest, hedgehogs, bats and dormice break their sleep to forage for a while. Foxes nuzzle for earthworms among the harsh roots. Cold salmon lie torpid on the waterbed. Red holly fruit hangs in droplets over the white banks. Other days, though, the wind from the south-west goes rattling across the roof; wet it is: sleet runs down the stairs of timber, dripping from thatch and branch in the time of the black frost and raw grey rain. And the folk who stamp and beat outside their doors, nod to each other with their breath on the stinging air, knowing that the worst is still to come...

The year turns on a day of clear, windless frost, when all is calm and cold and placid under the bright sun. And then it comes. The wind veers back to the north, and it comes, it comes, the snow-wind that blows pitilessly from arctic lands, and the white bees swarm. January, month of the freezing...

Otter tracks beside the frozen burn filling rapidly, disappearing where a pool is turbulent enough to be still black and free; otter head ploughing its way through the snow, breasting the cold white as a swimmer of the waves. Bitter land, bastard land, cruel snow-whipping north-blown land that howls like all the wolves who are starving in it. This is the hungry time. Stoat shivers in his winter white, his stomach cleft to his ribs. Eagle and fox fight for the same small prey. Red grouse and ptarmigan shudder in the misery of it. Deer crop the ivy on the trunks; they stand on their hind legs to reach for a few mouthfuls more. Most creeping things are back in hibernation; the foragers have returned as the temperature falls again. In the warmth of the peat-stack earwigs guard their eggs. The white wings of the snow bunting fly among the pines. The snowy owl winters where the north wind blows; he hunts by day, savage talons staining the clean white world with red. Chaffinches and titmice shelter from his vicious beak among the village roofs.

Daylong, nightlong, the wind rages and roars, and living creation stays inside its various doors and huddles there: the folk around candles, by the wood and peat fires, warming themselves with the winter flame of their talk while the wind tears at their walls and shakes the very foundations of them with its power.

*Whooo*, says the wind. *Whooo. Everything changes.* Ochone!

And it rushes over the roofs, raking the thatch with its grey fingers. It yells down the smoke-holes and batters the creaking door on its latch until the wood snaps and the planks fly open. It tears everything that is not battened down, the wall with a draught in it will crack and tumble, the ill-fixed roof will fly heavenward, the shutters bang and wallop around the kye and in the barn. On the fringes of the forest it spins the fallen leaves, and the learig is a place where rotted branches dance in the arms of the rain, and slender trees crash in the corrie.

And the wind is there that was there always, beyond even the fingers of wood, beyond even the mountains;

beyond the coming of the daughters of song swift in the morning tide from the east, glowy in scales and fins with seaweed fronds for hair;

beyond the going of the sons of war fading westward to the gloaming of blood and hopes that spilled like blood into the crying earth;

beyond O beyond the meeting and mating of these two rivers, these two strange peoples that made you my Scotland my mother in the yellow time of promise.

*Whooo*, says the wind. *Whooo. Everything changes.* Ochone!

And to the seasons passing under the belt of stone, in the slow slow time-clock of rocks, deep hidden bones of the world;

and to the furrow of wooden prows and coracle-hide carving the brine, and of ploughs turning the brown skin of patient earth in the days of the planting;

and to the ruins of kirks and castles and the crumbling of flags and the rusting of weapons in the wet underneath of the world's flesh;

and to the voice that speaks for dead mouths, and the maker who plays on the mountains of sorrow;

and to the shadow that walks beyond the skeleton bearing the cry of centuries and the clash of chains.

*Whooo*, says the wind. *Whooo. Everything changes.*

(But then the wind has always said that.)

Ochone!

Then midmost in February, St Bride breathes warm life back into the mouth of the dead winter. The first dandelions open their flowers. The cold air trembles to the slow birth of Spring.

Now the roar of the tempest is heard again in the wood. Snow falls from the shuddering branches, but no more from the sky. The iron-hard leaves jump and leap along the forest paths. The returning rain spatters the trunks of pine and alder, loosens slivers of thin ice from the frozen shallows of the loch. Sheets of thin water spill over the ramparts of the sky. The first primroses appear. Catkins grow on hazel and birch. The corbies come to nest under sheltered eaves of rock. And slowly, slowly the days lengthen. The first warmth is in the sun; the moon goes walking in a cloudless sky. A smile of light is on the face of the land. Shepherd's purse opens in the melting frost, and the first spring days come out all fresh and shining like snails after the wet.

Listen.

It is the gradual turning of the twilight time, the green genesis of the seasons, when quiet pools lie beneath the trees and the clearness of cold after-rain is on the dawn hills. Then the deer rub loose their winter hair, and the red stags shed their old year's antlers. The door of the strath is opening. Soon the rutted tracks will be passable again. And in the black hours, the snipe are heard bleating like goats of the air. *Klick-kleck*, at dawn the heavy capercaillie sings, perching in the branches of spruce. *Twee-te, tee-tee*, call the willy-wicket sandpipers from the loch as the last ice vanishes into dark waters. *Fraank*, answers the heron; *fraank*.

The song of the forest they call it, those who stop and listen.

Above the last lingering snowdrifts, new leaves start to appear on the birch. The last northern swans leave the strath as the first whaups return from the south. The heather is warm wine-red brown, the grass is fresh and green. *Tsiwick*, cries the woodcock, flying in the evening light over the canopy of trees. The night is raucous with the chorus of frogs. The swallow returns, oaring the breeze with his forked tail; *weet-a-weet*, he cries, *weet-a-weet*. The great hunger is over, and the darkness! The badger wakes in his sett and sniffs the air.

The Song of the Forest they call it.

*Surrexit Dominus de sepulcro.*

# Postlude

## *The Field*

On a morning when the first fine sun had already melted the overnight frost, the folk prepared to break the fields with the ploughing. They dragged the cashroms out into the open, they stropped the blades and cleaned away the rust. They harnessed two oxen to the big plough, and opened the seed urns, filling bags for the planting. The strath girls were singing. They were singing with frank contentment as all such folk know. The mild spring breeze was in the greening branches. Rooks were gathering to follow the ploughs. From nearby came the sound of a woodpecker hammering a tree.

And Mungo took up his bag of seed and went singing into the field.

# Author's Note

Central to this story is the Jewish legend of the Golem which I have taken the liberty to adapt and set in a somewhat fantastical and certainly long-vanished Scotland of great forests. Call it a city-dweller's pastorale.

I would like to acknowledge my indebtedness to Isaac Bashevis Singer's short story "The Golem" for the original idea; also to Marian McNeill's famous compilation *The Silver Bough* for its description of the manners of bygone ages. Students of folklore will doubtless also recognize some familiar episodes among these pages.

The ballads quoted here and there in this book belong to the later English-speaking era of border minstrelsy, but because their rhythm is more familiar to modern ears I have used them rather than attempt my own feeble versions of the Gaelic work songs which these people would have known. The women's lullaby on page 41 was suggested by a fragment within *The Gododdin*, the 7th-century epic tale of the riders of Lothian. Mungo's blessing on page 164 is an abbreviated version of the Reaping Blessing collected and translated by Alexander Carmichael in the *Carmina Gadelica*.

Until I was about ten years old the only trees I had ever seen were those that grew in Princes Street Gardens, and I thought they were a huge forest.

Yet as late as 1800 a squirrel could travel branch to branch from Caithness to Cornwall without ever touching the ground.

# Tim Parks

# Loving Roger

'A tight, disturbing novel . . . mordantly illuminating on the way love contains the seeds of vindictiveness and hatred.'
*Observer*

'Extremely compelling . . . the human observation is witty, acute and sensitive . . . absolute authenticity.'
*Sunday Telegraph*

'With his chillingly elegant prose and frighteningly deadpan narrative, Tim Parks has written, not a whodunnit, but a brilliant whydunnit.'
*Today*

'A tale that is cruel, upsetting and compellingly credible.'
*London Standard*

**Flamingo**